ASHES
TO
ASHES

Atlas Books
11271 Ventura Blvd, #520
Studio City, CA 91604

Printed by Atlas Books, in the United States of America.
First printing edition 2021

Book cover design by Jerry Todd
Book Layout by Chrissy Hobbs

Library of Congress Control Number: 2021912080

ISBN: 978-1-7374297-0-8 (Hardcover)
ISBN: 978-1-7374297-2-2(Paperback)
ISBN: 978-1-7374297-1-5 (e-book)

www.alanllee.com

ASHES
TO
ASHES

ALAN L. LEE

For my brother, Ronald.

I've reserved three copies of *Ashes To Ashes* in heaven's bookstore. One for you. One for Mom. One for Dad.

Not seeing you or hearing your voice has been difficult. You left us much too soon, Big Brother. If there's a positive, I know I now have three of the best advocates ever looking out for me in heaven.

Rest easy, Family and take my dogs out for a walk.

ALSO BY ALAN L. LEE

Sandstorm

CHAPTER 1

JAFAR KARIMI WAS no errand boy.

He told himself that several times—like he had the day before, and for the past month. But the large brown paper bag he carried under his right arm suggested he was an errand boy on this occasion.

A portion of the food staining the bag was nourishment for him, but mostly it was for Navid. Whatever Navid wanted, he got. He was the one Tehran had placed in charge, the more seasoned one. By Karimi's assessment, Navid was skilled at exaggerating his effectiveness. When not chasing the weakness of flesh, Navid rarely left the comfort and safety of the multi-storied flat in London's Notting Hill district. If Navid were to gather any useful intel, it would have to fall from the sky. Karimi didn't rule that out since Allah had so far awarded the man with a charmed, undeserved life.

Navid reveled in telling stories of his exploits from the days of pursuing a computer science degree at Michigan State University in the United States. He was fond of wearing the school's insignia-laden clothing. When he felt uninhibited in a public setting, watching a Spartans sporting event on television, Navid would often chant ad nauseam, "Go green! Go white!" The airhead European women he bedded thought it was cute. Their superiors in Iran had never seen his exuberance for all things Western. Karimi surmised if they did, they'd applaud him for immersing himself so thoroughly in their culture. Such was the blessed life of Navid Javadi. Many times Karimi had drifted off to sleep, comforted by the thought of besting Navid's privileged life. Today would be that day.

Karimi walked along Hereford Road with an air of confidence not usually a part of his DNA. A few days had changed his attitude. Tehran would soon note his potential. The best part would be the look on Navid's smug face. Thinking of the moment made Karimi smile. He planned on forwarding his vital information after Navid went to bed tonight.

Hunger made Karimi quicken his pace. He hadn't eaten for hours, his mind preoccupied by what he'd stumbled upon days earlier. In his report, he'd refrain from emphasizing that you had to drag your ass out of the apartment to garner results.

In a few minutes he would sit down to eat, enduring all the misguided insults Navid would throw his way while dining. Karimi had been close to home when he'd received Navid's text to pick up food at a favorite Persian restaurant. Karimi's objection had been the expectation that he get the food since he was "out."

Karimi paused at the end of Hereford Road. Satisfied that everything seemed okay, he crossed over to narrow Ossington Street. Their flat was on the west side of the one-way street, indistinguishable from the other white, multi-story dwellings. Black wrought iron decorated second-level terraces, and each building had a gate that allowed entry to a lower level. Keys out, Karimi hurried inside. He didn't announce his arrival, as was the norm. Worried about the bag leaking, he headed straight for the kitchen to grab plates, napkins, and utensils. Then he took everything to the dining room. There'd be no retiring to their respective corners this evening. They would sit down face-to-face, and Navid might start to realize they were equals on this assignment. Suspecting Navid had his headphones on, Karimi called out, raising his voice several decibels.

After Karimi yelled twice, the man had yet to come downstairs. A frustrated Karimi skidded his chair back from the table, scratching the wooden floor. He headed for Navid's room in a huff. The door was ajar, and Karimi swung it open with such force that it returned to hit him in the shoulder. Navid sat with his back to the desk and computer screen, sans headphones, a blank stare on his face.

"Did you hear me calling you?" Karimi uttered.

He waited for an explanation. The room had an odd smell, like someone had relieved himself. Karimi glanced down to see that Navid had wet his khaki pants. He took a step closer and noticed the man's face was puffy with fresh bruises.

"What the hell?" Karimi said, shaking his head, unable to make any sense of what he was seeing and why Navid remained silent. When he moved further in, Navid shifted his eyes. Karimi followed his huge hazel orbs to a corner of the room. He almost peed his pants too when he saw the slumped figure lounging in a chair, though he focused more on the menacing, silencer-equipped weapon aimed at him. There was no mistaking who the man was. An 8x10 photo of him hung on the wall next to two others. Here now, in the flesh, was Karimi's surprise.

"Hello, Karimi. So glad you brought dinner. Navid and I have worked up quite an appetite, and there is so much to discuss," the man said. He then referenced the wall of photos with a wave of his weapon. "I love what you've done with the place."

Karimi couldn't do anything but listen. He had not considered this scenario.

"Oh, before I proceed—" The man returned his full attention and the weapon to Karimi. "Let me ask, how's your medical?"

Karimi searched for understanding. "My what?"

"Your medical plan. Does your plan cover occupational hazards?"

Karimi glanced at Navid, who was no help at all. In fact, he sort of looked him off as if to say, "you're on your own."

"I'm afraid Navid is not too happy with you at the moment. You're supposed to be a team, and you've been keeping secrets from him."

Karimi wanted to convey he was sorry, but Navid's chin was on his chest. More than likely he was praying.

"I'll ask again because it's important. How's your medical plan?"

Karimi still didn't understand, but he blurted out, "It's fine. Total coverage."

"Excellent," the man responded. He fired a round into Karimi's right knee, sending the young Iranian to the floor with slobbering pain. He then rose from the chair to stand over Karimi.

The man wondered if he was doing the right thing by not finishing the pair off. If it weren't for the photos on the wall, this would have a different ending.

"Patch him up," he instructed Navid. "Like I said, we have much to discuss."

Equipped with towels and bandages, Navid did what he was told. Karimi stared back at the imposing figure. The man known as Dr. Mueller seemed to be penetrating his soul with eyes that didn't give a damn whether he lived.

CHAPTER 2

"SURE YOU'RE NOT hungry?"

Navid declined the invitation with a cautious shake of the head. Karimi was in so much pain from the bullet to the knee that he wouldn't have been able to keep food down, anyway.

Dr. Mueller, as they knew him, sampled a small plate of food at the end of the dining room table. "I heard the food at Hafez was good, but this exceeds my expectations. Delicious. Can I make you a plate? I mean, you bought it."

The Iranians had no interest in eating. Self-preservation superseded hunger.

Disappointed, Dr. Mueller wiped his mouth clean with a napkin.

"Well, your appetite might return later. I don't want to be too rude, barging in here unannounced, eating some of your food. Shooting poor Karimi in the knee." Dr. Mueller picked up the gun that had been resting next to his plate. He got up and examined the room in silence, stopping at the front windows. Peeling back the curtains, he tapped the glass.

He turned to address his captivated audience. "I wasn't kidding earlier when I said I love what you've done with the place. Thick, double-pane windows to offset eavesdropping. Soundproofed walls. And a very sophisticated, high-tech computer system upstairs. Impressive on a small scale. Someone has made this place quite cozy. To be honest, what screws it up though is you two. Well, let me change that statement. Navid, I get your contribution, but Karimi? Guys, what gives here?"

Navid and Karimi locked eyes, wondering who would be the betrayer.

"Listen, I'm going to be honest with you," Mueller said, dropping the weapon to his side. "There's a way you both walk away from this. And there's a way you don't." Confident he'd made his point, Mueller sat back down at the table. "Karimi, why have you been following me, taking pictures?"

The younger Iranian thought about concocting a story, but Dr. Mueller had already seen his photo on the wall upstairs. Plus, he valued the one good knee he had left.

"Orders," he admitted.

"What orders?"

Karimi paused when Navid cleared his throat, then grew distracted as Dr. Mueller's fingers started tapping the handle of his gun. After a moment of reflection, Karimi spoke. "We were dispatched, along with others, to various locations."

"To what end?"

"Our top priority was to be on the lookout for you, and the other people in the photographs."

"And what was to happen if you spotted one of us?"

"We're supposed to report it immediately," an agitated Navid offered.

"That's all? Just report?" Mueller said, seeking assurances.

"Yes. Take no action to intervene," Navid said, more lecturing Karimi than supplying an answer. "And without risking exposure, try to find out where you were staying. Your movements."

"Nice work, then." Mueller produced a sad face. "Except, Karimi withheld his discovery from you, Navid, and your superiors."

Karimi opened his mouth as if to explain, but Navid, having none of it, turned away.

"I caught you taking pictures three nights ago, Karimi, while I was having dinner," Mueller pointed out. "Most people take one or two pictures of their surroundings, but you took several. You had no dining companion, and you weren't taking selfies. I was going to dismiss it until I saw you in the crowd the next day at Piccadilly Circus. Coincidences make me very suspicious, so I ditched you and then followed you. And tonight, here we all are."

Karimi retraced his steps. He understood the restaurant mistake. But how could Dr. Mueller have picked him out of the busy, jam-packed crowd at Piccadilly Circus?

"The question I have for you now, Karimi—and make no mistake, it will determine whether you live or die. What did you do with the photos you took while I was at dinner? I want those pictures. All of them," he demanded, knowing his female companion had to be in them.

Navid grew more nervous, sweat lining his forehead as Karimi stayed silent. Mueller's mood was changing with each passing second. He no longer attempted to be jovial. He stood and came to Karimi's side, pressing the silencer against his head.

"Karimi, if you think those photos give you leverage, I assure you they don't. This is the last time I will ask. Where are the pictures?"

"Tell him, damn it. Tell him," Navid screamed.

Karimi blinked as he sought more air. He saw Dr. Mueller position his free hand as a shield against the expected blood splatter.

"On my phone. They're on my phone!"

Mueller fetched Karimi's phone. Given the password, he found what he wanted. Photos of him at dinner with Lauren, a different man altogether. He cared deeply for her, but so far had not dared tell her what he did for a living. It was too early in the relationship. The truth would likely scare her away. If anything were to happen to her because of him, all trace of humanity within him would be lost.

"These are all of them, Karimi?"

"Yes."

"If I find out otherwise, you'll die a slow, horrible death."

"There are no more."

Mueller lowered his gun. "Relax, gentleman. We're almost done. For your pain and suffering, I'll put you in good standing with your handlers."

Navid and Karimi produced baffled stares. They wondered if this was a twisted form of cruelty before Dr. Mueller sentenced them to death.

"I made it very clear to your government that I would help them, provided they didn't pry into my background or attempt to get in my business," Mueller said. "This charade has violated that treaty. I assume this is the work of President Shahroudi and the Quds Force. I'm sure they have questions about Natanz, as I do. I want to set up a meeting. I'll choose the location and time."

Mueller headed for the entrance. "I'll be in touch. Smile. Promotions may be in order. And, I strongly suggest you get somebody to take a look at that knee."

He'd make the Iranians wait before detailing a sit-down location. The time would allow him to do some digging of his own.

Exiting, Mueller thought about the photographs on the wall in the computer room. They'd made this ordeal go in a different direction. He knew the faces. One belonged to Nora Mossa, a CIA operative whose mentor he'd killed. The other was a man he'd almost killed before it was necessary to elicit his help. If that man's picture was on the wall, that meant he must have made it out alive too. Mueller only knew his name to be Alex. Both of them, he guessed, were in the dark about this witch-hunt, like he'd been. As for his photo being on the wall, he wanted answers before taking action. They still referred to him as "Dr. Mueller." His cover was still intact.

If the Iranians suspected he was the shadowy, deadly Mossad assassin nicknamed "The Devil," orders would have been to execute on sight. With Lauren's safety now assured, Nathan was pleased that he didn't have to kill anyone.

At least, not yet.

CHAPTER 3

ALEX KOVES WAS running late. That wouldn't make her happy.

From what he'd been told, you wanted to keep Karina Marchenko in a good mood. Alex did his best to offset his tardiness, texting her that he was minutes away. He didn't get a response. The Berlin night air was cool; his black, long-sleeved mock turtleneck provided a level of comfort. The heat generated by his increased movement helped.

Having traveled several blocks on foot, Alex gathered his breath before entering the B-Flat Jazz Club. He gave thanks, because the featured attraction had yet to take the stage. The hostess informed him that due to the headlining act, the venue was now standing-room only, and there wasn't much of that left. Alex told her he was meeting someone already seated.

Engaging and boisterous, the crowd was anticipating a special evening. The wait staff were in for a long and profitable night of delivering drink orders. Alex made his way through the crowd, searching without looking desperate. She would spot him before he located her, though he'd familiarized himself with women's fashion. The elongated bar area was packed, but he doubted she'd be there, considering the anticipated nature of their conversation. He expected to find her sitting alone. That would make the process quicker. He fixated on a woman sitting at one of the small tables along the wall. Shoulder-length dark hair, distinctive red lipstick. If his research was accurate, she wore a light grey cowl neck tunic sweater. She seemed locked on him as well with each step he took toward her. Standing next to her, he made his final assessment. As informed, she was wearing dark grey leggings, partially covered by knee high black leather boots.

"Karina?" Alex asked, waiting for one final piece of confirmation.

Casually, she brushed aside some hair from the left side of her face. He saw what he needed to see. Alex didn't stare and didn't dare ask. Marchenko's long, stringy hair sometimes concealed the inch-and-a-half scar to the left of her eye. It no longer bothered her when she looked in a mirror or when men who approached her from the right side were surprised when they engaged her full-on. If she had moved a fraction of a second slower, she would have lost an eye. The way she came to accept it, a scar was ten times better than a patch. When asked, she was known to reply with raspy seriousness, "You'll never see the other guy."

Prior to the scar, Marchenko had answered to superiors. She'd since rid herself of that dynamic. As a freelancer, she picked what worked best. The jury was still out concerning the American. His request was serious. He looked capable, but already had a strike against him.

"You're late," she said before shifting over to let him move a chair to sit closer.

There were two drinks on the table. The potency of straight vodka filled Alex's nostrils. "My apologies," he said, settling in. "I miscalculated how long it would take to get here on foot."

"Miscalculating can cost lives. Mine included."

"Point taken."

"I hope so, because this is a very dangerous undertaking." Marchenko chased her words with vodka. "I've taken a tremendous risk just by being here. You don't get close to a man like this without raising suspicion. Your tracks must be covered prior and after. So before we proceed, are you sure you're up to the job? The only harm in walking away now is that your bank account will be a little lighter."

There was a round of generous applause as the headlining act made their way to the stage. "You like jazz?" he asked Marchenko, joining the crowd by softly clapping.

She shot him a look in the dimmed lighting, wondering if it was best to just keep the down payment and ensure her safety by killing him.

"Maybe you didn't hear me. I asked . . ."

"I heard you just fine. I have doubts you're up to the job at hand."

"I picked this place because I couldn't pass up the opportunity to see Pat Metheny. This intimate space! Priceless." Alex grinned. "Doesn't get any better than this. So, do you like jazz?"

She considered his question and drew an intellectual blank. "It's good to fuck to," she offered.

With a raised eyebrow, Alex nodded. "There's that, yes."

After some brief remarks on how great it was to be here, Pat Metheny got the session started. Most of the audience chatter either stopped or shifted into a respectful hum. Alex and Marchenko sat in relative silence. He knew the song being performed by heart. With the crowd glued to the stage, Alex leaned in toward Marchenko so his words wouldn't be drowned out by the music.

"You question whether I can pull this off," he said. "To safeguard your identity, you asked for a one-on-one meeting outside of Russia. No handlers, no bodyguards, no stragglers."

Marchenko's lips parted to chime in, but Alex didn't give her a chance to interject. "So what's up with the two guys in the blue BMW parked across the street? Let's also not overlook the guy with a blue jacket folded across his lap sitting at the bar. I'd bet good money you have a matching earpiece in your right ear. Checking on your trustworthiness is the reason I'm late."

Marchenko finished one of her vodkas. She then pulled an envelope from her purse and handed it to Alex, telling him it contained the outline of a plan.

"We go three days from tonight. Your lodging information is in there too. I have connections at the hotel. After you've checked in, we'll do a dry run. The only reason you should attempt to contact me before then is to cancel. If you don't show up in Moscow at the appointed time, consider our business done."

"Got it. Now come on, admit it. The music is getting to you."

Marchenko's thoughts teetered on a ledge of uncertainty. For now, the American was intriguing. She reserved the right, however, to kill him if at any point she changed her mind.

CHAPTER 4

#BORED.

Nora's closest friends had responded with playful condemnation to her tweet from over a week ago. The post contained a photo of her from behind, having breakfast on a Paris balcony with the Eiffel Tower in the background, her face strategically hidden.

She had added, "On to Monte-Carlo next. Hopefully things will pick up." As punishment, a few friends found it necessary to unfollow her for a day. Nora didn't expect most of her friends to understand. The ones she worked with were off limits. They'd see her postings, but any form of return communication was forbidden. Her less knowledgeable friends, who thought she was taking a hiatus from her global corporate job, didn't know she was dealing with a life that had gone from doing a hundred miles an hour to crawling in a school zone.

Her boss, George Champion, had laid out the reality of the situation months ago. "You can either accept this suspension or resign."

The director of the National Clandestine Service got the answer he hoped to hear. He then told Nora off the record that she'd done a hell of a job under intense pressure. His praise wasn't meant to be a bandage covering her neglect of following protocol. She got the message without admitting she'd do the same thing again under the circumstances. A woman from human resources, devoid of personality, had explained what a paid two-month suspension entailed. Walk a straight line, keep your nose clean, and no communication with active agency personnel unless authorized. Essentially, she was on double-secret probation. They also froze her agency-funded financial accounts until her return to active status.

So be it, Nora had thought. She had demons to exorcise. Avenging her friend and mentor had taken her to a very dark place. Plus, after the hell she'd endured, two months off sounded ideal.

Free of stress, she returned to the nurturing arms of her mother in Oregon. Two weeks of lying around, sleeping late, and waking to the smell of a robust breakfast every morning made her feel like a kid again. She even got through the "when are you going to settle down" talks unscathed. She cleared her head, jogging around the Eugene campus of her alma mater. The fresh young faces, full of energy, took her back to a time of her own innocence. She couldn't have imagined then the path her life would take.

Reminiscing was nice, but she had to move on. Satisfied that her mom remained a pillar of strength and was in good health, Nora said goodbye. She calculated she could spend a reasonable portion of the unexpected financial windfall deposited months ago by Alex into her personal account. Her former apartment in Rome no longer an option, she needed to find a new place to live anyway. They'd also barred her from the Rome office. The city itself was off-limits temporarily.

Seeking discovery and excitement, she sampled the hotspots in Barcelona, London, and Paris. To relax, she opted for a change of pace in the quiet coastal town of Honfleur, France. Thanks to her "exotic" features, Nora attracted a fair share of interest from virile young men and a smattering of George Clooney-wannabes during her travels. She politely passed on all. It was hard to believe, but she still only had feelings for the one man who filled her heart with joy. After no contact for years, when she needed him the most, Alex had been there for her. He'd helped to save her life. They'd made love again, and then being realistic in not rushing into a relationship, gone their separate ways once more—this time, though, on good terms.

Sitting on the balcony of her suite at the Hotel de Paris had become an evening ritual during the past week. It offered a breathtaking view of the Mediterranean Sea, and the coastline that snaked around mountains. The sea and Port Hercule danced with activity every day. Yachts, tall ships, cruise ships, and people engaged in various water sports enjoyed this carved-out slice of heaven to the fullest. For her, it had been a week of sunbathing, swimming, and exploring the best of Monaco. She slept late to have enough energy to survive well into the wee hours. Re-instatement to the CIA was on the horizon. The time was right to embrace fun in a big way.

From every angle in the mirror, her outfit made a statement. She'd ventured into the Escada store on a shopping adventure and hadn't left empty-handed. The short-sleeved dress with ruffles at the hem above the knee was all about sophistication. The short slit at the neckline gave a hint to what was underneath. The dress's color mimicked the blue hue of the sea. She accented it with matching strappy sandals and a shoulder bag. After giving her image one final inspection, Nora headed to Le Grill.

The maître d' checked her off his list. He led Nora to her table on the open-air terrace with an approving smile. There were two seats. Expecting the question upon sitting down, Nora informed the maître d' that she'd be dining alone. She got a wide, mysterious grin, as he if he knew something she didn't. Exiting, he informed her that her server would assist her momentarily. Nora took in the view, the sun setting to form a perfect picture.

There was a good reason why Le Grill came highly recommended.

It was one of Europe's best rooftop establishments, and the view of the French Riviera was breathtaking. The interior had a retractable roof that was open under the stars. Seated patrons looked polished, with jackets required for all the men.

Nora's waiter arrived with an ice bucket containing a bottle of champagne. With a pleasant demeanor, he announced his name was Marcel. Puzzled, Nora informed him that she hadn't ordered champagne. Marcel opened the bottle anyway. He poured a glass, and set the bucket on the table.

"Complimentary," Marcel replied, promising to return shortly.

Nora recognized the champagne label. Over the counter, it'd set you back nearly three hundred dollars. It had to be a nosebleed amount here. She'd dropped a fair share of money at the hotel and casino during the week, but "complimentary" seemed a stretch. Did the staff somehow think it was her birthday or a surprise engagement? She shrugged off the gratis and returned to the view. The champagne was worth every dollar she wasn't spending.

Nora let the gentle breeze and atmosphere take her away. A cruise ship docked in Port Hercule blasted its horn prelude to departure. Various yachts scattered about were in party mode, their night lights constellations for fun. They reminded Nora that she was on such a yacht months ago. As an uninvited guest, her reason for being there had nothing to do with fun, but the outcome was satisfying. To this day, no one suspected that one of the richest men in the world didn't die because of natural causes. She raised her glass in a toast to that.

"Glad to see you're enjoying the bottle," said a man in a tailored black suit.

Startled by his presence, Nora set her glass on the table. Another George Clooney type. Rugged looking and well groomed, she had to give him that.

"I take it I have you to thank for the champagne?"

"A small token."

"An expensive token, but I'm afraid it won't make the seat across from me available."

The man disregarded her claim and sat down.

Nora protested with a wry smile, "Please, don't make me have you thrown out of here."

"Beautiful view, isn't it?" he said, pouring himself a glass.

"Okay." Nora searched for her waiter.

"Miss Mossa." The mention of her name brought Nora's attention back to the table. "I'm assuming you know a man named Alex?"

Her eyes narrowed.

The man continued, "I only know his first name. Muscular. Dark hair. Capable fellow."

"Suppose I have such a friend. You are?"

"My name is Nathan. He and I had an interesting introduction at an underground location. I'm the one who led you to a certain billionaire. Coincidental, I'm sure, that he passed away not long after. I have a message for you and Alex."

"Concerning?"

Nathan Yadin smiled as if the two were sharing an intimate exchange.

"Your lives are in jeopardy. You're being hunted."

CHAPTER 5

"SHOULD WE TAKE this conversation someplace more private?"

"This works just fine for me," Nora responded, seeing no reason to trust her unexpected companion.

Yadin played with the stem of his glass, measuring the noise quotient around them. He nodded. "Have it your way, but I assure you, I mean you no harm. I've already taken a chance by being here. It would be much easier to just let events play out."

Nora chuckled. "The only reason I haven't had you thrown out yet is because, as a means of introduction, you offered some details few people know."

"Makes me legitimate then, doesn't it?"

"Means you're connected somehow. That doesn't translate into trustworthy."

"Cautious. In our line of work, that's a very good thing."

Nora watched as the cruise ship pushed away from Port Hercule. "What exactly is your line of work, Nathan?"

"At the moment, I'm on a sabbatical," he offered. "Though I

suppose, given the present circumstances, that's somewhat disingenuous. Let's say I was on break until this fell into my lap."

"I'm at a disadvantage here. You seem to know a little about me, but I'm in the dark about you."

His knowledge of Nora Mossa ran deep, but he dared not reveal that yet. If she hadn't gone off grid a while back, he would have likely been her executioner. But that was in the past. He was here to offer an olive branch, partly because he harbored a great deal of guilt for killing her friend.

"I'm in the light now," Yadin said, his hands open.

"Oh, what a treat for me then." Nora raised her glass in a toast. "How did you find me?"

"I'm good at what I do."

"And modest, too."

"I assume you're riding out a suspension or on leave. Explains why you're so visible and not watching your back. That needs to change," he said firmly.

"You seem like a dangerous man."

"I'm not dangerous to you."

"One chance encounter and I'm supposed to believe you've gone through all this trouble just to give me and Alex a heads-up? That must have been some exchange between you two."

"There's more, but my motivation is not important at the moment."

"You say we're being hunted? By whom?"

"That should be obvious now that you know there's a threat. Aside from the embarrassment, your efforts weakened several people who are not used to being put in that position. They see payback as a way of saving face."

"If that's the case, you have a lot to worry about too."

"I'll handle affairs on my end. I'll leave it in your hands to contact Alex. Over time, this might go away. Political climates change. But for now, the threat is very real."

The last time Nora and Alex had talked, it seemed like he was trying to avoid a lengthy conversation. Based on past encounters, she'd assumed that meant he had something pressing in his life. That had been weeks ago, post notification of her suspension.

She'd try another avenue to communicate. Besides, it gave her a good reason to get in touch with a dear friend to both of them. But first, the promise of an enjoyable night was in the air—despite the ominous news she'd just received.

"You're welcome to stay for an appetizer," Nora offered, picking up the menu.

Yadin finished his glass of bubbly. He placed enough euros on the table to cover anything Nora ordered.

"Thank you for the invitation, but spending any more time with you publicly could have grave consequences. I have enough complications to deal with already. Good night, and good luck, Miss Mossa. I'll be in touch. This may require us to touch base again later."

CHAPTER 6

THE COMICAL CONTRAST of the large man walking a dog he could crush with his bare hands led Karina Marchenko to express what for her was a smile. Even when not cloaked in the shadow of darkness, she was a difficult woman to read. Her results, though, spoke volumes. There was no such thing as walking a straight line for her, but she knew the world would be a better place without one of her countrymen.

For a hundred thousand dollars, she would have gladly disposed of Dmitri Nevsky herself. However, that wasn't what she was being paid to do. The American had made it clear he wanted the privilege of doing that himself. Marchenko was present in part because, if he failed, she'd have to intercede. The thought of Nevsky surviving was the stuff of nightmares. He had the clout and means to exact retribution in the most barbaric of ways.

Nevsky wasn't a creature of habit. The same didn't hold true for the family Australian terrier. It required a late-night elimination stroll before resting until mid-morning. Nevsky had no one to blame but himself, since he often kept late hours on a disjointed schedule. He didn't protest the 2 a.m. walk because it gave him the chance to sneak in one or two cigarettes away from the constant nagging of his wife, who campaigned incessantly for him to quit.

Nevsky savored a long drag on one of those cigarettes, sending smoke upward, waiting for the light to change on Tverskoy Boulevard. At this hour, he normally didn't wait for the light to be in his favor, but there were enough vehicles still motoring through to make one cautious.

The Australian terrier sat patiently. Beyond the crosswalk lay the entrance to the spacious boulevard park. They would have the expansive kingdom pretty much to themselves at this hour, save for a harmless straggler or two. Nevsky had a friend in his pocket for anyone stupid enough to challenge him. This was his home turf, both a strength and weakness at the same time. The area was safe, and residing a couple of blocks away, he knew every inch very well. Familiarity also lulled him into letting his guard down. He'd dismissed his bodyguards hours ago so they could start fresh later today.

From her vantage point, Marchenko saw the man who'd paid her a sizable amount of money sitting on a bench to the right of the boulevard's entrance. Lampposts positioned throughout the park offered measured security to those squeamish about what darkness potentially hid.

Alex looked over his shoulder to see Nevsky shrouded in a puff of smoke. If true to form, he and his dog would make a right turn upon entering the park. Alex had no expectation he'd go unnoticed. Nevsky would have him on his radar the moment he entered the park. However, inadequate lighting at such a distance would make identification impossible. The plan Alex and Marchenko had rehearsed at night in the park was simple. Get noticed, then disappear. Give Nevsky something to think about. Make him search for what he couldn't find. A distraction from the shadows would shift his attention, allowing the real threat to get in position. The potential hiccup involved the method of execution. Nevsky wouldn't hesitate to drop a threat. The logical thing to do was attack first. But that wasn't how the man on the bench wanted it go. For him, this was personal. Marchenko had her reasons for being here, but she also wanted to wake up tomorrow.

She had been adamant in advising, "Get the drop on him, and take him out. End of discussion."

For months, Alex had prepared for this moment. A near-death altercation had convinced him to enhance his skills. His physicality and martial arts training weren't enough to get the job done. Though he dabbled in the finer aspects of mixed martial arts, no-holds-barred fighting tested him the most. During the final weeks of preparation, his instructors flipped the switch on him. He paid the price for being hesitant—a vital lesson learned. Even now, when he moved a certain way, slight pain pinched at his right side from where "Smash" Sanchez had caught him flush with a blazing kick. He watched a recording after so he could slow down for confirmation of what she had done in the ring. He'd earned Smash's respect by staying upright. He declared himself ready a couple of weeks later when Marchenko got back in touch.

Killing is never easy for a man of conscience. Dmitri Nevsky wasn't that type of person. He had committed many atrocities in his lifetime without remorse, and without reprisal. That was about to change.

The streetlight clicked to yellow. Nevsky looked down at his demure companion as he flicked his cigarette nub airborne. He paused before placing a foot in the intersection, then backed away a step as a car raced to make the yellow light. Right on its tail, less than a car length behind, was a nondescript minivan. Their roaring engines were loud, but when each applied their brakes, the screeching was deafening.

The minivan stopped in front of Nevsky to cut him off. Alex rose from the bench and saw two occupants of the car exit on the passenger side with what looked like guns drawn. The minivan blocked

Nevsky from view. Alex heard the men from the car shout in Farsi, "Hurry! Hurry!"

Alex sprinted toward the crosswalk opening that Nevsky should have been walking through. The commotion led a confounded Marchenko to step out from the shadows. The minivan rocked several times, and the two men rushed back to the open doors of the car. Doors shut, the vehicles burned rubber tearing down Tverskoy Boulevard.

When Alex reached the crosswalk, the Australian terrier, its owner nowhere in sight, greeted him. Bending to calm the nervous dog, Alex tried to decipher what had taken place.

He also wondered what to do with the dog.

CHAPTER 7

ALEX KOVES SAT on the hood of the vehicle he'd been provided, staring across the Moskva River at the structures and lights of the Moscow International Business Center. He didn't turn to acknowledge Karina Marchenko's car pulling up. The vehicle crawled to a stop next to his. Alex didn't bother confirming it was Marchenko. This was the planned rendezvous location. He should have been euphoric, but the complete opposite boiled inside him.

Marchenko exited from the rear of the car, and a burly man from the front passenger side joined her. Alex could no longer keep his frustration under wraps. He slid off the hood and confronted Marchenko. "You want to tell me what the hell that was back there?"

The man in front of her frowned and extended his big stop sign of a hand, tacking it to Alex's chest. Without hesitation, Alex angled his chest so that the man's hand followed. Alex delivered a swift, fierce downward blow, the force of which nearly broke the man's arm. Then Alex placed a kick behind the man's knee. Rather than let him fall to the ground, Alex grabbed the back of his head and slammed his face against the hood of the car. Alex released his grip, letting the man drop. Alex stood directly in front of Marchenko. The driver got out in a hurry, but Marchenko pointed her finger his way.

"Stay in the car," she ordered. She looked at her fallen colleague. "That was uncalled for."

"He put his hand on me, and right now, I'm a wee bit touchy. Nothing broken except maybe his nose. He'll be all right."

"To answer your concern, like you, I don't know what the hell that was back there."

"A complete surprise?"

"Yes!"

"You were on Nevsky for about a month. You claim you know the man. Hard to believe this comes as a shock."

Marchenko flipped her hair back. She strode to the sidewalk, resting against the railing separating her and the river. Alex followed.

"This is on me," Marchenko reluctantly said.

"Ya think?"

"Fuck you. This is my reputation on the line here."

"And my money."

"Your money's not the issue. I'll give your money back, if that's what you want. But, either way, I will find out what this is." Marchenko shook her head. "They knew, just like we did, where to take him. Where he was most vulnerable. They must have been watching like we were."

Alex thought about the possibility. "Did you take photos? Video, during your surveillance?"

"Yes. Of course," Marchenko responded, her irritation at the question clear. She then registered what he was getting at. "Damn it," she blurted out, rushing to her vehicle. She called out over her shoulder, "Go back to your hotel. I'll be in touch."

Marchenko sidestepped her slow-moving employee, who was being helped to his feet by the driver.

"Stop bleeding and feeling sorry for yourself. Get in the car. We have work to do."

CHAPTER 8

DMITRI NEVSKY HAD lain motionless for about a half hour on what was an uncomfortable mattress for a man his size. Zip ties secured his hands and feet. He was conscious, the fog of confusion lifted. Pretending to still be knocked out had let him learn little details about his captors.

Iranians.

He didn't have to hear a spoken word. The smells gave them away. They were from delicacies he had no passion for but that he knew all too well, having worked with the people who indulged. Preparing Haleem was time consuming and often symbolized a special occasion. Nevsky assumed his apprehension qualified. The aroma of fresh-baked Lavash bread also filled the air. The meal was being washed down with sweet tea based on what sounded like sugar cubes being sucked. Nevsky had identified three different voices. With his anger growing by the minute, it was time to discover why he was here.

The springs underneath the thin mattress squeaked as Nevsky stirred to sit up. His movement caused chairs to scrape over a hard surface. The voices and eating came to an abrupt stop. A figure hurried out the door, leaving two muscular men who stood balanced, guarding against the unexpected. Their level of concern said a lot considering his hands and feet were restrained. There was much to gain by being patient.

Minutes of silence passed before the man who ran out of the room returned, flanked by two more people. The guards in the room monitored the immobile Nevsky as if he were a bear emerging from hibernation, dangerously capable of anything.

Nevsky swallowed, the act difficult because he only had a sliver of saliva in his throat. The last man to enter the room was in charge. He was more relaxed than the rest—lean, neatly groomed, and dressed in expensive clothing. His shoes glistened from a recent shine. He consulted a folder held in his manicured hands. Closing it, he examined Nevsky's alertness.

"Free him," the man ordered, a hint of dissatisfaction in his voice. The smallest of the men, the one who'd run out of the room, nervously cut Nevsky loose with a pair of scissors.

Nevsky massaged his wrists to aid in circulation. The well-dressed man offered him bottled water. Looking through bloodshot eyes, the Russian took it.

"I apologize for my colleagues' disrespectful treatment," the man said, his voice polished, confident. "There was, regrettably, a lack of communication."

Nevsky wanted to test just how remorseful they were. "I'm not surprised. I've seen it before from you people."

The man didn't flinch. "We deserve that one. My name is Shahbod Gilani." He extended a hand, only to pull it back when the gesture was ignored. "I arrived in town just a short while ago. This should have been handled differently, I assure you."

"And what exactly is this? Do you know who I am?"

"For sure, Mister Nevsky. As you can see, the men behind me have much respect for your reputation. I'd offer you food, but I know it's not to your liking. I can have someone go get you something if you'd wish."

Nevsky felt stronger by the minute; the drug injected to apprehend him was wearing off. "I don't intend to be here long."

"And we don't want to keep you, either."

"So?" Nevsky said, an unimpressed look on his face.

"Yes, now that you're awake and responsive, we'll get right to it." Gilani requested a chair. He began speaking again before sitting down. "Let me take you back to an airfield outside Tbilisi."

Nevsky knew every detail about the night in question. He and his men, in several trucks filled with designer centrifuges, had waited on the tarmac of a remote airfield while a bevy of Iranians loaded cargo onto a transport plane. The transfer had gone according to plan. What happened afterward had been a surprise to all parties. Regardless, this was too much a one-sided conversation for Nevsky's comfort.

"Who are you?" Nevsky asked, his eyes covering everyone in the room.

"We represent certain interests of the Iranian government," Gilani paused, a sour look on his face. "Make that certain angry elements of the government. So please, walk me through that night."

Nevsky understood this was not unlike a test in school. The key to getting a good grade was showing the instructor you grasped material he already understood to be true. There was no room for interpretation. The facts were absolute, as there were plenty of witnesses present that night to corroborate the details.

"The sooner you answer my questions, Mr. Nevsky, the sooner you walk out of here."

Gilani was a pretentious little asshole, Nevsky surmised. He could reach out and snap his neck before the guards had a chance to react. The only thing that held him back was the uncertainty of what was behind the door.

Nevsky addressed his dry mouth with another drink of water.

"We waited for Mr. Green to show up. He was late. As per pre-arranged instructions—from your people—they couldn't load anything until he inspected and approved the merchandise."

"Mr. Green was late. Why?"

"You'd have to ask him, but I guess it was because he brought along an associate. The instructions were for him to come alone."

"Mr. Green said this Mr. McBride was a colleague?"

"Yes. Again, you should ask him. Mr. Green was your middleman."

Gilani wrote a shielded note in the folder. Nevsky felt the Iranians were having the same problem he'd encountered. Mr. Green was off the grid, a ghost in hiding with a sizeable windfall. He should have died that night, but Nevsky was sure he had Mr. McBride to thank for that.

Gilani stopped writing. He pulled a photograph from the folder and handed it to Nevsky. "Tell me more about McBride."

Nevsky stared at the photograph with hidden anger. McBride had to be the reason three of his men had died that night. Just like Mr. Green, his name was an alias. Earnest efforts to locate him had hit a black hole. The organization Nevsky worked for had uncovered Mr. Green's real name, but McBride remained a mystery. Anonymity like that came at a high price, often shielded by either large corporations or government agencies. Until located, McBride was a fairy tale.

This was where Nevsky told the instructor what he already knew in order to expedite his departure. There were many Iranians on the tarmac that night; any of them could have relayed what had happened.

"He didn't seem to fit the job description, so I tested his qualifications," Nevsky said. "Instead of Mr. Green, I initially had McBride inspect a centrifuge to sign off on. Mr. Green protested, but I insisted. I tried to trick him, but McBride knew the specifics, the technology. Mr. Green then completed inspection on his own. At that point, from my understanding, all was as it should have been. Does that match with what you have in your folder?"

Gilani retrieved the photo from Nevsky. "One more question. You and McBride have no prior relationship?"

Nevsky had pondered that as well. Their encounter had left him with an uneasy feeling. When the men sent to get rid of them turned up dead, Nevsky had thought harder. Too many faces over the years clouded his memory. They could have crossed paths anywhere. Hours of concentration failed to stir up a name or situation.

Nevsky rose to his feet, forcing the two big Iranians behind Gilani to shift into readiness. "None that I can think of," the Russian said, a dare in his eyes. "Now, if there's nothing else, we're done here."

Gilani sat back. "Yes, we're finished for now. You may leave."

Nevsky took a step closer to Gilani, and his bodyguards inched closer too. "We're done for good. Don't forget where you are," Nevsky said. He walked toward the door. "One other thing."

"Yes?"

"My dog better be okay."

Gilani addressed the others with a raised eyebrow after Nevsky's exit. "What damned dog?"

CHAPTER 9

KARINA MARCHENKO TOOK the equivalent of a catnap in the backseat. The Do Not Disturb sign in her brain blocked out the stop-and-go jerks of the sedan as it navigated through some of Moscow's busiest streets, horns blaring with irritability. The stolen minutes would hardly erase the nearly twenty-four straight hours she'd been awake. Her associates did their best to give her space to rest. They sighed every time someone cut them off in traffic, resisting the urge to pound the horn in protest. Each tap of the brake had the driver take a sneak peek in the rear-view mirror, fearing it would awaken the fiery dragon.

They'd scrutinized hours of video and photo surveillance of Dmitri Nevsky. Finally, Marchenko had spotted what should have been obvious, considering her team's expertise. The oversight was inexcusable. They had missed it during real-time surveillance because they didn't consider anyone else to be stupid enough to have an interest in the Russian thug.

The sedan turned off Lubyanka Square onto Maly Cherkasskiy Lane, squeezing into a tight parking place midway down the block.

The bruised-faced man in the front seat waited two songs on the radio before waking up Marchenko.

"Karina, we're here."

Marchenko's fatigued eyes came alive. She cleared her throat and got out with backpack in hand. It was approaching noon on a sunless, rain-threatening day, the kind of cloudy, dark day most of the world probably had in mind when they thought of Moscow. Marchenko welcomed the cool slap of air on her face. The entrance to Coffeemania was a step away. She pressed a forearm against her left side to keep her lightweight overcoat from flying open. The weight of the semi-automatic pistol strapped into the lining had a tendency to pull. She glimpsed her employee's blue and dark purple face as he opened the door for her. Sergei was talented, but in an instant, the American had taken him down. Once again, she rethought her opinion of the foreigner.

Alex watched them drive up from his seat next to a bank of tall windows. He'd chosen this place not for any strategic reason, but because he enjoyed sightseeing and experiencing new places. He saw nothing wrong in mixing pleasure with business if the opportunity presented itself. He'd seen photos of Coffeemania's grand café and wanted to try it in person. The decor of marble and wood flooring, with art deco chandeliers and latticework, gave the expansive establishment a rich and classy feel while maintaining comfort.

Two things stood out as his expected party approached. Marchenko had that "cramming for finals all night" look, and under daylight conditions, Alex saw his handiwork. Sergei, he believed was the man's name, had taken the full brunt of a momentary lapse of control. Alex hadn't meant to be so rough, but he wasn't about to apologize. He would bet Sergei was here, without bandages, to prove he had taken his best shot and was still functioning. Fair enough.

Marchenko mumbled a greeting before settling in next to Alex. Sergei sat where he had a clear view of the sedan parked on the street. He also had the interior covered should anyone questionable approach from the next room. Marchenko reached into her back-pack to retrieve a laptop.

Alex referenced the large pot of coffee surrounded by cups on the table. "Help yourself. I figured you might have had a long night."

Marchenko accepted the offer. "It was a long night, but worth it."

She drank her coffee black and took a sip before setting up the laptop.

"Show and tell," Alex said, finishing a croissant.

Marchenko was learning to ignore the American's flippant remarks. "I owe you an apology for last night. We should have been better prepared. I expect to have more details on the other party involved within the hour, if not sooner. Let me show you what we discovered this morning after going over photos and video. They went to great lengths to stay concealed," she pointed out, referencing the day and night footage. "Rarely did they use the same vehicle or same people. Two faces were present more than others, though. I assume they ran point. We blew up the video and photos to get license plate numbers. They came back registered to people with Arabic names."

That made total sense to Alex, since the men who'd grabbed Nevsky had spoken Farsi. "If I had to guess, I'd say they're Iranians."

"You don't seem surprised."

"On one hand, no. On another, it's puzzling. He's a man who's worked in many corners of the world, not exactly making friends at every stop."

"True, but this could also be a local dispute. Nevsky is second in command of a powerful crime syndicate. They have their hands in black market business all over Europe, the Middle East, and even in your country."

"I've seen his work."

"Then you know, as I've been telling you, he's a very dangerous man. Enjoys getting his hands dirty, which is why I've suggested you keep your distance by just using a sniper rifle and be on your way."

"Told you, I want him to know who's putting him down."

"Fine. Call him on the phone right before you blow his head off." Marchenko looked away. It was stupid to take this risky route. "Our plan has to change. After last night, he'll be extra careful. Probably change his routine, and might have his well-armed detail provide extended security for a while. Damn Muslims."

The reference got Sergei to snicker in a way that was both mocking and disapproving. Alex spoke to him for the first time. "I take it you don't approve?"

Sergei looked as if he'd unexpectedly taken a bite of some bitter candy. "On Russian soil?" he uttered, the taste getting worse. "No. They don't belong here. Where is their history of making this country better? They're like that fish of your country." He snapped his fingers, trying to remember. "Catfish. Bottom feeders. They come here, many undocumented, take jobs, send the money back home, and want all kinds of rights. They want more mosques in the city. And in the North Caucasus district, there's a king-sized bed of Islamist militants. Stalin is probably turning over in his grave."

Alex was positive he was staring at the Russian equivalent of a redneck. He glanced at Marchenko to see if she was in agreement.

"Sergei is a fourth-generation Russian," Marchenko said with a sly smile. "A part of him embraces the old ways."

"Moscow must be Slavic," Sergei chimed in. "These immigrants influence our life, not in a good way. We don't go to live in their homelands, but they come here, are quick to bitch and moan about living conditions and rights. If things are so bad, stay home. Make where you're from a better place." Sergei gave up with a flailing of hands.

"Much like your country, we have an immigration problem," Marchenko provided, sensing Alex was trying to grasp an understanding of Sergei's deep-rooted feelings. "When we were under Communist rule, it oppressed Islam and other religions. Now that we're not, it's opened the gates to commerce and enterprise, but with those gates open, other things rush through. I guess it's just one more thing we can blame the West for. Nearly two million Muslims live in Moscow alone. This is unfathomable, but I read it's estimated that by 2050, Moscow will be predominantly Muslim. Let that sink in for your image of Red Square."

"Somehow, I don't foresee the Slavs ever relinquishing total control," Alex said.

"Or the powerful men who run this world," Marchenko added. "The one-percenters will always come out on top."

It was important for Alex to understand the sentiments of both enemies and friends. Present company were neither. Marchenko came highly recommended, but she was being paid to do a job. In terms of trust, reputation played high on a resume. Alex was about to ask Marchenko what the next move was when her phone buzzed. She answered without hesitation.

The conversation was mostly one-sided as Marchenko listened. She checked her watch and said, "We'll be there within the hour. Good work." She listened for a few more seconds. "Interesting. No reason to stay on top of him. Might be too dangerous at this point. Again, good work." She ended the call and put the laptop away.

Alex waited for the update. Marchenko drained the remnants of her coffee cup.

"We need to go," she addressed Alex. "My men have detained two people who should be able to shed light on last night's activities. As for Nevsky, he just returned home, unharmed."

CHAPTER 10

THE SEDAN TRAVELED east away from Moscow, crossing the snaking Moskva River more than once. The monotonous ride continued on a two-lane country road until the sedan turned onto a patchy mix of concrete and dirt.

Thick forest blanketed both sides of the road, offering natural security. Nothing on this stretch of road said, "welcome" to strangers. The sedan eased to a stop, its progress impeded by a closed, rusty gate. Sergei got out to swing the gate open. The sedan pulled ahead, leaving him to relock the gate and follow a short distance on foot. A bend to the left revealed a circular drive and unassuming one-and-a-half-story house. The house was in desperate need of a paint job. Weather-beaten shutters framed dingy windows. There was a two-car garage, but the sedan parked behind a minivan with tinted windows.

Casual inspection revealed the house and property were in the late stages of neglect. Out of the sedan, Alex discovered contradictions. Camouflaged high up, in a big, leafy tree next to the driveway, was a security camera. Climbing steps to the house, Alex noticed more cameras dotting the roofline, angled toward the entrance, moving as he did. In a house like this, you'd expect the door to be brittle and worn. Instead, Marchenko slid a box open to access a panel requiring her to input a code. A click of mechanisms and the door unlocked. Marchenko had to lean against the door to open it because the material was thick wood on the front and reinforced steel on the back.

The interior décor told a different story than the neglect outside. The entry fed into a large family room, complete with sofas, chairs, a wood-burning fireplace, and a big-screen television. The room flowed into the kitchen area equipped with a small table and chairs. A narrow hallway off the kitchen led to the back of the house, where two bedrooms were located. The partial second level was accessed via a stairway to the right of the family room. Next to it was a carbon copy of the main entrance door, complete with entry code box.

Dressed in a tank top and jeans, a man emerged from a bathroom. His face bore fresh scars, and judging by the flexing of his right hand, his bruised knuckles were from recent use. Marchenko greeted him halfway. She held his face in her hand, inspecting the damage.

"One of them protested rather vigorously," he informed her. "I had to restrain him."

She patted his face with care and pressed on to one of the bedrooms, motioning for Alex to follow. There was a queen-sized bed wedged against a corner wall, but it was hardly the focal point. Eating up most of the space was a two-tiered desk that housed seven monitors with corresponding recorders. A demure, middle-aged man took off a pair of headphones upon seeing Marchenko enter. He slid his chair back, giving her room to view what he had been monitoring. Five of the monitors kept watch of the outside perimeter. They sufficiently covered the gate area Sergei had opened, the circular drive, and the front and back of the house. The other monitors captured scenes from identical rooms. The occupants in them were a study in contrasts.

The two men looked to be of Middle Eastern descent. One breathed heavily into his bloodstained shirt, his body appearing to have given up resisting any further. The other man seemed untouched. He sat rigid, trancelike. His eyes were closed, his breathing controlled. The words he uttered were based in prayer.

Sergei chuckled, "Allah doesn't know about this place."

"Are we ready?" Marchenko addressed Tank Top.

"You say the word," he responded, drying off his hands with a towel.

"Let's get started, then. Hopefully, this won't take long."

CHAPTER 11

THE ORDER HAD been precise. Nora was to stay out of Rome. To the best of her recollection, not a word was said about Venice.

One could grasp that since Rome was specifically mentioned, the order implied Italy altogether was off limits. Nora didn't see it that way. Since she was serving a strict suspension, they should have specifically detailed the limitations. Venice hadn't come out of anyone's mouth.

She embraced the pastel-blue sky, slow-moving white puffs swiped across its landscape. The sun felt invigorating. It was a good day to be alive, and the day was about to get even better. Nora bobbed in unison with the moored, twenty-two-foot runabout that danced to the wake created by the Grand Canal. She'd paid a gondola operator a pretty steep price to use the prime boat slip spot for a short period.

To pass the time, she watched boisterous, fashion-challenged tourists canvas the Rialto Bridge, a checkmark of must-see attractions. Easy to find and navigate, it was the ideal meeting place. The precise rendezvous point was near the water adjacent to the Hotel

Rialto. Her appointment was late, but that was fine. Nora was only a few weeks away from having to go back to work. There was no rush on her part. Besides, she had also paid a small fortune to rent the boat. The captain's hat was thrown in at no extra cost.

From the crowd of short shorts, some skin too pale and postures lacking an active lifestyle, Nora located what produced a satisfying grin. He stood out among the masses. Tall and muscular, he wore a light-colored T-shirt that struggled to contain his biceps. His sweatpants looked as if they'd been ripped away from an athletic store mannequin. Even though he concealed himself behind sunglasses, and walked to the beat of whatever music flowed through his earbuds, Nora could tell he was searching for her. He arrived near the water's edge, facing the Hotel Rialto to make sure. He glanced left and right with anticipation. Shouting to compete with all the surrounding noise was senseless, so Nora pulled out her cell phone and sent a text telling him to turn around. Message received, he did an about-face to see her posing with arms crossed. He took out his earbuds.

"Hey Sailor," Nora called out. "Want a ride?"

Duncan Anderson didn't hold back his joy. "My, my. You do travel in style. Permission to come aboard, Captain?"

"Permission granted, with pleasure."

Duncan boarded, giving Nora a huge bear hug. She planted a kiss and told him how great it was to see him. She had him untie the line to the dock, then backed the boat away to join the busy traffic of the canal.

Referencing a cooler in the second row of seats, Nora said, "Grab a drink. First time to Venice?"

"Yes, as a matter of fact."

"It's magical. Tonight, we'll have a fabulous dinner, drink too much, and laugh a lot."

"Working?" he asked. "No, wait. You're benched for a while."

"That's correct," she acknowledged. "However, my sabbatical ends in a few weeks."

"So you just decided you needed a sight-seeing buddy?"

"No, Duncan Anderson, but if I did, I couldn't imagine any better company."

"Uh-huh. Well, your message was sugarcoated, and cryptic at the same time. What's up? Me leaving work on a moment's notice isn't good for business."

"Oh, please. You own the company."

"True that, but I try to set a good example for my employees." Duncan popped open a can of beer.

"You look exceptionally fit," Nora observed, swinging the boat a safe distance behind a vaporetto full of people.

"My new workout routine. Plus, I've gained an additional set of skills," Duncan announced with pride.

Nora gave him a sideways look. "Okay, Liam Neeson. New set of skills?"

"Yep. I've been learning Krav Maga."

Nora tried to hold back a giggle. "Duncan . . ."

"Laugh all you want. I bet I can give you a run for your money now."

Nora laughed through the wind. "Maybe you should put that beer back."

Disregarding her advice, Duncan gulped down a sizeable amount. Coming up for air, he belched and laughed with her. The boat ride gave him the opportunity to take in the city's ambiance. So many periods in time reflected and represented by Baroque architecture.

"Absolutely gorgeous. Amazing, when you think about it," Nora said, anticipating what he was thinking.

"Yeah, though a touch of paint wouldn't hurt here and there," Duncan offered, noting that several colors were no longer the vibrant hues of green, yellow, and red they once were. Whites had faded to various shades of cream. In the foreground, though, stretching out like the arms of metal stickmen, giant cranes proved progress had plans to make use of any available space.

They swayed forward, listening to the sounds cascading from the shore, a melting pot of dialects mixing like a disjointed symphony. Nora felt it was a good time to explore the matter at hand.

"When is the last time you've talked with Alex?" The look on her face let Duncan know it was not merely a question coming from her heart.

"A little over a month ago. I went down to St. Thomas to visit for a few days. Worried about something? You could have asked me this on the phone."

"It's been over two weeks since I've been able to reach him. We'd gotten in the habit of communicating. He hasn't responded lately. Hasn't answered my calls, voice mail, or texts."

"Well, people get busy. He has a job, you know."

"It takes just a few seconds to respond to a text message or email. You got back to me within ten minutes of getting my email, and you run a company."

Duncan had to give her that one. Now that she and Alex were on intimate terms again, he could see where the silence would raise concern.

"Maybe he's doing something for your boss."

Nora had considered that. If true, there was no way she could inquire about it. Work was off-limits. "How was he when you visited?"

Duncan had dismissed much of Alex's daily regimen as a former world-class athlete trying to stay in top condition. But now, he had cause to wonder.

"He worked out hard," Duncan recalled. "Sometimes twice a day, for hours. One night, he showed up for dinner with a few bruises. Said he was just getting into better shape, fine-tuning his martial arts training as part of the process. Other than that, he seemed fine. Again, you could have learned this without inviting me here. So, what's all this really about?"

"I wouldn't have given it this much thought, except I was in Monte Carlo a few days ago, and got a surprise dinner guest. He conveyed some fairly alarming news. Essentially, Alex and I have might have a price on our heads because of what happened in Iran."

Duncan considered getting another beer upon hearing that. "Great, people out gunning for you. How would this person who approached you know that?"

Nora overtook a waterbus moving too slowly. She smiled and waved back at the fares as she did so, looking every bit a native Venetian. "He claims he's a target too, and wanted to warn us. What's unnerving is that he could find me like he did. He was trying to locate Alex too, but didn't have enough information to go on."

"How does he know Alex?"

"He was there."

"In Iran?"

"Yes. He's the one who helped Alex escape. The one Alex thought was dead."

CHAPTER 12

IT WAS JUST the two of them, and despite floating on a wave of intense pleasure, she dared not scream out his name. He'd supplied her with one to use, but through their association, she knew it was an alias. He had many names. Passports and driver's licenses from different countries backed them up. Anything having to do with his origin was an enigma. That was fine with her; she didn't need to know everything. Didn't want to know everything. This relationship would not have a fairy-tale ending.

He liked refined things, which helped to explain her presence in his life. He always sought control, even now, as he thrust his pelvis into her from behind. Sometimes he was gentle during sex, like a man in love. Sometimes it was rough and distant, like a man paying for the night. He never said much. A less experienced, more emotional woman would have wondered if she was pleasing him, but his erection left little doubt that he was fully engaged.

They had started in missionary position, and then he'd placed her on top. She could tell he was near climax. He held her buttocks tightly, quivering as her back arched, her body tingling and her mind on the edge of a cliff. Whenever she was with him like this, her persona was light years away from the person she was normally. He had done that to her. Over time, she'd tried to convince herself that she needed him, but the truth was she lacked the desire to walk away. A part of her, the part only he saw, wanted this. As long as it wasn't full-time, and she could maintain her other life without the two intersecting, it was therapeutic.

He rolled out of bed without saying a word. She guessed his age to be late forties. His body easily passed for that of a much younger man. Traces of gray wove through a thick crop of well-groomed black hair. He had blue eyes that mesmerized like a magic trick. They smiled when his mouth didn't. When needed, they also warned to proceed with caution.

He put on one of the hotel's lavish robes that accompanied the equally impressive suite. For her, experiencing comforts like this used to be the stuff of vision boards. She caught him glancing at the bedside clock, and casually, she did the same. It was past one in the morning in New York City. He poured himself a scotch, neat. From the ice bucket, he retrieved a bottle of white wine, filled a glass, and brought it to her along with a robe as she sat up. She smiled as she took a sip of the wine before getting out of bed and sliding into the robe. He headed for the terrace, his movement silent on the plush carpeting. Opening the terrace doors let in all the noise associated with the city that never sleeps. He rested against the stone balcony, the night air drying his sweaty body. He nursed the scotch while soaking up the majestic glow of lights from structures of different heights and shapes.

She joined him, the wind flapping her robe open. The rush of air gave her goose bumps, and tousled her long hair, adding to her sensuality. She took a seat at the round, heavy steel table.

"As always, thank you Erik," she said. It was the name he responded to this time around, "Snow" being the surname on the hotel reservation.

His eyes answered, *You're welcome.* His voice switched the subject. "Your impressions?"

Michele Orsette was prepared to provide context from a week of travel and meetings on his behalf. Much had changed since Erik entered her life. She now lived on a quiet street in upscale Birmingham, Michigan. That had previously been a dream she would drive by to keep her motivated.

"These are not nice people," she said.

"Nor am I, occasionally."

"You at least hide it well. These men have little respect for women outside the home. They weren't happy about not dealing with you in person."

"And yet, they deposited half the funds. So you must have been impressive."

Orsette shook her head. "More like insistent they could find someone else if they didn't approve of the terms."

"I never doubt your ability to be persuasive when the time calls for it." He joined her at the table. "The Iranians, or at least President Shahroudi, are on a timetable that's winding down quickly."

"They seemed desperate and nervous."

He let out a polite laugh. "They should be. They're forking over a large sum. If something goes wrong, I may have to consider retiring."

This marked the first time Orsette had heard him bring up the subject of quitting. Doing so would undoubtedly put an end to their relationship. She grasped it had to happen one day.

"If it's too dangerous, perhaps you should pass," Orsette advised, wondering if she had chosen the right words. "I mean, is constantly looking over your shoulder worth the trouble?"

"I can handle myself," Erik said, putting her at ease. "Now, did they get what I asked for?"

"They assured me all your requests are being met."

"Good, because if I feel one thing is out of place or not addressed, I'll walk away—with the money they've deposited. There are no refunds."

"I stressed that to them."

"I'm all set then. I'll arrive in Geneva after my business in Kentucky."

He raised his glass in a silent toast. He could be so caring. Earlier, he'd reminded and encouraged her to make a bedtime call to her children in Michigan. She thought he enjoyed seeing her nurturing side. Perhaps it gave him a sense of comfort having her around. She didn't know that often his nights were restless, filled with uneven sleep. But when she was around, he soundly got through the night. It was hard not to fall in love with him. He was every woman's dream man. Successful. Educated. Attractive. Warm. Caring.

The perfect catch.

That is, if you were willing to overlook that he killed people for a living.

CHAPTER 13

DURING HIS CIA days in Iraq, Alex had seen his share of torture. The public and political outcries of the practices at Abu Ghraib prison were understandable. However, the worst abuses never saw the light day. For extreme cases, the workaround to a potential public relations nightmare was rendition. Outsourcing torture to countries where enemy combatants had zero rights either produced valuable information or eliminated a problem. The interrogators' methods had no limitations. Waterboarding, nails pulled, electrical shock to the testicles—any form of humiliation, including sodomy, was at their disposal.

Alex discovered that the set of heavy interior doors at the house led to a basement containing two soundproof cells. Each was equipped with a camera, a speaker, and monitor mounted out of reach. The concrete floors graded toward a drain centered in the room. The two detained Iranians had to know they were in a desperate situation. The flip of a switch provided each room with the capability of seeing and hearing what was happening in the adjacent one.

"Adds to the pressure for the poor bastard not being worked

on yet," said the middle-aged man to Alex. He manned the control board in the bedroom. "Sit back. It's about to be a good show."

For several minutes, the unmistakable sounds of a man being beaten came through the speakers. Once a question didn't get a satisfactory answer, the man in the tank top wailed away with his fists. Still somehow conscious, the bound man was tougher than he looked.

Standing over the crumpled figure, Tank Top peeled off layers of black tape he wore over his knuckles. He turned to address the camera. "I need to ice my hands before we start on the other one."

The restrained man in the other cell saw and heard everything. He adjusted his posture, eyes glued to the monitor in his cell. The control board operator hit a button that unlocked the cell door so Tank Top could exit. Marchenko entered shortly after, holding a pistol in her right hand.

"I don't have time to play games, Saeed," she said, not an ounce of emotion in her voice. "We'll get answers, eventually. It's not worth dying for. Now, I'll ask one final time. What business did you have with the Russian, Nevsky? Why was he taken?"

The Iranian remained silent, a stream of blood dribbling down his chin. "I know nothing," he spat through bubbles of blood and saliva.

Marchenko raised the gun and fired. The wall behind the Iranian was splattered with brain matter. The force of the blast toppled him over, his body landing in a lifeless thud.

In the other cell, the remaining detainee's pupils were as wide as they could get. He saw Tank Top re-enter the room along with another man he'd never seen before.

"Dump him in the river," Marchenko ordered. "Next we'll see if Qasim has any answers."

Alex watched Tank Top and Sergei drag the dead Iranian out of the room. He addressed the Russian on the control board. "Tell her this has gone too far. We'll find out another way."

"Relax," the Russian responded. "She knows what she's doing."

Alex was about to protest vigorously when he heard Marchenko's voice again. She was in the adjacent cell.

"Qasim, I'm out of patience. We could spend the next several hours making you less of a man, if you get my meaning." Marchenko waved the gun at the Iranian's crotch. "You have two choices. One is to leave here like your fellow countryman. Or—or, you can leave here unharmed, and no one but us will know you spoke of anything. It's a small thing we're asking, Qasim. Die for a cause. Don't die to protect a Russian asshole."

Considering what Qasim had witnessed, the woman was not bluffing. His restraints seemed tighter, and his throat was dry. Qasim sought guidance through prayer. This was not how he saw his life ending.

"Time to decide, Qasim," Marchenko urged. Tank Top slithered into the room, affixing new layers of tape. Sergei followed, pushing a rectangular metal cart that displayed various knives, pliers, small liquid bottles, and a bowl to place discarded items.

Qasim squeezed his clammy hands. He was a decent-sized man. He could take a beating as much as he could dish one out, but this was different. He internally reached out to Allah, but received no response that would help solve his predicament.

Marchenko exhaled. "Have it your way." She picked up a curved, serrated blade and handed it to Tank Top. "He can still hear with one ear."

Tank Top approached Qasim's side. The Iranian stomped his feet to halt him. "Okay! Okay. What do you want to know?"

Marchenko smiled. "Well, you are the smart one. My guy will stay behind you, just in case a tiny lie comes out of your mouth, forcing us to make an adjustment to your appearance."

The Iranian gave Tank Top a concerned look. "There won't be any lies." He turned back to face Marchenko. "Ask your questions."

Still lacking sleep, she wasn't in the mood to drag this out to the extent it could take. For the moment, she holstered the pistol. "Why did you grab the Russian?"

"Orders."

"Qasim, this isn't twenty questions. Whose orders, and why? Be specific."

"Orders from Tehran," Qasim said. Interpreting the look on her face, he added, "I don't know specifically from whom, but someone higher for sure. The Russian was never in any danger. Under no circumstances were we to hurt him. Tehran wanted to know how well the Russian knew someone."

"Who?"

"A man named McBride. Has something to do with an exchange at an airfield in Tbilisi a few months ago."

Without looking away from the monitor, Alex asked the board operator, "The name he just said. What was it?"

"McBride." Alex's interest was noted. He'd pass that along.

"Who is this McBride?" Marchenko probed, now leaning against the door that led to Qasim's freedom.

"That I don't know. They didn't inform us of that. But they want to find him."

"What did Nevsky say? Does he know him?"

"He said he had no prior relationship with McBride. Claimed he met him that night at the airfield, that another party brought him there."

"And that's it? That's what grabbing Nevsky was all about?"

"Yes."

Marchenko rolled her eyes. "This story is so damn boring I believe you, Qasim. You no longer interest me, but you've bought your freedom. We'll knock you out with a sedative. When you wake up, you'll be someplace safe and sound. If you say a word about this, your people will probably kill you for talking. They'll praise you for your honesty, but kill you just the same for what they'll see as betrayal. On my end, we never had this conversation. But remember"—she pointed at the camera—"we have you on video."

Alex greeted Marchenko and Sergei when they appeared from the basement. It was written on his face that he had concerns. Marchenko avoided direct contact and headed to the family room. She opened a cabinet to take out several glasses and a bottle of Zhouravli vodka.

Recalling what had happened the night before, Alex curtailed his emotions. "You took that a little too far, don't you think?"

Marchenko ignored his observation and filled each shot glass, offering one to Alex. When he didn't accept, she shrugged and emptied the glass. Sergei followed suit.

"We needed answers. We got them," Marchenko said, refilling her and Sergei's glasses. "You learned what the Iranians wanted with Nevsky."

Alex made sure his body language gave nothing away. He'd keep the McBride revelation to himself for now. He only knew Marchenko through reputation, and her associates' backgrounds were totally off grid. He didn't want to test the temptation of possibly handing him over to Nevsky or the Iranians if they discovered he was the McBride they were after. A big payday would be in order for such a find. Better to maintain his displeasure with the methods used.

"It went too far," he chided again, declining another offer of vodka.

"I did what I had to do," Marchenko rebuked. She caught Alex off guard by laughing. Unable to refrain, Sergei joined her.

"I really don't see what's so damn funny about this," Alex pointed out.

Marchenko downed another shot and laughed harder. She pointed a finger beyond Alex. "You talking about that dead man?"

As Alex turned to see what she was referencing, laughter erupted from the middle-aged control board operator and Tank Top. Behind them, bloody, but also laughing, and very much alive, was the Iranian Alex saw take a beating and get his brains blown out. They all congregated in the family room.

Marchenko put a robust arm around the bloodstained Iranian. His brains were very much intact. Close up, his battered face revealed a skilled makeup job.

"Meet Sanjar Namazi. Quite the actor, wouldn't you agree?"

Alex raised an eyebrow in appreciation. "You got me."

They all laughed again. "More importantly, we got Qasim," Marchenko clarified. "Sanjar helps us out from time to time. He's a special effects artist by trade."

Quite the production, Alex admitted. "Just curious, why would Sanjar here help you out in this way? Sergei, I gathered you didn't like Muslims."

Sergei looked at Sanjar with affection. "This Muslim. This Muslim I love," he said, raising his glass in a toast.

"Sanjar is also family," Marchenko added. "His sister is married to one of my cousins."

The patter of feet moving across tile distracted Alex. Racing to Marchenko was Nevsky's little dog, its tail excited to be part of the group.

"I'll take that drink now," Alex said.

CHAPTER 14

NORA GOT HER evening started with a Vesper martini. She promised to pace herself. Partaking in a drink made famous by James Bond seemed appropriate. Contrary to belief, spies could be such nerds. She sat behind one of the marble columns in the lobby area of the Hotel Danieli. Duncan wasn't late this time. Out of habit, she was early. People watching, though, had a limited shelf life, especially when mundane conversations didn't have volume control.

She spotted Duncan making his way through the lobby like it was the red carpet at a Hollywood premiere. An entourage of one, he wore a lightweight dark suit. Each stride made an impression. He added extra swagger to his gait when Nora presented herself.

"My, you sure clean up nice," Nora said. "And quite the entrance to go along with it."

Duncan gave her the once-over. "Well, you always set the bar rather high."

"Speaking of the bar, want a drink?"

"Uh, no. I had to take a nap after hanging with you on the boat." Duncan observed the privacy of where Nora had been sitting. "You trying to keep a low profile?"

"Always."

"Anything I should be cautious about?"

"Not at the moment," she answered truthfully. "Were you able to find anything?"

Duncan's head dropped to the side. "You didn't have me come all the way here just because of my good looks."

Nora locked arms with him. He meant the world to her. She knew a few hours after Alex introduced them that he'd become someone special in her life. Not even the breakup with Alex had undone that bond. She didn't see Duncan during that period, but when they reconnected months ago, it was like riding a bicycle after years of inactivity.

"It's a five-minute walk to the restaurant over in Saint Mark's Square." Nora put her head on his muscular arm for a moment.

Outside the hotel, a number of tourists were trying to take artistic selfies and group shots with the setting sun as a backdrop. Vendors were pushing to sell as many of their "Italia" themed merchandise as possible before calling it a night.

"I'm all ears," Nora announced.

"First off, he hasn't responded to my texts—or emails either. But, I can tell you where Alex's phone is. There's no guarantee he's with it, but assuming he's like most people, they'll be together. A few days ago, he was in Berlin. Phone on, easy to establish location. Shortly after, he went dark. Totally. Given that, we have to deal with last points of contact."

"So, you're telling me you don't where he is now."

"Since my people started monitoring twenty-four seven, at considerable overtime pay mind you, Alex has turned his phone back on a few times. That allowed us to run a remote exploit, giving us the ability to establish a backdoor into the baseband processor."

"Sounds very illegal."

"I'll plead the fifth on that. Besides, it's Alex who we're hacking, so no big deal."

"You can tell him that."

"Oh, no. This one is on you. You started this, remember?"

"Screw it. I'm used to taking the heat. Quit burying the lead. Where is he?"

"The last point of contact shows Moscow."

Nora came to an abrupt stop, separating from Duncan. He kept walking and talking and then realized he was alone. He turned to see Nora pull out her cell phone and punch the screen at a stenographer's pace.

Backtracking, Duncan caught up and asked, "What's up?"

She engaged Duncan with a concerned look. "If he hasn't already, I think Alex is about to put himself in harm's way. How much longer can you hang with me?"

"A few more days. I can do business on the road."

Nora returned to her phone, speed punching again. When she finally put her phone away, she grabbed Duncan's hand. "Let's go eat and enjoy the evening. Take my mind off this for a short while." Nora's tone was relaxed. "And you're right, not too much drinking tonight. Maybe just a bottle of wine. We'll have to catch an early afternoon flight to Moscow tomorrow."

"Hold on. You just can't go waltzing into Russia. You need a visa, and usually that's not a turnaround process."

Nora ran her fingers through her hair. "There are several types of visas. The most expeditious one requires an invitation. I have to work the phone while we eat. Someone in Moscow owes me a huge favor. We'll be okay."

CHAPTER 15

NATHAN YADIN WORE a patterned flat cap and reflective sunglasses on a nearly cloudless, warm Saturday afternoon in Hyde Park. He achieved the desired effect. No one gave him a second look.

He started his reconnaissance by renting a paddleboat from the boathouse. He made a point to stay clear of fun seekers navigating the Serpentine River. The Solarshuttle ferry, packed to near capacity, passed him more than once. He mustered a nonchalant wave as some passengers captured the ambiance with their cell phones. The photo would generate likes or favorites on various social media sites. Yadin found it humorous that people largely had no qualms about advertising to total strangers virtually everything about their lives— locations and even the mundane, trivial sharing of what they were eating. It was a sobering, modern-day reality that the most advanced eavesdropping software, and satellite monitoring, didn't produce the detailed intelligence people freely exposed. Yadin imagined, had Twitter been around during World War Two, some idiot, in a moment of self-proclaimed cleverness, probably would have posted on the eve of D-Day something like, "Beautiful night. #Normandy."

Back on shore, Yadin strolled through the park, a copy of today's *Daily Mail* folded in his hand. He found nothing that disturbed him. He expected his party to arrive early despite minor inconveniences. Dr. Mueller had been specific about the instructions to follow, keeping the location secret until a phone call two hours before. They'd be anxious, so he purposely set the meeting for 1 p.m., guaranteeing they'd run into lunch-hour traffic. He wanted them on edge as much as possible.

A half hour later, Yadin watched from a comfortable distance as two shiny four-door sedans rolled across the Serpentine Bridge, heading for the nearest parking area. Finding two available spots, a man from the front passenger seat of each sedan advanced outward in opposite directions. Their scan of the immediate area complete, they returned to their vehicles. Three more men got out. The smaller man in charge directed two of them to follow a much larger one back toward the bridge. The man calling the shots took off down a path that would lead him to his destination in the park. He separated himself from his trailing bodyguard, who kept close watch.

Yadin was satisfied to see three figures making their way to the middle of the bridge. One man slowed the rest down, because despite using crutches, he hugged the railing for support, his right leg in a thick cast. The bullet Yadin had put in Jafar Karimi's knee was debilitating, as planned. The leg would heal in time, but he'd probably walk with a limp for the rest of his life.

Standing next to Karimi was Navid Javadi. With no computer attached, he looked totally out of his element. The muscle accompanying them tried to separate, leaving ample space between the pair. The well-dressed, slender man emerged from the path, searching for the bench he was told to occupy that bordered the water. Seated, his back was to Yadin, his hands purposefully in plain view. One rested on his lap, while the other hugged the top of the bench.

Yadin waited for a group of young people. He fell in line several paces behind them as they headed for the bridge's underpass. When the trio passed the man on the bench, Yadin altered his approach, closing in from the left. The seated figure's attention hung with the joyful youngsters. Yadin was now within arm's length on the man's flank.

"Dr. Mueller, punctual as expected," the man on the bench said without flinching or turning around. "Please, take a seat."

Yadin glanced up toward the bridge. The bodyguard stiffened his stance upon being recognized. Yadin held his position. "I'd prefer not sit with my back to the bridge," he stated.

"As you request. Don't want you to feel uncomfortable. We have much to discuss." He slid to the other side and extended a hand. "Dr. Mueller, my name is Shahbod Gilani."

"I know who you are," Yadin said, completing the handshake. Gilani's name had popped up in the background during preparation for the Natanz operation. They'd never met, but according to Mossad's synopsis, Gilani was a high-ranking member of the Ministry of Intelligence and Security, or MOIS. Directly or indirectly, he was responsible for the deaths of Jews and a logistics supporter for the likes of Hezbollah.

"You are well informed then. Unfortunately, there is much I don't know about you," said Gilani. "Despite my protests, there were strict orders not to vet you regarding the Natanz project." Pausing, Gilani measured his words. "Most unusual set of circumstances." The Iranian studied Dr. Mueller for any sign of uneasiness.

"For what I do, privacy is a necessity," Yadin assured. "Imagine my surprise when I stumbled upon an operation of yours."

"I merely follow orders, but there are questions, Dr. Mueller. Your picture being circulated doesn't have the same meaning as the others you saw. Not at the moment, at least."

Yadin's gaze intensified.

"Just being transparent," Gilani responded to the non-verbal query. "Until days ago, we assumed you were buried in a deep, sandy grave. Imagine our surprise that you had surfaced."

"I barely made it out of there."

"Yes, but you did make it out. Countless others were less fortunate."

"If I hadn't turned off the reactors, your country and some of your neighbors would have endured a far greater and harsher reality. I also got President Shahroudi out in time."

"A fact not lost on him, I assure you," Gilani said. "Several technicians back up your story of staying behind to deal with the reactors."

Yadin had to commend the Iranian's initial intellectual approach. Let the subject know he was held in high regard, give him his due respect. Test him at intervals and measure his responses to find a blip on the radar.

"But, you have some doubts." Yadin let Gilani play the cards he wanted to show.

"I need answers to help fill the gaps on gray areas."

"Ask away. Hopefully, I can provide some clarity."

"Very well. You are being most cooperative."

"I sense the stakes are high," Yadin replied, not wanting to come across as too comfortable or confident.

"Let's start by going back to that fateful day at Natanz. Dr. Mueller, I am a true believer. I wouldn't be in this position if that weren't the case." Gilani now addressed his bench mate with firmness. "If need be, I'm prepared to give my life for my country and beliefs."

Yadin had heard those exact sentiments before. When driven to the brink of existence, few remained so loyal. Perhaps Gilani was the exception. Yadin hoped he'd get to find out one day.

"I sense, Dr. Mueller, that you aren't motivated by such ideology," Gilani continued. "I presume money and personal gratification are what get you up in the morning. We paid you millions for your work on Natanz, respecting your insistence on total anonymity and secrecy. What I can't wrap my mind around, given your motivation, is why you would risk your life to save others?"

"I wasn't successful in saving the facility."

"No, but as you said, you prevented a far greater tragedy from happening. The death toll and destruction to the area could have been cataclysmic. My country, in particular, would have suffered the worst. Most, if not all of it, would have been uninhabitable if you hadn't shut down the reactors. Why then, Dr. Mueller? Why risk it all?"

"The answer isn't complicated, and it might disappoint you. There was no other option. Had those reactors remained active, the radiation released into the atmosphere would have guaranteed a slow, painful death."

"Your answer is self-preservation then. The acts of a desperate man," Gilani observed. "That is plausible. How did you get out? Even with the reactors secured, the facility continued to crumble from explosions."

"I extensively helped with design modifications. Structurally, I knew where the strongest points were and prayed they'd stay intact long enough for me to reach the surface."

"Not your time and place. Praise to Allah."

"Someone was watching over me."

"Salvage teams are still digging at Natanz. Investigators are sorting through every item discovered, trying to find a cause for what went so horribly wrong. Have you formed any speculation? Natanz was built with some materials you helped to procure. Your blueprints were vital."

Yadin switched into prickly Dr. Mueller mode. It was the right avenue to take with Gilani, since he was trying to get a rise out of him by questioning his expertise. "I inspected a lot of the essential shipments prior to their arrival. I mandated that once they were on site, technicians thoroughly do the same. Not once, but several times. I even insisted said materials get tested on a rotating schedule once installed."

Yadin was sure Gilani already knew that to be true, but he wanted to gauge the doctor's response to the inquiry. Again, another clever attempt to discover a piece that didn't fit.

Dr. Mueller eased off the throttle. "Without examining physical evidence, I can't pinpoint blame any more than your investigators have. I know for a fact, though, that there was a malfunction in the centrifuge housing area. A large enough event could have triggered a domino effect."

The country's remaining top-notch technicians and engineers had told Gilani that without concrete evidence to rule it out, such a scenario was conceivable. "I'm correct in pointing out that you oversaw the centrifuges?" It wasn't so much a question as it was an accusation.

"I helped to specify what kind of device to construct, and even directed the Natanz team on where they could get it done away from prying eyes." Dr. Mueller was aware that Gilani thought he was on to something. "I didn't, however, inspect or approve the last shipment delivered."

"Why didn't you? Quality control was your responsibility."

The circumstances were fresh in Yadin's mind. The appearance of a stranger had startled him. Inspecting the centrifuges and clearing them as operational was his responsibility, but Mr. McBride, or later Alex, had done that for him. McBride was now the perfect scapegoat.

"I was prepared to inspect the centrifuges as a final check before declaring everything operational. I was told it wasn't necessary. You can verify that with President Shahroudi. Something tells me you already have."

Gilani didn't enjoy being predictable. The good doctor exhibited above-average intelligence for more things than just engineering and blueprints. "Yes, a Mr. McBride approved the installation. He even cleared the shipment beforehand. I'm told they introduced you to him at Natanz. You'd never seen him before?"

Yadin hunched his shoulders for effect. "Never. I found his presence on site for the first time puzzling on such a pivotal day. But, your people vouched for him, so I let it pass. Shahroudi was in go mode."

Gilani couldn't press that issue. Though weakened and unlikely to win re-election, Shahroudi still wielded power. This witch-hunt was proof of that. Gilani couldn't go back to Shahroudi and tell him, "If you weren't in such a hurry, this might never have happened."

Gilani clasped his hands. "Dr. Mueller, you've been able to provide useful insight. I appreciate your cooperation." Turning his attention to the bridge overpass, Gilani offered a smile. "A favor, please. Don't shoot any more of my people. I admit they shouldn't have been in the field to begin with, but as you well know, one can't oversee everything."

"Glad to ease some of your concerns. Any luck in finding this McBride? If I can be of any help, let me know. I may have contacts that might be of assistance with your search."

Gilani produced a blank stare. "I will accept all the help I can get on this matter. Your credentials have checked out."

"My credentials?"

"Yes, sorry. We were forced to break our agreement once you were officially missing. We exhausted countless resources to find you. None of your former colleagues or employers had heard from you, either."

Yadin remained outwardly calm. A background check into Dr. Mueller being authenticated could mean only one thing. Mossad had kept his cover story active. They would speculate now with questions of their own. One of the deadliest assassins in their storied history, the man who had earned the nickname "The Devil," might still be in play. Why hadn't he checked in? Did his absence have anything to do with the death of his handler and mentor, Yosef Ezra?

Mossad would definitely seek answers.

CHAPTER 16

DANIEL SHARON WAS not in a good mood. He bypassed the smells of bakeries, coffee, and a cheese shop without hesitation. It was a true test of will since he had a proclivity for all of them. This particular Parisian afternoon, Sharon had blinders on because his short fuse was lit.

Summoned!

What the hell was that! He wasn't a damned civil servant. People who worked in corporations with a HR department got "summoned." Not him. Not a member of Mossad's elite Kidon division. There weren't many of them, and for good reason. They operated in secrecy. They killed that way and sometimes died that way. Because of the intense nature of their work, they also burned out faster. The job offered certain privileges and demanded respect, which was why you didn't get "summoned" out of the blue.

For effect, he lingered to admire the abundant floral offerings on display outside Les Floralies flower shop. Enough time wasted, he marched inside, encountering a female clerk stemming roses behind the counter.

"Bon après-midi, monsieur," she cheerfully greeted.

"Bonjour."

"Comment puis-je vous aider?"

Sharon relayed he was here to pick up three-dozen yellow roses. The clerk informed him she was still working on his order. He could wait in back if he liked.

"Merci," Sharon responded, heading for the door she'd gestured to. Behind it, a stairway led to another door on the second floor. He was about to apply a second soft knock when the door swung open.

The familiar face of his Mossad case officer invited him in. The protesting started the moment Sharon entered. "Shit, Jeremy, is this necessary? Totally against the norm." Sharon stopped bitching when he noticed they were not alone. Seated on a sofa by the window was a fellow Kidon member, one he'd worked an assignment with before.

Jeremy stayed by the door. "Introductions aren't necessary."

Lisa Neril acknowledged Sharon's presence with a nod. They had worked together—about three weeks, if memory served her right. She had been brought on board an operation when it looked to be heading in the wrong direction. Most of the other men had resented the implication that they needed her. Sharon hadn't shared their sentiment. His attitude had been to try anything to make the operation a success. Neril's role of seductress wound up being a difference maker. And, she did it without complaining or roasting the dissenters. The other men on that operation discovered she was not someone to second-guess.

Sharon waited for Jeremy to start filling in the blanks. He didn't hear what he expected.

"It doesn't happen often, Daniel. Next time, do as you're told," Jeremy chastised.

"I'm here, aren't I?" Sharon responded defensively.

"Always a pleasure. Now if you'll excuse me." He opened the door. "Neril." He bowed his head in respect, then exited.

Confused, Sharon turned to Neril, who offered no explanation.

Movement from the kitchen distracted him. He couldn't see the person, but when the man holding a cup of coffee revealed himself, Sharon bristled.

For security reasons alone, Yariv Rozen, the chief of Mossad, hardly ever left Israel, and certainly not with such an apparent lack of security. One could reason that with two of Kidon's best in the room, there was at least an expectation of safety. Regardless, it was a risk. Judged by those who did the job, Rozen was the perfect person to occupy the position. He wasn't just a political appointee who had kissed all the right asses. He'd spent the better part of his life getting his hands dirty, working his way to the top. Rozen understood the trials and tribulations of the people who risked everything. He was considered a master strategist; rumors flourished that when he was in the field, he liked to work up close. Huge, thick hands gave the tale credence.

"Daniel, I'll try not to use up too much of your time," Rozen said between sips of coffee.

"Sorry . . . had I known," Sharon mumbled, moving to sit next to Neril, who fought the urge to smile.

Rozen handed them sealed folders from an end table. "In the time we have here, you must familiarize yourself with the contents. You'll discuss them with no one. Should this meeting ever come up, I expect you to have a very selective memory. If that in any way gives you concern, you may leave now."

Sharon and Neril peeked at each other to establish a mutual understanding of compliance.

"Good. We can proceed. Open the folders. Consume the contents while I highlight the specifics," Rozen instructed.

The folders contained photographs, copies of emails, and summation notes. They'd seen similar ones many times. One thing was very different, however.

"Yes," Rozen acknowledged, catching the furrowed brow that bounced from one to the other upon reading certain sections. "A lot of the file has to do with Yosef Ezra. I'm sure you've heard the whispers. As far as intelligence officers go, he was one of the best. Devoted to his homeland. One could surmise he was overzealous in establishing his legacy. You're well aware of the outrage his death created. Not since Rabin has such a high-ranking official been assassinated within our borders. That there was so little evidence makes matters even worse. Those responsible remain at large. An operation carried out with such precision has people on edge. It's like something out of our playbook."

Sharon looked up. "You aren't suggesting . . ."

"It's on the table. Ezra solely handled one high-value asset. He handpicked him and molded him into a lethal, cunning operative. Worthy of his folklore status, The Devil."

Neril's mouth moved with no words. She glanced back at the folder, stumped. "Surely," she found her voice, "I mean . . . we all just assumed he was a fictitious entity designed to spook the Arabs. Propaganda at its best. You're implying that one person—not a team—accomplished all the carnage attributed to him?"

"He's definitely real. His name is Nathan Yadin." Rozen let the information take hold. "You'll see photos of him as a teenager. Beyond that, nothing we can trust. He's undergone plastic surgery. The only person who could identify him today is now dead. Ezra had all his photos destroyed. Once he became a very wanted man by the Arabs, Yadin insisted on secrecy. Ezra supported that and convinced his superiors to sign off on it. Yadin's results got people promoted. Ezra was happy to remain in the lofty position he'd carved out for himself. He got carte blanche status and a hefty budget. We were all guilty of being too eager to use his attack dog when needed.

"So why the focus now? What's changed in the investigation?" Neril asked.

"Until recently, there was sufficient reason to believe Yadin didn't survive the Natanz implosion. Ezra had a small team in place that, for years, worked to facilitate Yadin's various activities. No one knew about the unit, and thus it remained active after Ezra's death. A short while ago, an operative from that unit with sufficient clearance pops up at headquarters. He gave assurances there was nothing to worry about concerning recent inquiries into 'Dr. Mueller's' background. His cover was intact."

Sharon turned pages as if he'd missed something pertinent. "I don't believe I saw anything pertaining to a Dr. Mueller."

"And you won't. Not on paper. Anywhere," Rozen assured. "All matters pertaining to Dr. Mueller fall under plausible deniability."

"Where did the inquiries come from, sir?" Neril asked.

"From Iranian interests, it seems, and from what I've been told, they were seeking validation. So, what does that tell you?"

Neril gathered her thoughts before speaking. "To me it suggests that Yadin is unaccounted for or eluded a desert grave."

"If he's alive, and hasn't checked in, it could mean the Iranians have him stashed away and are questioning his validity," Sharon stated.

"If the Iranians had him, I doubt they'd go through the trouble of checking his background," the Mossad chief speculated. "Better to throw him in prison and interrogate him until he broke, or worse. No, I suspect they aren't sure about what went wrong at Natanz. As for Yadin not checking in, maybe that's how he wants it."

"How so?" Sharon asked.

"According to encrypted files found on Ezra's home computer, Yadin may have reached his tolerance level. You aren't at that point yet, but there's a limit. A line. The egregious work he's done." Rozen, with understanding, shook his head. "Painful, thankless work. Isolating. It takes a toll. Ezra's notes suggest a highly trained, deadly machine was developing a conscience. In his case, that could lead to orders being questioned. There's a concern with that. In addition, we've learned Ezra had an extraction team in Tehran. It looks like Ezra intended for Natanz to be Yadin's last mission. When he didn't show at the rendezvous point, and no contact came for weeks, Ezra assumed he didn't make it out. If Yadin got wind of Ezra's plan, long-time mentor or not, he would have felt betrayed."

"Can't say I'd blame him," Sharon observed, wishing right away that he'd kept the thought stashed away.

Neril came to his defense. "What is it you want us to do, sir?"

Rozen fought off the urge to torment Sharon. He didn't entirely disagree with him, however. "I asked for this meeting, here in Paris, because it's a starting point. According to travel documents, and expense accounts, this is the last place Ezra traveled out of Israel, presumably to meet with Yadin. Could just be a meeting place—or something more. If Yadin is alive, we need to find him."

Sharon asked, his forehead creased, "To what end?"

Rozen was firm. "Alive is how I'd like it. I understand that's no small undertaking, but there are questions that need answers."

"And if he's not in a cooperative mood?" Sharon shot back.

"Then exercise your best judgment. First, find him. And I can't stress this enough. Proceed with extreme caution. Don't think you have anything to prove here. Truth is, you're not as good as he is. That's a fact you should hold dear in the back of your head. You're to report only to me. I have cleared your schedules with your katsas. Questions?"

There were none.

"You can get started once you finish familiarizing yourself with the files. There is one more thing—might have some relevance. The Americans are brokering some kind of deal with Iran. Other countries are in on it too, but we've been selectively excluded. We're monitoring the situation, but if you have to switch gears, be flexible."

CHAPTER 17

THE NONDESCRIPT, MIDSIZE, American-made car lacked the latest high-tech options. The color wasn't exciting either. The car rental clerk at Louisville International Airport had offered an upgrade at a discount price, but there'd been no interest.

Erik Snow only cared about driving a reliable vehicle that got excellent gas mileage and had functioning air-conditioning. The air outside was sticky hot, like standing next to an open oven set on broil. Water mirages popped up on the roadway while bugs chose the better option of crashing into his windshield rather than frying to death.

He'd traveled without incident on US-60 West, paying special attention to the speed limit and mostly staying in the right-hand lane. He passed a fair share of state troopers, who, even in this heat, wouldn't mind handing out speeding citations. He gave them no reason to give him a second thought. They seemed determined to make quotas, hiding behind underpasses to catch unsuspecting speeders. He didn't see any trooper or sheriff's vehicles taking State Road 261 South into Hancock County.

Tall green trees and heavy brush framed by utility poles guarded the bending two-lane road. Every couple of miles, a home, shed, or idled tractor would break up the monotony. His cell service was spotty, forcing him to consult a hand-drawn map for guidance. Confirmation came that he was on the right path when he drove by the nearly rundown red barn highlighted on the map. He made the next available right turn onto Paul Baker Road, then slowed down about a half mile later. A dated house with a pond behind it came into view. Buildings of various sizes dotted the property. Rolls of hay, the hallmark of farmed land, outlined the other side of the road. Even further back on the spread was a barn. Had to be the place. Snow pulled into the driveway, parking next to a white pickup truck. Turning off the ignition, a man emerged from the house, looking every bit the part of someone whose occupation centered around rising early to put in a full day's work. Snow got out to greet the approaching man. Their contrasting hands met; Snow's were perfectly manicured, while the farmer's were rough and hardened, dirt lodged under his fingernails.

"I'm guessing you didn't have any problems finding the place," the man said, his skin reddened from long hours of sun exposure.

"Your map helped a lot," Snow replied.

The man flashed an impressive, symmetrical set of glowing white teeth. The financial windfall Snow had provided over the years had gone a long way. Aside from those teeth, two kids were put through college and a major health scare with the man's wife was under control. That was a good place to start before addressing business.

"Marlene doing all right?" he asked, removing his sunglasses to show his sincerity was real.

The man scratched the silver stubble on his face, appreciative for more than just the money the slightly shorter man provided. "She's a strong one, and praise God, it looks like she's in the clear. The cancer is in remission. Nice of you to ask, Mr. Beach."

Snow patted the man on the shoulder. "Bob, I've told you before, no need to be so formal. Scott is fine."

There was a high probability that Scott Beach wasn't the man's real name, but several jobs later, Bob knew the money was real, and that was what really mattered. Bob walked to the driver's side of the pickup. "Hop in. I know you're a busy man. We have to go across the street. You sure picked a helluva week to drop in. Been so hot I saw the devil down at Home Depot buying an AC unit."

Maybe it was the discomforting heat, but Snow found the joke amusing. "You ever think about getting out of here?"

"Me?" Bob backed out of the driveway. "Naw, born and raised. Bluegrass is in my blood. Land of fast horses and beautiful women. Now, my kids, that's a different story. They're getting opportunities I never had. Creating their own path, and that's the way it should be."

They headed through a makeshift road carved into the grass by repeated trips of the pickup. It led to a rectangular clearing about three football fields long. On either side, the forest cut in, but mostly the land was clear and quiet. They passed another pond and a building that at one point might have housed horses or livestock. A broken-down fence defeated that purpose now. Bob came to a stop near picnic tables butted together, positioned short of the tree line, which provided unobstructed views of the field. Heavy tarp blanketed the tables, fastened to the ground with large metal stakes.

Bob instructed his visitor to pull up the stakes at the other end. The items on the table were revealed with each undressing of the tarp. Snow leaned in close but didn't touch anything.

"Gotta say, this one was a real challenge," said Bob, admiring the finished product. "Lightweight. Some assembly required. Deliverable in multiple pieces, and capable of getting through customs."

Not understanding the mechanics yet, Snow still realized quality workmanship when he saw it. "You always come through."

Bob flashed a humble smile. "I aim to please."

There were three items on the table, each made of hard plastic.

The tallest one was around thirty-six inches. Assembled, there was no mystery what they were—freestanding weapons, complete with a trigger mechanism. But they were much more complicated than what the eye could see. Snow picked up the largest piece. He was surprised at how effortless it was to lift.

Bob opened a box on the table containing rows of ammunition. "As requested, 308 Win, Ruag Swiss Tactical. These will penetrate a window at least an inch and a half thick without bullet deflection. I've tested them frequently. Consistent MOA (Minute of Angle) up to three hundred yards. Given the mass you specified, not once did I encounter overpenetration."

Since the Civil War, farming had been the family business. It was honest work, but a hard way to make a living. Bob had watched his grandfather and father wear down from the predawn to after-sundown workload. Bob dreamed of breaking the cycle for future generations. He had spent many restless nights deflecting boredom and despair by tinkering with weapons and creating gadgets. Bob's hobby caught the attention of local gun owners. Hunters sought added stopping power, accuracy, and distance. Word of mouth garnered business from military types, snipers mostly. They marveled at Bob's expertise of invention. The side jobs afforded Bob the luxury to end the drudgery of full-time farming.

Seeking to have a special order filled, Scott Beach got in touch one day. A sizable check accompanied the introduction. A satisfied customer turned into a business relationship that paid dividends for both parties. This, by far, was the most ambitious order to date.

Bob picked up several bullets, showing how to load them into a makeshift magazine. He slid it into place and pronounced, "That's all it takes."

Snow remained impressed because even with the magazine attached, the build didn't appear menacing. The device now in his hands, Snow hung onto every word Bob spoke, especially whenever he pushed a button or loosened a part. Sliding a bolt in one direction released a barrel that, when extended, locked into place by screwing clockwise. Next, a tube resembling a kaleidoscope got attached along rails and secured in place. This sturdy plastic design was now a fully functional sniper rifle.

"You can use this manually by affixing the tripod on the table as a stabilizer, or"—Bob was beaming now—"attach this baby." In his hands was a device similar to what professional video photographers used to keep a camera steady. There were handles on opposite sides, requiring the use of both hands. Bob explained the trigger mechanism was a button above where the right thumb rested. He pointed out you could go traditional and use it with the scope, or take advantage of a three-inch monitor he'd locked into the side of the rifle that relayed every detail displayed within the scope. "It adds some bulk," Bob warned, "which is why you'll probably want to lock it down. You wanted it to work on a boat, so obviously, it's a gyroscope-leveling device."

"Oh, obviously," Snow said, fascinated that something so crude looking could work.

Bob continued his walk-through, running his hands along the bottom of the device as he explained, "It has strong magnets here that secure to metal surfaces, or you can use the grooves at the bottom to lock it into place. Either way, it won't move once secured. If, as I suspect, you want to trigger this and the other device remotely, you can use a smartphone or tablet to zero in on a target and fire once the levels are to your liking. They'll be able to communicate with one another as long as the distance isn't over eighteen hundred yards. But you know, talk is cheap. Let's put it into action."

Bob handed Snow a pair of binoculars. He guided him toward the building they'd passed on the way in. He hadn't noticed before, but now Snow saw fully dressed, life-sized mannequins standing inside behind a row of windows. Adjusting the binoculars, there were more behind the ones in front. Ample lighting inside made each figure distinguishable.

"They're bolted to the floor so they won't go flying," Bob pointed out. "Ready?"

Snow's otherwise stoic face was grinning with anticipation. "Let's see what you've done here."

"Excellent. And after this"—Bob motioned to the other device on the table—"I will show you what the rocket launcher can do."

Snow shook his head. For the first time all day, the heat didn't bother him.

CHAPTER 18

MICHELLE ORSETTE WANTED to lean on her car horn. Her children had forced her to refrain from cursing, so it was the only aggressive recourse available. The two bundles of joy strapped into their booster seats in the second row had called Mom out over the potty mouth she used in such situations.

The focus of her ire was the mom in the black Navigator three vehicles ahead, holding up the car line. Time was precious each morning for school drop-off. The frustrating part occurred when a seemingly simple process rarely worked. You roll up, get in line, and drop off your kids. That blanking simple. If you had to have a conversation with a parent, or your kid needed extra time bringing items to school, you found a parking spot. That was the rule. Too often, certain people exhibited a "rules don't apply to me" attitude. That was the mom in the Navigator. She might as well have raised her middle finger to the other parents in line while she conversed with another mom walking back to her parked vehicle.

"Bitch, come on!" Did she say that out loud?

"Mom!" came the admonishment in unison from the backseat.

"Sorry. I know. I know."

The children weren't astute enough to recognize that Mom always was more agitated right after an extended business trip. Orsette had explained to her parents, and the children, that business trips could get intense. Her boss was a stickler for detail, and often very demanding. Aaron, who now liked to wear his blond locks long, fixated on "stickler," thinking Mom's boss traveled around the world applying stickers to things.

What Orsette couldn't tell her family was that she worked for a corporation of one, and its CEO killed people. Her job description didn't call for it, but she also sometimes slept with the boss. She was developing a strong attachment to Erik Snow, or whatever his name really was, and that contributed to a frustration she couldn't share with anyone but herself. He had changed her life in countless ways. He'd first approached her mid-tears as she sat alone in a darkened corner of a coffee shop, trying to make the financial numbers of her life make sense. After the murder of her husband, she had become the sole provider for their two kids. The amount her husband had left in insurance and investments from a modest job would only last so long. There was a mortgage to pay, mouths to feed, a car payment, and credit card debt. Her dental assistant job had sufficed with two salaries coming into the household, but now, reality had taken a firm hold around her neck. Her goal of going back to school to become a dental hygienist looked bleak. Her parents didn't have the monetary reserve to lend her without putting their financial future in jeopardy, and she wasn't about to ask. Everything had closed in on her. Then, he happened.

Snow had offered her a handkerchief, coaxing his way into a seat by declaring, "Things don't have to be as bad as they seem. There are options."

She'd been distraught, but his soft features and demeanor had been calming, reassuring in fact. It didn't take long to realize this was no chance encounter. More than once, her intuition had told her to get up and leave, but he'd offered her two things that kept her feet firmly planted—a lifeline and retribution. He explained that if she came to work for him, she could expect a six-figure income, and spend plenty of quality time with her kids. He pointed out the obvious: Doing so would prove beneficial in helping them cope with their father's absence. The job demanded secrecy, some travel, and potential danger. He promised, though, that he'd assume the majority of risks.

Then came the grand prize offer. She'd get the opportunity to punish her husband's killers. She was stunned at the possibility and also the brashness. The police investigation had come up empty, and offered little hope of catching the killers. Here was a stranger, not a law enforcement officer, pledging a bandage for her open wound. How could he have solved her husband's murder? Skeptical, she'd been vulnerable enough to listen.

Once she confronted and questioned the men, there'd be no doubt about their guilt or his credentials. She'd then have a choice to make. There'd be no calling the police. Either he killed them, or she could.

Two nights later, Orsette found herself inside the massive, abandoned structure of a former steel plant in the downriver city of Trenton. A short distance to the east was the Detroit River. She didn't have to be a genius to understand the logistics. The cavernous darkness was beyond eerie. Noises, imagined or otherwise, came from unseen spaces. Maybe it was the wind that rustled the corroded, worn-down building, or maybe it was her inner voice trying to reason that this was the dumbest thing she'd ever done in her life. She rubbed her slippery palms against her jeans as she took measured steps toward the unknown. Three men were in front of her, spotlighted by the single source of light available, the high beams of a dated, dented, and rusted minivan. Orsette recognized the man from the coffee shop. His presence was comforting, but she was still disturbed.

Snow stood behind the other two men. Duct tape kept them

secured in chairs, their mouths covered to insure limited noise. They'd been moaning in protest until they saw Orsette. The man to Orsette's left looked like the type of person you'd cross the street to avoid. He had hard, uncaring eyes and bad skin shielded by a scraggly beard. He gave off a vibe that, if not in this predicament, he'd likely rape her and leave her for dead. The other man gave Orsette momentary pause. He had a baby face, seemed soft and innocent. She found herself wondering where his mother was. Snow had expected her bewilderment. Without warning, he ripped the duct tape away from the young man's mouth.

"What the fuck, man!" he cried out. "You better let me go. This is some bullshit."

Snow addressed Orsette, "See, not so innocent." He then moved in front of the older man, removing the tape from his mouth just as hard.

"You recognize her, don't you?" Snow inquired.

The man raised his eyes to meet Snow's, one dangerous man to another. "Yeah, I seen her on the news or some shit like dat."

"I also believe you know her from the picture in her husband's wallet, and the ones on his cellphone."

The man seemed unimpressed. "How many times we gonna go over this? I found the wallet and phone."

"Really," Snow said, knowing the answers already. "Then how did Baby Face here end up using her husband's ATM card?"

"Fuck I should know. Ask him."

Baby Face laughed. "You ain't got shit, man." He looked past Snow to Orsette. "This is a crime. You're going to jail for this shit, bitch."

In an instant, Snow shut him up with a blow to the face. The young man's eyes tried to fight back tears. Bleeding from a broken nose, he said, "That's some punk-ass shit right there."

Orsette jumped when Snow added an exclamation point across the younger man's cheek. His head snapped around as if on a swivel.

"You killed a man for a hundred and thirty-eight dollars," Snow said. The other man kept quiet, his eyes fixated forward into the darkness. Snow shifted his attention back and forth between the prisoners. "I get it now. Baby Face here got out of control. Wanted to see what it was like to kill someone." Snow squatted next to the seasoned man. "He screwed things up for you. You just wanted to rob her husband, maybe rough him up. Put a scare into him so he wouldn't talk. But Junior over there, Junior wanted to prove how tough he is. He brought all this heat down on you. Hell, why didn't you just kill him when you had the chance?"

Snow was surprised when he got an answer.

"Unfortunately, the dumbass is family."

After that admission and other undeniable facts spelled out by Snow, Orsette at some point held what she learned was a 9mm pistol. She had never fired a real weapon. Her only experience had come while joining her husband in one of his Call of Duty games. She'd always died. There'd be no reset button tonight.

The gun shook so badly in her hand that even at ten feet, she'd miss hitting the stationary target. Snow helped her by putting both his hands around hers. When her aim was on point, he told her it was the only way she could move forward. It'd be impossible to turn back after seeing them and hearing how they had shown her husband no mercy. A senseless killing.

There was no explosion of noise as she'd expected. The suppressor attached to the 9mm took care of that. Orsette heard the life of the hardened criminal extinguish with a sickening guttural exhale. Call of Duty had never felt like this. Standing in front of the young man, she looked into his then-pleading eyes. She didn't think she could take another life. Not that life. So young. He was someone's child. But this child had taken her husband's life without the slightest regard for him being a loving father who'd provided for his family. She recognized the young man for what he really was: a chameleon. If she let him live, he'd come after her—and worse, her children.

Orsette's hand didn't shake this time. She resigned herself to making eye contact. Grasping the finality of his situation, the young man begged with full emotion. A squeeze of the trigger returned the warehouse to its hollow, nothing-lives-here-but-memories state.

Afterward, Snow had directed her to leave, promising to take care of everything and that she had nothing to worry about. He'd also reiterated that he wanted her to work for him. As she thought about her life and what the promised future could be, the deciding factor had come down to what was best for her kids. She'd accepted his offer.

Now, Orsette's children exited, backpacks in hand. She smiled when the expected "Love you, Mom" goodbyes came flowing from their mouths. It never got old. They were happy, and that meant she was too. The kids now attended Detroit Country Day Lower School—one of the best private educations money could buy. The family lived in a modest home in the upscale suburban neighborhood of Birmingham. Her parents were close by, the perfect babysitters when she had to travel.

Driving away, Orsette had no time to accept the text invitation to mingle with other moms at the nearby Starbucks. She had work to do. There were large sums of money to transfer for her employer, and packages to move from Kentucky that were complex to transport without drawing suspicion.

A busy day ahead, but at least she'd be able to pick up her kids from school.

CHAPTER 19

NORA HAD SAID little during the trip from Venice to Moscow. Her relative silence spoke volumes to Duncan. Other than stay by her side, there wasn't much he could do to comfort her. She checked her phone often for a possible missed message, having called Alex's phone countless times.

The Aeroexpress train from Sheremetyevo International Airport into Moscow ran on a continuous schedule every thirty minutes. Nora paced back and forth on the platform. Duncan gave her a five-minute sign. Frustrated, she ran a hand through her hair. The warning from the mystery man in Monte Carlo sounded more cryptic with each non-connection. Nora tried dialing Alex one last time. She'd stopped leaving messages. She was about to hang up when the voicemail greeting sounded different.

"Hello? Nora?"

"Alex!" she said, loud enough to get Duncan's attention several feet away. "Oh my God, where have you been?"

"What the hell? I've got like eight voice messages from you, even more hang-ups, and a novel of text messages."

"You ass! Why haven't you called me back?"

"I've had my phone off. Been using burners mostly," Alex said. "I'm in the middle of something."

"Where are you?"

"I'm about to go into my hotel room."

"What hotel?"

Alex frowned. "You taking a survey or something? What difference does it make what hotel I'm at? Trust me, geographically, we're not close."

He entered his hotel room.

"Yeah, smartass, during my hiatus I'm picking up some extra change by working for Trip Advisor. Just answer the question, please."

Alex didn't understand her insistence, but better to give Nora what she wanted. "I'm at the Hotel Metropol in Moscow. Room 5517. It gets four and a half stars."

"Don't go anywhere. We'll be there within the hour."

"What are you talking about?"

"We're in Moscow."

Alex didn't know what to say. He thought about the possibility. "You're funny. Okay, I get it. I'm sorry. I've missed your messages, didn't return your calls, but I don't have time to fool around, Nora. In all seriousness, I'm on a job." Alex thought about what she'd just said. "What do you mean, 'We'?"

Nora smiled, looking at her traveling companion. "Duncan is with me."

"Stop trying to punk me. There's no way."

"Way, baby. See you in a few. But listen, we have to talk. According to your newfound friend Nathan, you might be in danger," Nora said, moving into position as the Aeroexpress train pulled up. Her happiness at finally making a connection turned in a different direction. "Alex I know what you're up to. Do nothing until we get there. You understand?"

"Nora, listen . . ." Alex never finished the sentence. The phone dropped from his hand while he tried to defend himself. The large forearm wrapped around his neck cut off circulation. The other hand inserted a needle into his neck. Alex tried to elbow the man's side, but the drug pumping into his system moved fast, reducing his resistance until he fell unconscious.

Passengers bumped Nora by accident when she abruptly stopped before entering the train. Through the surrounding noise, she thought she heard a struggle on the other end of the phone. Her fear became pronounced when Alex stopped talking.

"Alex," said Nora, wondering if it was a bad cell signal. "Alex. Alex!" Duncan pushed her into the train ahead of the doors closing.

In the hotel room, Alex was out cold on the floor. Sergei stood over him with a wide smile. He reached down for the cell phone. A woman's voice kept calling the American's name. Sergei silenced the phone and handed it over to Karina Marchenko.

She looked at Alex, pleased with the way things were working out.

CHAPTER 20

NORA LOOKED PAST her reflection in the window to the street below. Teatralny Proezd was full of headlights to Revolution Square. She wanted to shove her fist through the glass. She had been so close to catching up with Alex. His smell lingering in the room added to her feeling of despair. Terrible outcomes tormented her, and paramount among them was the reason she knew Alex was here—Dmitri Nevsky. He was a danger under any circumstance. On his home turf, that threat was magnified tenfold. And considering the warning from Nathan, Alex may have blindly walked into an Iranian trap.

Duncan didn't get an answer from Nora on his first attempt. He tried again. "Have you come up with anything? I went through his clothes in the dresser, the closet. Nothing. You check his carry-on?"

"Sorry," Nora replied, snapping out of her trance. "I'll do it now." She grabbed Alex's bag and rifled through it on the bed. There was nothing out of the ordinary: boarding passes, earbuds, a writing pad, pocket change, and a smartwatch instruction pamphlet.

One item got Duncan's attention. "What kind of smartwatch?"

Dumbfounded, Nora said, "What kind? You mean, like, the operating system?"

"Yes. Well, no. Who makes it?" Duncan rushed to her side, asking for the manual before she could provide the answer. He scanned the room with purpose. "No phone, right?"

Nora fed off his energy. "No, it's not here. They must have taken the phone. What are you thinking?"

He thumbed through the manual. "No watch in the bag either?"

Nora shook her head.

"There's a good chance he's wearing it then. Who bothers to take your watch during a struggle? The phone, yes. The watch, maybe not. This one looks like a regular, typical chromatic watch."

Nora wanted to scream waiting for Duncan to offer clarity on what he was thinking. He pulled out his cell phone to make a call. Nora was about to interject with a question, but he connected with someone on the other end.

"Stu, I need you to track a GPS signal, stat. Get whoever you need to assist you," Duncan barked. "And listen, hack into whatever server necessary. I'll send the device's serial and model number. The target's name is Alex Koves. Try to link it with his cell number. You might get lucky. As soon as you're locked on, clone the map to me. Time is a definite issue." Duncan hung up and forwarded the promised information halfway across the world to an office in Washington, DC.

"Okay, that sounded impressive," Nora observed.

"Thanks. Alex's smartwatch has a standalone GPS sensor. Runners love that shit because you don't always have to drag your phone along to measure your run or plot your course."

"So it's like those Garmin devices and trackers golfers use?"

"Exactly. Provided Alex is still wearing it, and there isn't too much crap in the sky, we should be able to pinpoint his location. Plus, if his phone is nearby, and not turned off, we'll be able to cross-reference the two signals, which will increase the accuracy."

Nora pushed off the bed and planted a huge kiss on Duncan's lips. "You are amazing!"

"True, but hold that assessment," Duncan said. "We still have to find him."

Nora headed for the door. "Let's get some transportation then."

CHAPTER 21

ALEX FOUGHT HARD to combat a wave of nausea as the drug that had been shot into his system began tapering off. His head felt like it weighed a ton. He had limited range of motion due to being bound to a chair bolted into the floor.

Boating excursions on Lake Michigan and the waters around St. Thomas had educated him enough to determine that he was in a stateroom below deck. The boat seemed to have ample power. Alex guessed twin diesel engines, at least 460 horsepower each. Above him, intermittent footsteps suggested an upper deck and bridge. It looked to be a fully equipped trawler design with two bulkheads—size wise, about fifty feet.

Alex established his general whereabouts by staring out the starboard windows. River trams had surged along, and when the trawler passed the light-infused Radisson Royal Hotel, it confirmed he was traveling along the Moskva River. The ride soon bounced less, progressing to a gentle roll. A series of footsteps sounded on deck. One of the last things Alex remembered was having a conversation with Nora. He still couldn't wrap his mind around her saying she was in

Moscow, and with Duncan no less. Was he thinking straight about what they'd talked about? Did she mention Nathan? She had said his name too casually. Perhaps the fogginess in his head was playing tricks. That would have to wait. Heavy footsteps were now heading in his direction.

A key unlocked the door. The flick of a switch illuminated the room, causing Alex to squint. The first person he identified was Marchenko's right-hand man, Sergei, who displayed a contemptuous, in-your-face smile. Behind him, her hair pinned back, a confident Marchenko stepped into the room. A fresh, bulky frame of a man followed, holding a briefcase, his one-size-too-small navy jacket threatening to come apart at the seams. They filtered into the room, making way for the man who walked through the door next, careful to duck his head.

The man displayed the frozen look of a child on Christmas morning, seeing everything from his wish list under the tree.

"Mr. McBride," the man said, gutturally pushing the words out. "Wonderful to see you again."

Alex smiled at the image. Like the night at the park—a huge, bulging muscled man, accessorized by that small little dog.

"Dmitri Nevsky. I've been looking for you."

CHAPTER 22

"KARINA, YOU HAVE outdone yourself." Nevsky stroked his cradled pet, his eyes fixated on Alex. "Two most welcomed gifts. And Mr. McBride, or Alex as Karina says you call yourself, I've been looking for you too."

Alex raised his head. "Well, lucky for you, I'm not going anywhere."

Nevsky's chest heaved with laughter. "Humor must be your coping mechanism. Interesting, the human condition, Mr. McBride. You get to see a person's real makeup when they're confronted with primal fear or unyielding pain. Some eventually plead for the pain to stop. That type will offer you anything. Disappointing to witness that kind of weakness—it literally takes the fun out of the process. Others are true believers in whatever cause or calling they have embraced. Harder to break, but over time, break they do. And then, there are people like you, Mr. McBride. You are the hardest kind to break. Mentally and physically sound, I suspect. You're pre-wired, conditioned to push through. Pain gives you confidence because it reinforces that you're still alive. My intention though, Mr. McBride, is not to break you. I don't relish the time it would take. And besides,

I really have no interest. Ordinarily, we would not even be having this conversation. But this is not an ordinary situation. Not by any means. You represent a nice payday, and a few favors to pocket. Truthfully, knowing what will happen after I inform the Iranians and turn you over to them is where I take delight. But before that, you will endure some pain."

Alex produced a sour look. "I hate to break it to you, but you talk a lot. And you aren't that interesting."

Nevsky's burly associate put the briefcase on the floor. Then he slammed his fist full throttle into Alex's stomach. Alex flexed, trying to offset the blow, but it still hurt.

Marchenko rolled her eyes, moving to prevent Nevsky's man from throwing another punch. "All this testosterone is too much to bear," she said. "Dmitri, you do not get ownership until I get paid. I came through as promised. Now, if you will, my money. I have better things to do than stay here and watch bad theater."

Nevsky instructed his man to hand the briefcase over. "You used to be a lot more fun, Karina."

"We all used to be a lot more things," she responded, inspecting the briefcase's contents of stacked bills. Satisfied, she closed it and, as an afterthought, walked over to Alex. She looked him squarely in the eyes. "I'm not sure which of you I should thank," she said, talking loud so Nevsky could hear.

Alex chuckled. "So this was your play all along?"

Marchenko put the briefcase down and placed her hands on his bound wrists. "Dmitri can be a pain, but he's our pain in the ass. I would never betray a fellow Russian for an outsider like you."

"Doveryai, no proveryai," was Alex's retort, his disappointment and anger evident.

Marchenko retrieved the briefcase. "It was a pleasure doing business with you, Alex. Unfortunately for you, the clock starts now."

She gathered Sergei to exit, but Nevsky stepped in front of the door to block her. Karina stared up at him. "Is there a problem?"

"No problem. You delivered as promised. Just most unexpected. Usually, Karina Marchenko is not so charitable."

Karina tapped the briefcase. "It's hardly charity. And a gentle reminder that I am entitled to a cut of what the Iranians give you for him."

Nevsky stepped aside to let her and Sergei leave.

Once topside, Marchenko quickened her pace in case Nevsky changed his mind. She collected her other crewmember, who had been engaged in a protective stare down with two of Nevsky's men. They stepped onto the dock and breathed a sigh of relief when the boat pushed away to resume its course along the winding Moskva River.

In a moment of rare reflection, Marchenko watched the vessel drift off, wondering if she was doing the right thing. A strand of hair broke free from its tied-back position. Brushing it back, her fingers skimmed the scar on her face, reminding her that if one lived a dangerous life, odds were it would eventually catch up with them. There were really only two choices.

Survive, or become a casualty.

CHAPTER 23

TIME HELD THE key to ending what made Alex ache. He'd traveled a long way to kill the man who stood near him.

Alex took another jarring blow to his side. His method in the room for dealing with pain was the luminous clock on the wall. The more it moved, the closer he got to his goal. Dmitri Nevsky's anger and frustration were rising. So far, Alex had refused to answer any of the man's questions. It was akin to adding lighter fluid to a flame. The Russian was not accustomed to being played for a fool. Those who defied him usually stopped breathing.

Alex glanced at the clock again. Time was the only friend he had on this boat, and he had to keep the relationship going.

"The moment I laid eyes on you in Tbilisi, something didn't register," Nevsky said, shaking his head. "But it was in the middle of nowhere, late at night. I wanted to be done with those damned Iranians and their precious cargo. I was not as focused as I should have been. You killed three of my best men. No small feat, I assure you."

Trusting the clock's accuracy, Alex knew he needed fifteen more minutes.

"What makes you think it was me? It could have been my associate," he offered, knowing the observation was implausible.

The response annoyed Nevsky. He put the dog on the floor and scurried over to Alex to hammer a missile of a right hand to the midsection. Alex choked for air, and his eyes watered. The difference in strength between the enforcer and Nevsky was measurable.

"You insult my intelligence," Nevsky followed up, regaining his composure. "That little cockroach Mr. Green had neither the stomach nor skill to take out men of that caliber. He is still in hiding, but I will find him. In the meantime, I have you, Mr. McBride. You represent quite a problem for me. My men, like Viktor here, want nothing more than to torture you to death. The Iranians, though, will pay a large sum for you. Getting my men to understand the win-win of this was difficult. But, I told them, turning you over represents a financial windfall, and the Iranians will eventually kill you. So everyone goes home happy."

Nevsky retrieved a chair from a nearby desk and sat a measured distance away from Alex. He had a faraway look in his eye when he spoke. "What I cannot figure out, Mr. McBride, is the utter stupidity of this. To somehow pull off what you did in Tehran takes no small measure of intelligence and help. My gut suspects you're CIA, but they would never sanction this mess you've gotten yourself in, trying to kill a respectable Russian businessman like me in Moscow."

Able to breathe again, Alex said, "I see humor's not lost on you either."

Nevsky gave Alex the once-over. Fit. Able to take a beating. Smart. Not overly concerned about his current situation. Something was off. "No, Mr. McBride, this feels personal, and that has me puzzled."

Alex shifted to minimize the pain creeping up his right side. "Oh, it's personal," he confirmed.

"See, I knew it," Nevsky excitedly said. "We're finally getting somewhere. So what is it, Mr. McBride? Did I take away someone you love? Perhaps ruined you professionally? I'm dying to know."

"Oh, you will die," Alex responded without fanfare.

The bravado was surprising. Nevsky leaned back. "Considering your present situation, duly noted. Now, out with it, or I'll have Viktor beat on you until he gets tired. Two more of my associates are up top. They will gladly relieve him if necessary."

Nevsky had the look of a hungry wild animal within feet of its prey. And yet, experience had taught him to be careful. He paid heightened attention to every confined movement and word that came out of Alex's mouth.

"I'm here because of Ammar Handi."

Nevsky waited for more. He hunched his shoulders. "Ammar Handi?" he threw back. "The name means nothing to me."

"I guess when you've killed so many people, names and faces become unimportant."

"If I killed this Ammar Handi, I probably had a good reason. But, in the rare instance I am mistaken, please refresh my memory."

"Iraq. You left a lot of bodies in your wake."

Nevsky chortled. "If we are counting bodies, the Americans led the way in deaths by attrition. Compared to them, I was a choirboy. Weapons of mass destruction. Give me a break. Look at the domino effect that deceptive lie created. Didn't make the world a safer place!"

"No, it didn't, and we'll be cleaning up that shit show for years, if not decades. But whenever you can make a serious wrong a right, you don't pass on that opportunity."

With open hands, Nevsky asked, "So you are here to avenge this Ammar Handi?"

"Among others." Alex wanted to keep Nevsky engaged. His associate had already taken a relaxed stance against the wall.

"You are a poor man's assassin. And not a very good one, I might add."

"The jury's still out on that one."

"I have to say, your confidence almost has me believing." Nevsky laughed at Alex's words. "I very much want to kill you myself. But, as you pointed out, when you can make a serious wrong a right, and there is profit involved, you do not pass on that opportunity.

Alex refrained from offering a sarcastic retort. It was getting close to the point when he had to reserve his strength. Taking on more punishment was risky. "Let me take you further back," Alex continued. "If it were just Ammar, that would be one thing. He knew the risks. Felt they were worth it for the advancement of his country and the promises made. But you didn't stop with Ammar. You butchered his entire family. You killed his wife, his daughter and six-year-old son."

"Ah, that Ammar," Nevsky remembered with wide eyes. "You were his handler. You were the young CIA officer gaining a foothold in the area. I got a glimpse of you, but only once. No wonder I didn't remember you. But Ammar, and the others you recruited, I had orders from Moscow. Couldn't just let the Americans swoop in and lay down the future groundwork unchecked. There were business interests and relationships to maintain."

"You went too far."

"A message had to be sent." Nevsky used his right index finger for emphasis. "Brutality is the only thing that got their attention."

Alex felt the years of nightmares and frustrations boiling in his head. He had already taken care of the man who betrayed them years ago in Iraq. Now it was the executioner's turn.

Seven minutes . . .

CHAPTER 24

THE SPEEDING TAXI missed clipping the bumper of the car in front of it by inches, squeezing ahead into the next lane. The car driver hit the brakes and horn simultaneously in reaction to the idiotic move. The dart-and-dash ride through Moscow's jammed streets took on a heightened sense of anxiety once Nora dropped $200 in rubles on the passenger seat. A matching amount hinged on the success of catching up with a moving target.

"How much farther?" a restless Nora asked.

When Duncan didn't answer, she noticed the perplexed look on his face.

"What's wrong? What is it?"

Duncan looked at her and then to his left while the taxi searched for another opening, hugging the outer lane of the crowded Moskvoretskaya Embankment. He consulted with his phone one more time. "It appears he's just ahead of us over there."

Nora held on tight to the top of the passenger seat in front of her, combating the constant jerking. She tried to locate what Duncan had referenced. "On the other side?" she spit out.

"Nope. Right there." Duncan pointed with emphasis.

Nora's enthusiasm sank. "You're telling me he's on that boat on the Moskva River?"

"It would appear so."

Nora released her grip and pressed against the backseat. "How are we supposed to . . . ?" she exhaled. She knew the river snaked its way to the outer reaches of the city and then narrowed to areas where they either couldn't follow or risked losing the GPS signal. They could get screwed long before that happened if the boat made a port turn around the statue of Peter the Great to enter the Vodoot-vodny Canal. Since the statue was on the other side of the river, the nearest place they could cross would be the Krymsky Bridge. That would put them behind again, and in this traffic, catching up would be tricky.

Minor geographical details came rushing back into her head. She hadn't set foot in Moscow in years. Her knowledge stemmed from brief operations here and in the region under the direction of her former mentor, Erica Janway.

Nora gripped the front seat for stability again. She addressed the taxi driver in Russian so that there was no misunderstanding. His perilous driving reduced the conversation to a number of affirmative head nods. Nora said one final thing and then held on for dear life. Duncan didn't need to speak Russian to tell she had brokered an agreement with their aspiring Formula One driver.

"Okay, what is it?" Duncan wanted to know.

Nora had a devilish look on her face. "You can swim, can't you?"

"Yeah, I can," he replied, thinking it might have been better to lie.

CHAPTER 25

THE PLAN MADE sense, at least in Nora's head. She refused to listen to the inner voice that reasoned it was a bad, haphazard plan. Among other drawbacks, they didn't have any weapons, and would likely encounter trained individuals who did.

Nora had yet to fill Duncan in on her conversation with the taxi driver. The discussion's aftermath resulted in him driving more recklessly than before. Duncan saw they were getting ahead of the boat he suspected Alex to be on. According to the GPS signal, Alex's smartwatch at least was onboard. How they could stop the boat to find out, Duncan had no clue. He had a feeling, however, that Nora did. When they passed under a large bridge, she took particular interest in the structure.

Nora spoke to the driver once more. Excited, he nodded repeatedly, finishing up with, "Da."

Nora caught Duncan's blank stare. "Almost there. Is the boat still heading in this direction?" she asked, praying it hadn't veered toward the adjacent canal.

Duncan checked his phone. "Yes."

The taxi cut through breaks in traffic with ease. Nora was confident they'd make it to their destination in time. Unfortunately, that was all she felt strongly about. She hoped Duncan hadn't been just boasting about his newfound skills. They possibly were about to be in grave danger, and she might need him. Giving him the option, though, would only be fair.

The Krymsky Bridge grew larger by the second. The bridge provided the ebb and flow of Moscow traffic with another crossing point over the Moskva River. The taxi shot through the intersection just as the light turned green. It slid over to the shoulder, on the other side of the bridge, stopping at a light pole on the corner. The driver pointed to a set of stairs on the right, uttering some rushed words to Nora. She patted him on his shoulder and dropped a wad of rubles on the front passenger seat, then told Duncan it was time to go.

They raced to the bridge steps, climbing two at the time. Duncan had no idea what Nora was thinking, but he followed right behind, sidestepping people on the way up. As they reached the bridge level, multiple lanes of traffic impeded Nora's ability to see clearly, giving her pause. She rose on her tippy toes, jumping up and down to get a glimpse of the river on the other side of the road. The boat they'd been following was catching up. Nora tried to gauge whether her plan had a prayer of succeeding. She ran along the crosswalk to the middle of the bridge, trying to keep the boat in sight. With Duncan behind her, she blurted out, "Put me on your shoulders."

Duncan kneeled down to let her hop on his back, and then he lifted her up. His height allowed Nora to see over the traffic and past the other side of the bridge. She got a bearing on the boat heading their way.

"Move to the left," she instructed. "A little more. Stop!"

Nora hopped off his shoulders and headed for the railing, bending over it as she inspected the water below. Duncan joined to see what she was looking at—and then he knew.

"You must be joking," he said in disbelief.

"Afraid not, unless you've got a better idea."

"I don't, but this one is nuts."

"I understand your concern, and yes, there's a huge amount of risk involved. I can't make you do this, so if you'd rather not, I get it. But, it's the only thing I got. If Alex is on that boat, I'm going to at least make an attempt."

Duncan shook his head. "Friendship is so damn overrated. Let's do this."

Nora gave him a silly smile. "You're the best. And I deeply apologize ahead of time if you break your ankle or get shot."

CHAPTER 26

ALEX HAD BEEN constrained for a while. He rocked his feet and flexed his hands to stimulate blood flow. He couldn't afford to cramp up with the moment of opportunity approaching. He only had to buy a little more time.

"I noticed we passed the Kremlin. You don't have a lot of friends there either. You didn't leave the FSB on good terms. Now, you're just a common gangster."

"That would be a rich gangster," Nevsky corrected him. "As for the Kremlin, its reach doesn't scare me. I have information that affords me the luxury of doing what I please."

"You frighten some people, I see. You got to Marchenko, and she doesn't spook easy."

"She's no pushover. Perhaps too strong-willed for her own good. I was surprised to hear from her," Nevsky said, his eyes strolling the cabin.

Alex had to keep him engaged. "You'll never garner respect. Just fear."

"Fear works for me."

"The moment you become vulnerable, which of your men is going to turn on you?"

Nevsky's enforcer left his relaxed stance against the wall to slam a fist into Alex's face. He waited for Alex's head to come back around and then hit him again. Alex redirected his strength to his lower body, pressing his feet hard into the floor to remain stable.

Nevsky laughed. "You insult my comrade by questioning his loyalty. I suggest you do not make that mistake again."

Alex spat out blood. "I'll keep that in mind." The taste of iron reinforced why he was risking his life, thousands of miles from home, tied to a chair in the lower stateroom of a boat.

Alex counted down.

Sixty . . . Fifty-nine . . . Fifty-eight . . . Fifty-seven . . .

CHAPTER 27

NORA CLIMBED OVER the railing first, taking care to hold on. Against his better judgment, Duncan did the same. They timed it as best they could. The last thing they needed was intervention from strangers, mistaking this as a suicide pact between lovers. Leaning forward, they were in position. Nora had gauged the boat's path and calculated the alignment.

Feet planted, they held on to the railing with one hand, squatting low to maintain balance. The footing was tricky, but they wouldn't have to hold on for long. Nora trusted that her hasty analysis was on target. Judging where the boat would pass under the bridge was crucial. There'd be no second chance. Explaining everything to Duncan in a hurry got her adrenaline pumping, leaving less time to think about the absurdity of the plan.

The boat's upper deck stretched beyond its bridge. Nora didn't see anyone atop. The crew had to be in the bridge. She stressed to Duncan that they had to land toward the back of the upper deck. The drop was shorter, and it might provide an element of surprise.

"Any words of advice?" a concentrating Duncan asked.

"Don't get killed. I'd really have a hard time living with that."
"I'll keep that in mind."
Nora pushed away from the railing.

CHAPTER 28

TEN SECONDS. IT seemed like an eternity.

Alex had to steady himself to keep from jumping the gun. The beating he'd taken fueled him even more. He was stronger, quicker, and more skillful than he had been months ago. He rolled his wrists to get them loose, then did the same with his zip-tied ankles.

At six seconds, something unexpected happened. Two loud thuds from above caught the attention of all three men. Startled, Nevsky's man turned from Alex to focus on the noise. Nevsky had mentioned there were men atop. The sinister sound made him rise to attention, his ears and eyes on alert. The distraction gave Alex extra seconds to work his restraints. The unmistakable sound of the engines shutting down added to the Russians' confusion. Then the power went out, blanketing the room in darkness.

The designated time had arrived. Alex broke free. He didn't need to see clearly. The Russian enforcer hadn't moved from his position—he was easy to locate. Alex reached under the chair to rip away a pistol that had been taped in place.

He lunged hard, pinning the enforcer to the wall. One hand held down the man's holstered weapon. Viktor tried to rip Alex's hand away, but the angle left him at a disadvantage. The failed attempt was met with two shots to the Russian's chest. Alex pivoted behind the dying body, throwing him in the direction where he'd last seen Nevsky. Three shots rang out, all finding the falling Viktor. The shots betrayed Nevsky's location, and the dead man's body collided with him, knocking him off balance. Alex picked up a nearby chair and hurled it at Nevsky. The chair connected, sending a shot off target. The sound of Nevsky's weapon skidding across the floor made Alex advance in a hurry.

Images took form in the darkness. Nevsky's silhouette was bent low at the knees, his hands franticly sweeping the floor. Alex planted and kicked Nevsky under his chin, sending him onto his back. Alex was tempted to shoot, but that was too easy an exit for the man who had inflicted so much pain and torture on countless others. Alex closed in, keeping the option to shoot later if he lost the upper hand.

Considering his bulk, Nevsky was nimble. Crawling along the floor, he balanced on one arm, swinging his right leg around to whack Alex's gun hand. Nevsky locked Alex's arm in place and recoiled with a left-handed punch that propelled him into the wall. The unchecked flush blow clouded Alex's head. He wanted to lift his right arm, but it was tingling too much. The damage administered by Nevsky's bodyguard was taking effect. Nevsky's oversized hands were trying to gain control of the gun while his weight had Alex sealed.

Alex slid his left shoulder a fraction. The move freed his right leg enough to thrust the heel of his shoe against Nevsky's right instep. The strike made the Russian loosen his grip and step back. Free of pressure, the feeling in Alex's right arm returned. He folded his elbow and thrust it into Nevsky's neck, barely missing his Adam's apple.

The Russian grunted and stumbled backward, but cornered, his survival threatened, he became more aggressive. His hands found the chair he'd been sitting in and wasted no time throwing it at Alex. He rushed immediately after it. Alex was quicker, angling his body to make Nevsky miss. Gravity on his side, Alex slammed Nevsky into the wall so hard it cracked. The Russian didn't stay there. Expecting a bullet, he crouched to his right.

Alex's failure to fire told Nevsky something relevant. The American wanted him alive. Inspired by his discovery, Nevsky let fly a crazy left kick that glanced off Alex's thigh. Advancing, he followed with a right kick, keeping Alex on the defensive.

With his size providing an advantage, Nevsky liked to work close. There was a place for the efficiency and expediency of guns, but he defined the true measure of his talent when he could use his hands.

Nevsky didn't know his adversary felt the same way.

Gathering his footing, Alex found space to rebound. Shooting Nevsky in the shoulder or leg would serve a purpose without ruining his plan. He raised the gun to squeeze off a well-placed shot. Nevsky reacted in the most unexpected way—by throwing his dog at Alex. The animal bounced off, negating a shot. Alex blocked a right hand destined for his face, but doing so dislodged the gun from his hand. Nevsky tried to strike again, but Alex was light on his feet. He side-stepped two jab attempts that left the big man's side unguarded. Alex seized the opportunity with a left-right combo that punished muscle.

Angered by his clumsiness, Nevsky bobbed to avoid a third punch and locked his left hand around Alex's right wrist. He jerked Alex inward, delivering a series of full-fisted facial strikes. Alex let his weight drift back, making Nevsky lean over to maintain his strong grip. The opening Alex had hoped for presented itself.

He used the Russian's firm hold to rise, then brought a blinding-quick left hand with him, pinpointing the mastoid bone behind Nevsky's right ear. Alex added a jab and right cross to gain separation. He was amazed that the Russian hadn't gone down.

Equilibrium now a problem, Nevsky attempted a reverse kick, but there was nothing solid to connect with. What he felt next dropped him to his knees. Alex brought his full weight behind a fist to the lumbar vertebrae of Nevsky's spine. The nerves in his lower body went numb before a rush of unbearable agony—Nevsky couldn't talk or move.

"It's over, Dmitri," said Alex, exhausted. He retrieved the pistol and noted the time on the wall clock. There was a second schedule to worry about, and he had to deal with the two men up top. No doubt they would come to investigate after hearing the volley of shots. Dealing with the sudden loss of power would have gotten their attention and bought him some extra minutes. One of them at least would have to keep the boat steady.

"Get on your feet," Alex commanded, seeing that Nevsky was stirring. He was one tough a son of a bitch. "Slowly now. We're going up top. You have a decision to make."

The Australian terrier was at Alex's feet, seeking protection. Nevsky remained on the floor. The sound of wood squeaking outside the door prompted Alex to move. He positioned his body along the wall to be ready for whoever came through the door. He had to make this quick.

A new countdown, one a lot more dangerous, was ticking away.

CHAPTER 29

NORA DIDN'T PANIC, but she was off the mark.

She tried to compensate while falling, mindful that a muscular, two-hundred-pound-plus man was descending right behind her. She'd been several degrees left of the target when she jumped. Her ideal landing spot had been more to the right, and the added complication was that Duncan needed space to land, too.

By inches, she dropped just inside the upper deck's outer railing on the left-hand side. The pace of the boat rocked her backward and to the side. If not for securing a firm hold, the water would have been her destination. As it was, she was leaning over the rail, struggling to gain control.

Duncan had had a good vantage point to see her predicament as they'd descended. He'd attempted to give her room by adjusting his landing to the right. They announced their arrival by hitting the upper deck in a one-two thunderous touchdown. Duncan rejoiced for a moment that no bones broke. Then he saw Nora trying not to fall over the railing. He sprang to his feet to help when the boat suddenly jerked due to the engines cutting off. Perhaps the men on the bridge had shut them down to come deal with them.

Gunshots startled Nora and Duncan. Three more followed in rapid succession, but they sounded hollow and not directed at them. That caused Nora to worry even more.

If Alex was onboard, the gunfire had to involve him. Nora couldn't wait. She bypassed the stairs and slid under the back railing, holding on to lower onto the back of the vessel. Another shot rang out. She identified the sound's location as coming from below deck. Making her way, Nora stopped upon seeing a man at the helm in the cabin, working to keep the powerless boat steady in the middle of the river. He kept cursing at someone she couldn't see.

Nora stepped portside to discover a slender man urgently dropping anchor. The chaos provided opportunity. She crept low into the dark cockpit, lit only by an emergency spotlight directed at the helm. Training her eyes on the man there, she wished she had a weapon to make it happen faster. A sofa slowed her angle of approach, but it offered concealment. On one knee, she braced against a wood-paneled half wall a few feet from the helm. She was overjoyed to find a fire extinguisher—it would have to do. She unhooked it, the noise covered by the Russian's verbal sparring with his partner. Nora leveled the fire extinguisher in her hands. She then bolted up, her out-of-nowhere reflection caught in the cabin window. Startled, the Russian stopped his one-way conversation. He reached for his handgun as he spun around. Nora smashed the fire extinguisher into the side of his head, and the force knocked him out cold. But as she went to pick up his weapon, a voice from behind shouted out an order.

"Leave the gun on the floor and turn around, hands up," the man who'd been tending to the anchor said in Russian.

"You better pray he's not dead. That was you landing on top? Responsible for the power going out, too?" he asked, not caring if she answered.

They were the last words to come out of his mouth. A thick wooden oar broke apart from the sleeve as the spoon crashed across the back of his neck. Duncan stepped through to admire his handi-work, a satisfied grin on his face.

"Special skill," Nora observed. Gun in hand, she headed for the stairs leading below decks and inched her way down. There were a lot of things crashing, the faint tail end of a voice, and then silence. She was outside the door where the voice came from. Steadying the gun, Nora turned the door handle. The room was dark, too dark for her to make anything out. Throwing caution to the wind, she kicked the door inward, dropping and rolling into the room, ready to fire.

"Drop the weapon now!" Alex shouted.

Nora swung in the voice's direction.

"Alex!"

"Nora! What the hell."

"Oh my God. Are you all right? We heard shots."

"What are you doing here? How?" Alex said, lowering his gun. "You said 'we'?"

"Yes, Duncan's up top."

"You've got to be kidding me. I told you stay away."

"I think the phrase you're searching for is 'thank you.'"

Nora could make out more of the room. A man appeared to be dead on the floor. Alex raised his weapon at her as she got up.

"You need to move back toward the door now," he said.

It wasn't until she was in the doorway that Nora noticed the other man in the room. He was struggling to stand up. Everything about him was large. Big head, big chest, big arms, big hands—just big. She didn't need a proper introduction. It was Dmitri Nevsky. She had been right about why Alex was here. And she totally under-stood, having settled a score of her own recently.

"Like I said, Dmitri," Alex addressed his captive, "it's time to decide. Up top."

Nora led the way, backing up the stairs above Alex with Nevsky in between them. She stopped when Duncan called out.

"Nora, is Alex okay?" he shouted.

There was something in his voice she didn't like. "Yes, he's fine. We're coming up."

"Good. We've got a situation up here."

CHAPTER 30

NORA REACHED THE top of the stairs to see an apologetic Duncan. There was also a pistol braced against his temple.

The man holding the gun wasn't either of the Russians they had encountered. That pair remained unconscious where they'd fallen. But two other guns in the room each tracked Nora's movement. A woman sat relaxed on the sofa with her legs crossed. Making on-the-spot judgments, she used a flashlight to motion Nora to lower her gun. Then she waved for Nora to keep walking up the steps and hand over the weapon.

"Sorry," Duncan mumbled. "She came out of nowhere from another boat, asking if I needed help."

The next person to emerge from the stairwell was a bruised and battered Dmitri Nevsky. Seeing the woman on the sofa, he became euphoric. He let out a boisterous laugh of approval. Nevsky turned to show Alex a lot of teeth. Alex ignored him as he held up his hands, the pistol angled in a non-threatening manner.

"You're in store for a considerably larger stake, my dear Karina," Nevsky beamed.

"When I passed and saw this one on deck," Marchenko replied, referencing Duncan, "I had my doubts about whether you were okay."

Marchenko smiled when the Australian terrier hopped up the stairs, finding a spot next to her on the sofa. She showed the animal some love, but her playful disposition dissipated after checking her watch.

"We need to get this over with. I'm not comfortable being on board. You are cutting this close," Marchenko remarked, rising as she put the dog in her left arm, the gun in her right hand. "What do you want to do with"—she nodded at Duncan—"this one, and her?"

Nevsky folded his massive arms. "I'd bet she's the one the Iranians are looking for. That translates into a bigger payday for us both, Karina. The black one . . ." Nevsky shrugged. "No value. I'll get rid of him."

When Alex stepped forward, none of Marchenko's men tried to stop him. He lowered his arms as he spoke. "They're with me. Put them on your boat."

Sergei removed the gun from Duncan's head to acquire another target—Dmitri Nevsky. The sudden shift of loyalty left Nevsky speechless. Nora and Duncan didn't move either.

"Alex," Nora called out with restraint, "what's going on?"

"Go with them," Alex told her. "Do it now, please."

Nevsky's face held onto a bewildered look, watching Marchenko exit with Duncan and Nora in tow. Marchenko's men kept their weapons on him as they backed out.

The Russian that Duncan had knocked out begin to stir, muttering inaudibly. Marchenko stepped over him and nonchalantly placed a round in the back of his skull.

Unfazed, Alex stood a comfortable distance away from Nevsky, his weapon fixed on an object he couldn't miss. He ordered Nevsky to head for the deck. Outside, he made sure everyone had transferred to the boat idled next to the trawler. Sergei waited to untie the rope keeping them tethered.

"Ten minutes," Marchenko informed him.

"What the hell is this, Karina?" Nevsky shouted over the revving engines of the neighboring boat. "You double-crossed me? For this piece of shit?"

"You don't get it, do you?" Alex said, an air of satisfaction in his voice. He rested on cushions at the back of the boat, the gun on his knee, pointed at Nevsky. "She didn't really sell you out. It was her intention all along. The scar on her face, she got that when she came to the aid of her sister that one of your men raped. You didn't know it was her sister. But you remember your guy. Stabbed about twenty times. That was part of Marchenko's payback. This is the other. I said you'd have a decision to make. Well, here it is. You get to choose how you die. We're anchored in the middle of the river. The boat's disabled."

Nevsky assessed his options, searching for anything that might give him a fighting chance. For all the predicaments he'd endured through a violent existence, he'd always survived. "I can pay you a large sum of money. I can even get the Iranians off your back. I'll tell them you were killed trying to escape."

"This isn't a negotiation. It's a funeral."

The Russian dashed starboard, reaching the edge of the boat before halting.

"Go ahead, jump," Alex encouraged. "Oh, that's right. You can't swim. The rest of the bad news is, there are no lifejackets, no buoys, no dingy. You have a choice, though. Down below in a galley cabinet, attached to a timer, is enough C4 to blow this boat to pieces. It's been counting down ever since the power went out. Got to warn you, it's a tricky configuration. Try to move it, boom! You can try to defuse it, but there are a lot of wires and I'm told it's very sensitive. Pull the wrong wire"—Alex raised an eyebrow—"boom!"

"All this because of some forgotten, discardable people," said Nevsky with fire in his eyes.

"I'm giving you what you never gave them. A choice. A chance.

Hey, you might make it to shore without drowning. You might diffuse the bomb. But I'm thinking you're just going to die." Alex stood up and climbed into the waiting boat. Relieved, Sergei untied the connecting line.

Alex gave Nevsky a half salute as the boat began whisking away from the stranded craft. Exploring his options, Nevsky paced from starboard to port. He ran forward to the bow and back again. As they got further away, Alex saw Nevsky had entered the cockpit. By now, he'd be in the stateroom, taking his chances at diffusing the bomb, a problematic task in the dark.

Nora came to Alex's side. She wrapped an arm around him, resting her head on his chest. The darkness and distance reduced the boat to a shadow on the water. Seconds later, a deafening explosion lit up the night. Alex took a deep breath and exhaled.

"Karina, appreciate you not shooting my friend," Alex said over his shoulder.

Marchenko stepped up to join them. "I nearly did."

"What stopped you?"

"He's kinda cute."

Alex laughed. "He's okay. Where's the best place to get drunk in Moscow?"

"Exactly what I had in mind," Marchenko responded. She threw Duncan a flirtatious look. "Is he coming?"

Alex already felt sorry for Duncan. "He is. And I'm buying."

Now that all the excitement was over, Nora gave Alex a detailed inspection. "Oh, my, you look like hell."

"Well, I got my ass kicked on purpose," Alex shot back. "Most satisfying beating I've ever taken."

CHAPTER 31

FROM THEIR LOFTY perch, the gargoyles and chimeras of Notre Dame Cathedral kept watch over the city. Half man, half beast. Grotesque and misunderstood by some, a savior to others.

Nathan Yadin could relate. Like them, he made some people feel uneasy. But even staunch detractors had come to acknowledge the need for those like him—people who had the stomach to do what others found morally reprehensible. Being a constant victim was an ill-advised survival plan. Sometimes you had to strike back.

Paris had become Yadin's adopted home. Though he was overjoyed to be back, it saddened him to avoid his Ile Saint-Louis apartment. His address remained a guarded secret. He'd yet to share its location, even with the woman who unknowingly was forcing him to question his way of life. For now, for her safety, best that she stay in the dark. There were way too many skeletons in his life, and not all of them were in the closet.

A warm day loomed on the horizon. Yadin's dark-gray, moisture-wicking T-shirt was soaked from early-morning exertion. He was pushing himself again. A therapist would tell him he'd been attempting to achieve personal bests since age ten. Had he been faster, he might have arrived in time to prevent his father's murder. The fact that he hadn't been physically strong enough to ward off the two assailants, taking a knife to the back, didn't alter his feelings of guilt. Years later, stronger and filled with rage, he found the killers, and avenged his father's death. That act of retribution began the transformation into what he saw himself as today. Half man, half beast.

Yadin liked to get his run in before most of Paris awoke, and definitely before the tourist logjam sprang to life. He navigated the streets and bridges of the 4th Arrondissement with added purpose. If by remote chance someone had latched onto him, he'd spot the tail in no time. He took several narrow, one-way streets, heading against traffic to mix things up. He crossed sections like the Saint-Louis Bridge over the Seine because it was closed off to motor traffic. And to alleviate all doubts, he'd dart down a set of stairs to run along the river before returning to his temporary residence—a boutique hotel along Boulevard Saint Germain.

The hotel was an extra layer of caution. Yadin had left the Iranians in London with additional questions and suspicions. Shahbod Gilani was adeptly clever. Taking extra precautions wouldn't hurt. The Iranians, however, weren't what concerned him at the moment. His gut knew there was a much larger problem brewing. He couldn't remain dead forever. A check of his background cover would have Mossad thinking that maybe he had somehow survived Natanz. They would want answers. The killing of his former mentor, Yosef Ezra, had occurred with precision on home soil. His assailant had eluded justice, and one thing was for certain: Mossad would never stop looking.

Operation Bayonet served as the best case study for Mossad's persistence. Members of the Palestinian terrorist group Black September were systemically hunted and put down by covert Israeli assassins for their involvement in the 1972 Munich Olympics massacre that killed eleven Israeli athletes. The operation was rumored to have stretched out for nearly twenty years before the final conspirator was blown up. You could run and hide, but every day would involve looking over your shoulder.

Why run a background check on Dr. Mueller if he was supposed to be dead? Yadin was amazed that the small, secretive department Ezra had set up to assist with the validity of his various backgrounds was still operational. The right people would be sent to investigate the underlying question of why, if he was still alive, he hadn't checked in by now.

The truth, in this case, was not in his favor.

Tonight, he'd purposely fall into a Mossad trap and do what the situation called for under extreme measures.

He'd lie.

Dying wasn't an option.

Not in Paris.

CHAPTER 32

ALEX OPENED HIS eyes mid-morning to a jarring amount of discomfort. His eyes watered, but deep inside there was a smile. Mission accomplished. He recalled the play-by-play of every punch that led to the climatic finish. For what transpired after, he consulted Nora to fill in the blanks. He questioned the accuracy of the video playing in his mind.

Nora joyfully informed him that yes, she and Karina Marchenko had kept him and Duncan upright after a night of intense drinking.

"And, were we singing?" he apprehensively followed up.

Nora laughed. "Yes, loud and badly."

Concerned, Alex asked about Duncan. Nora told him that Marchenko had gotten them a room.

"Them?"

Nora smiled like an adolescent schoolgirl privy to a naughty joke. Alex wanted to laugh, but it would've hurt too much. He hadn't put away liquor that heavily for years, but given the circumstances, the excess was understandable. He spent most of the day trying to recover, falling in and out of sleep.

A late-afternoon room service meal revived him enough to passively take part in a conversation again. Nora had taken care of the travel arrangements and packed his clothes. When she mentioned the destination was Paris, Alex didn't bother to ask why. Instead, his mind drifted to the events of the night before. Watching Nevsky suffer with the realization of his impending death was gratifying—he must have felt the same despair of his victims. Discovering that Marchenko had aided in his demise served as icing on the cake.

The Russian Railways train bound for Paris left on time at 10:15 p.m. Once clear of the Belorussky terminal, Alex shifted his focus to Nora. She was reading the latest Patricia Cornwell offering.

"Why are we going to Paris, again?" he asked in passing, slouching in the seat cushion of the VIP sleeping compartment.

"I told you over the phone. Your newfound friend," Nora answered without leaving the pages of the novel.

"What friend?"

"Your Natanz buddy, Nathan."

Alex lowered the book to Nora's lap. "You talked with Nathan?"

"Yes, in Monte Carlo. That's the name he used. He established himself as credible."

"And how did he do that?"

Nora wondered why Alex seemed hesitant. "He referenced where you two met and said he was responsible for the lead on Daniels. Who else besides us would know that? I'll admit, he was a little creepy at first, but something about him seemed legit."

"What did he want?"

"He wanted me to get in touch with you, since he hadn't been successful in doing so. He said because of what happened in Iran, we're on a high-value target list." Lifting the novel again, Nora added, "Feels good to be wanted, doesn't it?"

"Make jokes all you want, but the Iranians are serious about this. They had the balls to grab Dmitri to ask him about Mr. McBride."

"So you know?"

"Not exactly. Just bits and pieces."

"Well, if I found you, Nathan wanted to meet with us in Paris. It could be a setup."

"Why do you say that?"

"You trust him after meeting one time? Under dire circumstances?"

"He sort of saved my life."

"If memory serves, he sort of almost ended it too. Besides, something bothers me."

"What's that?"

"How he found me. I'd been traveling all over Europe, never said where I posted some pictures on social media, never with my face in them, and not under my real name. He said my postings helped him locate me. Careless, I know," Nora said, shaking her head, "but, it felt like he knew me. Like I said, a little creepy."

Alex turned his attention to the sights outside the window in the passing darkness. He couldn't bring himself to tell Nora the whole story. She wouldn't understand why he'd kept the truth from her for this long. Paris would take on a whole different tone if he did—she'd likely kill Nathan on the spot.

Finding the right path and time to tell her everything was the problem, with them being emotionally involved again. It was a dark secret you didn't keep from someone you deeply cared about. Not from her.

For now, he'd continue holding on to the knowledge that Nathan was the man who'd killed her dear friend and mentor, Erica Janway. Alex also couldn't say that the reason he was so acquainted with Nora was because she had been on his target list.

CHAPTER 33

MOST DAYS, CONSUMING a quality meal was high on Daniel Sharon's agenda.

Today was an exception.

The full plate of food in front of him got colder by the minute. Being toyed with ran a direct line to his appetite. He sat at the outdoor café as instructed, fuming for nearly thirty minutes, sweat running down from his armpits. Sharon's back stayed glued against the chair so that the worst part of his soaked shirt wasn't visible. When he did lean forward, it was to let the coolness of fresh air tickle his back.

The chilled glass of water on the table came in handy. He ran it across his forehead before gulping the contents down his throat. The waiter had already refilled his glass twice. Sharon didn't order the food before him, but the hanger steak, French fries and nothing green had arrived within ten minutes of him sitting down. He hated to admit it, but the meal was on point. The drink ordered for him at the pub prior to this location was close enough to warrant appreciation too.

The test had begun before sunset. The parameters were to navigate from one spot to another with no discernible timetable. He never knew when he'd get a few minutes to rest before receiving instructions via email to move along. The first order had come while sitting in the open on one of the green chairs around the circular pond at The Tuileries Garden. Sharon had to hop on the Metro to visit an art gallery in the 18th arrondissement. Next came a bookstore trip in the 6th arrondissement, followed by a visit to the Eiffel Tower.

The reward for his diligence and sweat had been that drink at a pub. His overheated body had relished it to the final drop. He then had fifteen minutes to make it to the restaurant on foot. When he arrived, a table was reserved in his name, along with a glass of iced water.

Sharon's butt had been in the chair, stewing, ever since. How long someone had been keeping watch during this journey, he had no clue. He'd tried to pick out a repetitive face, but other than a family of four, no one had crossed his radar with any degree of repetition. Each stop had its own characteristics. The art gallery had been isolating. The bookstore was the same, but to a greater degree. The Tuileries Garden had been vast and spread out. The Eiffel Tower, a mixture of young and old, with plenty of places to disappear or blend into the background. The pub had been boisterous, a meat market of youthful bodies that made him stand out like bacon at a vegan convention. He'd protested when a waitress had brought him a drink he didn't order. She'd told him the drink had been paid for. Noting his curiosity, she'd added that they'd been told to look for someone who matched his description, down to the clothes he was wearing. Twenty minutes later, the email directing him to the café had buzzed his phone.

Part of the reason for running Sharon around was punishment. The other, that Nathan Yadin wanted the full scope of what he was up against.

CHAPTER 34

THE MAN DRESSED in a black suit, fidgeting in a green chair at Tuileries Garden, had made Yadin remove his eye from the viewfinder of the SLR camera. From just under a hundred yards away, what he'd seen through the telephoto lens was a man who didn't look capable of handling the physical task of what was in store for him. The humidity alone didn't favor dark clothing, and there'd be a lot of movement required to get from point A to point B under fluctuating times. Just when he was about to feel sorry for the man, Yadin remembered who the "pushing portly" individual was—a trained assassin in Mossad's elite Kidon unit. Killers came in all shapes and sizes.

Yadin had plenty of photos to work with back in his hotel room. He ran his main subject's face through a database provided by his former handler, Joseph Ezra. Having access to the information represented a major security breach, but Ezra had often operated outside the lines. The rules were bent when doing so served, according to Ezra, the greater good.

Though he was a brilliant strategist, Ezra's greatest achievement had led to his downfall. He had partnered with the wrong people, chasing legacy instead of being satisfied with pulling off an operation that derailed Iran's nuclear ambitions for years. His fatal mistake, however, had been betraying the person who regarded him with the utmost respect. Had it been an act all along? A lengthy recruitment? The intense training, praise, and secrecy. The unbridled freedom not afforded to other Mossad agents. There had been nothing Ezra wouldn't do for his prized asset. Nothing, except let him willfully walk away. The signs had surfaced that Yadin was growing tired of the killing and leaning toward tackling the biggest fear of all—a normal life.

Yadin had held back his reservation over disposing of Erica Janway because he trusted Ezra's decision-making was based on sound judgment. In studying his target, Yadin had concluded there was something tranquil and non-sinister about the CIA operative. Having shadowed and stalked prey for years, he had become an expert in examining the human condition. Janway had a purity of purpose. He'd carried out his orders, but her death stayed with him. When the reactors didn't shut off at Natanz, Yadin knew it wasn't due to a design oversight. The final confirmation had come from monitoring his extraction team. The operatives in place had nothing to do with smuggling people out of country. Their expertise was leaving bodies behind. Only one man could have put that in motion.

Presumed dead, Yadin had figured there was nothing to worry about. That feeling lasted long enough to spend quality, carefree time with Lauren. She was compelling. She offered tangible proof that the fairy-tale life he dreamed about could happen.

One night at dinner with her in London gave him pause. Yadin had noticed a man taking photos of them with his cell phone. The man had seemed harmless enough to make Yadin think he was being overly cautious. He had let it go to enjoy the time with Lauren. When he spotted the same man at Piccadilly Circus the next day, Yadin fought the urge to act right away. The possibility of putting Lauren in harm's way enraged him. He'd considered sending a violent message, ending Karimi and Navid's dog and pony show. Discovering the Iranians had started a large-scale manhunt that included not just him, but also Alex and Nora Mossa, was the only thing that stopped him from killing the two clueless, low-level worker bees.

The depth of the Iranians' probing had created a more dire threat. One such threat, named Daniel Sharon, barely touched the hanger steak dinner ordered for him. He'd done better canvassing the city's arrondissements than Yadin thought possible upon first glance hours ago. Yadin had only kept eyes on Sharon at Tuileries Garden, the Eiffel Tower, and now here. Sharon didn't know that, so he had to assume he was being watched the entire time. He couldn't contact anyone using his personal phone because Yadin had possession of it. Sharon had been forced to exchange his phone with a co-ed on her bicycle at Tuileries Garden. She'd promised he'd get his phone back later if he were a "bon garçon."

Yadin let Sharon bask in anger a few minutes longer. The body language spoke volumes, but the eyes were darts of fire as they canvassed.

CHAPTER 35

THE TAP ON his right shoulder from behind caught Sharon off guard. The contact was not the courtesy of a waiter politely announcing he was passing by with food or drink in hand. The pat was unnerving in that it was friendly. Sharon turned to look. There was no one on his right. He reversed attention to his left side, coming up empty again. A person slid into the seat directly behind him, momentarily bumping into his chair. The lack of an "Excuse me" or "I'm sorry" didn't help Sharon's mood. He wanted to educate the offensive patron on manners, but he had to exercise restraint. Another sip of ice water cooled his emotions. Sharon's fingers played a rough melody on the edge of the table, causing ripples of water to dance in his glass. He stared at the burner phone given to him, waiting for a new notification. This run-around-town, follow-my-orders shit had gotten old by the Eiffel Tower visit. With no new message of instruction, he sighed and leaned back, making contact with the chair behind him.

A proper upbringing made him exclaim, "Excuse me" while scooting his chair forward. He was upset at being so cordial, given he hadn't gotten an apologetic response from the man prior. Sharon realized his anger was getting the best of him. Not a good demeanor by any account.

"No problem," the man behind him said, a trace of sarcasm in his voice.

Sharon shook his head. The nerve. He didn't like the man inching back so close, either.

"You should eat your steak, Daniel. It's been an exhausting day."

Addressed by name, Sharon froze.

"Don't turn around," the man insisted. "My goal is for us both to walk away from here tonight."

Over the shock of being played so well, Sharon said, "Seems like you've been trying to kill me all day."

"Perhaps you should consider a healthier lifestyle."

Sharon nodded. "Pot, meet kettle."

"I assume because you're sitting here, it was your idea to hack my mother's email and send that bogus correspondence?"

"Yes."

"Well done."

Sharon hunched his shoulders. "I had faith you'd see it for what it was. Worth a try. You're not exactly on anyone's contact list."

The seating arrangement frustrated Sharon. He wanted to be face-to-face, but he was in no position to demand anything, not from this man. It troubled him that Nathan Yadin knew his name. Director Rozen had stressed that this operation was being run under a tight microscope. How then could Yadin know his name? They'd never met. Director Rozen had been adamant about Yadin's skill level. Fantasy was reality, and the legend was sitting directly behind him. Reckoning with that, Sharon felt compelled to add to his last sentence. "And as I stressed in our correspondence, I'm here in a non-threatening capacity."

"You're alive. Take that as a good sign."

Sharon shelved his clever reply as the waiter stopped to take Yadin's order of red wine. It gave Sharon the chance to sample the steak. He didn't give Yadin the satisfaction of letting him know, but the steak was flavorful.

The waiter moved on to place the order. "There are serious questions that need clarity."

"Questions or accusations?" Yadin asked with a hint of disdain.

"There are whispers. But, I'm here solely on the director's orders."

This was a moment to exercise caution. The tone and words chosen would receive heavy scrutiny. "The director taking a limited approach has its pluses and minuses," said Yadin. "He gets to frame the message, should he have to present it to the Prime Minister. On the other hand, if no plausible explanation is offered, he can close the books on supposition alone."

"I'm all ears if you have a theory surrounding Ezra's death. There's also your disappearance."

"Surviving Natanz was no easy accomplishment," Yadin offered. "I sustained injuries that required medical attention and prolonged rest. But first, I had to get out of the country. Not knowing whether I was alive or dead, the Iranians searched high and low to find me. I missed connecting with my extraction team. I managed to get out. I didn't risk contacting Ezra, because the region was a hot zone of finger pointing. Then, I heard the news."

"Surely there was a way to bring you in?" Sharon had to admit that so far, there was reasonable doubt. The explanation seemed plausible. This wasn't the place, however, to examine the intricate details of Yadin's story. Lucky bastard. Had he met up with the extraction team, he might not be here today.

"How's your steak, Daniel?"

Son of a bitch. This was infuriating. Mid-bite, Sharon replied, "It's fine." He stopped short of adding "thank you."

The waiter arrived with the wine. After a courteous "Merci," the line of communication resumed.

"Who would have brought me in? No doubt you've been over Ezra's files and been briefed by his superiors. He ran his own program without stringent oversight. I took orders from him, and him alone. I rarely worked with anyone in the field. Ezra even had his own dedicated tech support team." Yadin sipped his wine. "Who else has that kind of setup? So tell me, Daniel, who was I supposed to report to after Ezra's death?"

Based on the responses, there was a limit to how far Sharon could take this. "You're smart enough to know where this is heading. It's one thing to tell me the details. You have to convince the decision makers. They want that to happen back home."

Sharon delivered the message the director had instructed him to convey. The next move was not up to him.

"I'm afraid I have to decline." Yadin's tone was neither threatening nor apologetic.

Shit! His back to Yadin, Sharon had hoped to hear a different response.

"May I ask . . ." Sharon began, positioning his right hand closer to the knife in his jacket.

"Nothing to tell you at the moment," Yadin said. "Now is not a good time."

Sharon took a deep breath. The day had been challenging, and it wasn't over. "When, then? I have to give them something."

"This matter with the Iranians has gotten out of hand. I must resolve that first. Checking into my credentials and background raised a red flag. I have to get them off my back for good. Dr. Mueller's run must end."

"We can help you with that."

Yadin thought of the so-called extraction team that had been waiting for him in Iran. Sharon was no choirboy either. He also thought of Lauren and how life could move forward, if that was even a possibility.

"Thanks, but I'll handle the situation my way. Once it's done, we can revisit this misunderstanding."

"I'll pass your decision along. I advise you not to let this go unresolved too long. You were dead until a few weeks ago."

Yadin didn't reply. Perhaps he was reconsidering, going over his options. Or was he merely indulging in the wine? The waiter unexpectedly appeared at Sharon's side. He asked if everything was satisfactory considering he had hardly touched his meal. Sharon replied that all was fine. He wasn't too hungry, which was a definite lie.

The waiter gave an understanding smile and then raised a finger. "Oh, the gentleman that sat behind you thought you'd dropped this." The waiter held Sharon's cellphone, which he'd relinquished at Tuileries Garden. He spun in his chair. There was no Yadin.

"Is it your phone, monsieur?"

"Yes, it is. Thank you. The check, please."

"There is no charge, sir. Everything was taken care of before you sat down."

Sharon whispered, "Of course it was."

He hadn't felt Yadin get up and move at all. At one point, their chair backs had been touching. He felt foolish.

Adding insult to injury, Neril was probably laughing at him too.

CHAPTER 36

COME ON! COME on!

Lisa Neril watched Nathan Yadin get up and leave the café from a white Mercedes-Benz Sprinter van parked half a block away. Her hand rode the door handle, waiting for Sharon to give her a signal. He remained in his chair as if frozen in time.

Pick him up or let him go?

Metro entrances on both sides of the street made a decision urgent. Yadin didn't take either. In not doing so, he'd done a very smart thing, opting to head down a one-way street against traffic. Neril was on the verge of losing him in the darkness and the crowd if she didn't act. She needed an answer fast. Neril glanced at Sharon and saw the waiter hand him a phone. Sharon's reaction when he turned in his chair confirmed he had no clue Yadin had left.

Neril shook her head. "Shit!" She would bring it up later, but for now, her concern was abort or apprehend. Getting over his embarrassment, Sharon gave the signal.

She flew out of the vehicle and took off jogging in Yadin's

direction, speaking into her Bluetooth headset. She wasn't in the mood for the feedback she received.

"I don't know," Neril directed. "Figure it out. Take another street. I'll keep you updated on the location."

The Sprinter van swung out of a parking spot. The three occupants were armed and, because of Neril's agitated state, on high alert. The van's customized list of features included: soundproofing, bulletproof windows, reinforced steel panels on the exterior shell, and heavy-duty, self-inflating tires. The one major drawback was that the gas mileage sucked.

Neril wore a jean jacket, a breathable striped shirt, olive skinny jeans, and slip-on sneakers. The attire allowed her to blend in while offering flexibility of movement. That freedom came in handy as she picked up the pace, searching for a lightweight tan jacket and dark khaki pants. She cursed under her breath at the thought of losing him after such an exhausting day. There were many side streets he could have already chosen. That would be the smart play. She was about to blurt out the French equivalent for her anguish when across the street, a half block ahead, she spotted a tan jacket and dark pants, walking without fanfare.

The Mercedes crew got Neril's update. She analyzed the landscape ahead. If Yadin chose a quiet street, he would hear them coming. A busy street presented the unpredictability of bystanders, but offered a degree of protection. Because of past terrorist attacks, uniformed and plainclothes police patrols were increased. Neril had to avoid such a confrontation at all costs. Then there was the underlying reason for all this caution—the man she was trailing was utterly lethal.

Yadin approached an intersection but didn't cross the street with the light in his favor. Neril ducked into a small sandwich shop. She hung by the entrance to keep tabs on him. Yadin seemed to be weighing his options. Two right turns would lead him toward a busy intersection close to Notre Dame Cathedral. If he continued straight along Boulevard Saint-Germain, a number of food establishments remained open for business. He decided to go left on Rue Saint-Jacques, another one-way street. Neril exited the sandwich shop, relaying the development to her team. One occupant of the van familiar with Paris contemplated Yadin's next move. When the clarity of their location sank in, he told Neril that if Yadin maintained his direction and crossed Rue des Écoles, they could intervene in the next block on Rue Saint-Jacques. He stressed that even though the street bordered Sorbonne University, there would be fewer people around at this time of night. Neril gave her approval, but cautioned she'd call it off if the tiniest thing didn't feel right.

Yadin passed the first hiccup, electing not to take the street before Rue des Écoles. Neril worried as he continued on. It was his demeanor. He was too at ease. Had he spotted them while at the café or had he been aware of their presence all day? Who was setting a trap for whom?

Rue Saint-Jacques began a gradual incline, giving Neril a better view of what lie ahead. The street was mostly quiet. The Mercedes had pulled over to the curb a block away. They were in position to see Yadin if he walked across Rue des Écoles. If he decided to head in their direction, they wanted to know if they should intervene.

"Not unless you want to die tonight," was Neril's response. "Wait for my instruction."

She widened her stride, veering off to Yadin's side of the street. Her sneakers softened her movement, but in the quieter surroundings, he'd hear the steps.

The men in the van straightened up when the target strolled past Rue des Écoles. Neril followed in his path. She took one last look ahead and to her flank. She also made sure the van was in the right place. Content, she whispered in her microphone that it was a go.

The van crawled forward, making the left at the intersection and locating Neril ahead on the right. The driver kept his eyes darting between what was in front of him and checking the rearview and side mirrors. The other two men crouched near the door, ready to spring it open.

Closing the gap, Neril maintained a line to the right, staying as wide as possible to avoid being perceived as a threat. She wanted to come across as a woman who was not comfortable walking alone in the dark. She shielded the hand dug into her purse by sliding it to the back of her hip. Being advanced upon from the rear on a quiet street, Neril saw a swift glance over the shoulder acknowledging her presence. Barely noticeable, Yadin shortened his stride, moving closer to the street so she would have sufficient room to pass. Neril couldn't quite put her finger on it, but something felt out of place. Yadin seemed apprehensive and timid.

No turning back now, Neril told herself.

The van flashed its high beams and hit the horn twice as if trying to get the attention of another vehicle. This being a one-way street, there was no oncoming traffic, but the intended distraction worked. Yadin spun to his left. The van hit the brakes hard. The side door flew open, and the two men rushed out. Yadin reached out, more in protest than a defensive position. Leading with her shoulder, Neril shoved him forward into the arms of the two men, who locked Yadin down. His arms pinned and restrained, the men hoisted Yadin into the van, jumping back in themselves. Neril joined them, the door shutting behind her.

The driver shifted into gear and lurched forward. Yadin struggled, but couldn't free himself of the grips that held him in place. Neril duct taped his hands and feet like a mover securing a heavy piece of furniture. That feeling of something not being right grew even stronger. It shouldn't have been this easy.

Neril collapsed into a seat to face her secured prize. An interior light clicked on. The tinted windows assured no one from the outside could see in.

"Sorry it had to come to this, but the director wants to talk to you now, back home," Neril said.

Yadin looked disheveled, not the image she'd imagined. In fact, he didn't appear the least bit threatening. He kept looking around, taking in the other two men, focusing on one before moving on to the other. Then he settled on Neril.

"I'm afraid there's been a terrible mistake here," he said.

"Yes, the mistake is you wanted to do things your way," Neril added, scrutinizing him in return. "Play nice and this will go smoothly."

Neril stopped talking when a flesh-colored device dislodged from her captive's ear. She also noticed something dangling around his neck. She reached to rip his shirt open.

"Damn it!" Neril exploded.

The necklace held a small pendant of a camera that you could hold between your forefinger and thumb. Neril tore it free from his neck, covering it with a fisted hand. She picked up the apparatus that had fallen and put it up to her ear.

"Go ahead, say something," the bound man said, not sure how cool he should be at the moment. "He can hear you. I'm just a freelancer. I got paid to do a job. Show up at the café. Sit behind a guy and respond with what I was told to say."

Neril shut her eyes hard. She put the device up to her ear. "Hello. Nicely played."

"Don't beat yourself up too bad," a voice answered. "You're good. I didn't spot you until right before the cafe. But now I have your picture."

"You know how this looks?"

There was a chuckle on the other end. "That's rich, considering your actions. Like I told Sharon, there is a matter I have to take care of first. Then I will address this."

"I don't know how that will play back home."

"My worry, not yours. Do me a favor though and please release Mr. Charbonneau. He's played his part very well and has a wonderful knack for forgetting things. Oh, and I promised he could keep the camera. Goodbye for now."

Neril smashed the earpiece against the van and told the men to cut their captive's restraints. She instructed the driver to find a place to pull over, and they kicked Mr. Charbonneau out near Luxembourg Garden.

Neril slumped back in the Mercedes, knowing that when Sharon learned about this, he'd have a huge smirk on his face.

CHAPTER 37

ALEX LET HIS head clear before he stirred under the covers. He discovered Nora was not by his side. He was grateful that she'd let him sleep. His body needed all the time it could steal to recover. Nora had left a note saying she'd gone to join Duncan in the dining car. They'd save him a seat should he show up.

Alex's body ached, reminiscent of those Monday mornings following a physical Sunday NFL game. He used to bounce back much quicker. In his defense, he'd taken a huge risk with the strategy he used against Nevsky and his enforcer. Concussions had persuaded him to end his pro career prematurely. The blows to the face on the boat had been jarring, but he'd survived. While he waited for the shower to reach optimal temperature, Alex inspected the damage in the bathroom mirror. His face was bruised and swollen. That paled in comparison to the deep, discolored blotches across his torso. Every breath hurt.

He was in no hurry to end his shower, but he was hungry. Putting on clothes pinpointed which areas of his body hurt the most. After another check in the mirror, Alex realized the bruises weren't a good look. Reluctantly, he grabbed the flesh-colored makeup Nora had bought for him and smoothed over the worst parts of his face. Hopefully the lighting in the dining car would be bad.

Traveling the countryside by train was rolling melatonin for the soul, relaxing and nostalgic. Taking a plane would have been quicker, but it also would have exposed them to a multitude of interested parties—plus, the train gave Alex added time to recuperate.

He made his way toward a smiling Nora in the dining car, avoiding direct eye contact with the other seated passengers. Nora greeted him with a soft kiss on the lips.

Duncan winced. "You look a little like Ali after the Foreman fight."

"Thanks, Sunshine," said Alex, picking up a menu. "At least you didn't say Ernie Terrell. Anything good?"

"Can't screw up the basics," Duncan offered. "Stick with what you know."

"Eggs, bacon and toast it is." Nora poured him a cup of coffee. She kept a smile hidden upon noticing he'd used the makeup, managing to soften some spots without going overboard.

Alex quickly acknowledged the waiter and ordered, not wanting him to fixate on his facial bruises. If an explanation was warranted, Alex had an elaborate cover story about being a boxer, and how last night's winning fight had been a brutal one.

"Marchenko sent me a link to the morning papers," Alex said after the waiter left. "The authorities have more questions than answers about the explosion. Four bodies recovered. Not sure if there are more. Identities of the deceased unknown for now." Alex sat with that for a moment. "Oh," he continued, addressing Duncan. "Marchenko says 'hi.'"

Duncan threw Nora a disappointing look. "Had to tell him, didn't you?"

Nora hunched her shoulders. "Look at it this way. You made a lasting impression."

"I've known you for years, and you never, not once, mentioned a thing about wanting a Russian bride," Alex prodded.

"You two have jokes."

"Just messing with you," Nora offered. "Actually, she seems nice. Smart. Confident. Can drink with the best of them."

"You left out deadly," Alex chimed in.

Nora nodded. "Definitely marriage material."

"This going to continue all the way to Paris?" Duncan wondered.

"No, we're done," Alex conceded with a smirk. "I'll come back to this at a later date for sure." Changing focus, he tapped the back of Nora's hand. "When are we supposed to meet Nathan in Paris?"

"If I found you, Sunday evening," Nora confirmed. "He'll get in touch."

"That's it?"

"Yep."

"And you agreed to this?"

"We don't have to follow through. He had something to do with saving your life, not mine."

Alex refrained from correcting her on that point. He hadn't figured out a way to tell her the whole truth. Hopefully he would never have to broach the subject.

"I was around him in a very tense situation."

"You coming over to my side of thinking that this could be a setup? Both of us neatly wrapped in one place together."

"I'm not ruling anything out at this point. We'll take the meet, but be ready for anything."

Nora agreed, adding, "Problem is, we're a bit light in the hardware department, and I'm prohibited from contacting any Agency-related assets."

Duncan sat listening to his friends brainstorm. They complemented each other well. They'd gone through hell to get back to this point, but it was good to see them together again.

"This Nathan seems to have gotten your attention," Duncan observed.

"He's a dangerous person," said Alex, thinking back to their encounter. In the meantime, he intended to make what he expected to be a rather ordinary breakfast taste better by hearing a good story.

"Just so I'm clear," Alex said to Duncan and Nora, "you guys jumped off a bridge?"

CHAPTER 38

GEORGE CHAMPION TRIED to curtail his wife Jill's enthusiasm. A 2 a.m. call from the White House could run the gamut of possibilities. Most of the world's trouble spots were hours ahead, and what transpired in the dark would shine in daylight. As the CIA Director of the National Clandestine Service, Champion's insight might provide valuable background information if a decision for swift action loomed.

Still in the honeymoon phase of the job, the top man at 1600 Pennsylvania Avenue had shown an early penchant for validating his thoughts and edicts to everyone on a need-to-know basis. Champion speculated that was partly due to the president not yet establishing total trust with certain members on the Hill. Drawing conclusions wasted time—Champion would know soon enough. There was transportation en route to pick him up.

Groggy from having his sleep interrupted, Champion put on his socks at the edge of the bed. He assured his wife, "I feel confident it's not a hit."

The remark warranted a pillow in the back. "No, but you might become a made man."

Talk had begun that Champion was on the president's short list to become the next CIA director since Adam Doyle, the current occupant of the position, had announced he would soon step down. Champion also had an ally on the inside: Deputy Chief of Staff Amanda Jergens. They'd been friends since college, and later on, he and Jill had played matchmaker by introducing her to the man she'd marry.

There was one other thing about President Travis Hudson that made this hour not so unusual. The man was legendary for staying up late. A California native, Hudson often pushed sleep aside in favor of the three-hour time difference. Football season was underway, meaning he was in full "Fight On" mode for his alma mater, USC. He'd grown up a Dodgers fan too, and their night games were often seen on TVs that POTUS might pass in the White House.

Champion stood to let Jill finish knotting the tie she'd chosen to go with his dark suit and white shirt. She always took care of him without ever complaining. They had a great life together. She'd accepted his decision to serve his country when there were more lucrative opportunities out there.

Jill stepped back to admire her work, then handed him his suit coat as a way of saying, *You're complete now.* Champion put an arm around her and held up his phone for her to see. The fifth-ranked Trojans had beaten Pac 12 rival and seventeenth-ranked California, 37–20. Unfazed, she paused, then headed to the walk-in closet. When she returned, she undid his tie, replacing it with a subtle cardinal-and-gold one. Champion smiled. That she knew the Trojans' school colors was impressive, because she rarely paid much attention when he watched sports on television.

In the kitchen, Champion had to accept a Keurig cup of coffee. He gave his best pouting impersonation, but it wasn't going to work. Jill looked at him crossways. "I love you, but I'm not making you a fresh pot of coffee. Mrs. Prescot has spoiled you way too much," she said, referring to his do-it-all administrative assistant.

Expecting the doorbell to ring at this hour didn't make the sound less startling. Jill gave her knight in black armor a final once-over. "Maybe you can take a catnap in the car," she advised, delivering a kiss. "I know you can't tell me much about your job, but let me say, and it's not the first time—the hours suck."

"Thanks. Love you too. Go back to bed."

He opened the door to a waiting Secret Service officer. With obligatory pleasantries exchanged, there was no time wasted getting him into the back seat of the waiting vehicle. Jill watched him leave from a front window.

Her possibly soon-to-be made man had a meeting with the most powerful man in the world.

CHAPTER 39

CHAMPION SLEPT FOR most of the thirty-minute ride. A short nap, but welcomed just the same. For a moment, he thought he was back in his bed dreaming. Reality kicked in as the SUV pulled up to the White House West Wing entrance.

The marine on duty issued a welcoming salute and then held the door to the White House open. The Secret Service agent who'd greeted him at his house led Champion inside, announcing their arrival into his lapel while passing through the lobby. Champion stayed on his heels down the corridors like he had a string attached.

Champion's first visit to 1600 Pennsylvania Avenue months ago had been a tension-filled night. An unknown commodity then, he'd faced tremendous pressure to make his case before the most powerful members of the administration. His actions had interrupted sleep and disturbed a group of individuals who were looking for a reason not to like him. Thank goodness he'd risen above the "pissant" level the secretary of state had mentally assigned to him then.

President Hudson was not present when Champion entered the Oval Office. He encountered two men who rose off the sofa, only to sit back down when they realized it wasn't the occupant of the office. They acknowledged Champion with grimaced smiles. He took a seat on the sofa opposite them. The two men were familiar with each other, exchanging short, soft-spoken dialogue. They'd never met, but Champion was certain of the older man's identity. Awkward silence followed, neither Champion nor the men knew the protocol for introduction since they weren't clear on the circumstances of the meeting.

To ease his apprehension, Champion looked around the room. Everything was as he remembered, but the familiarity didn't lessen the intimidation. He was admiring the choice of artwork when the door to the outer office opened. Each man rose slightly from his cushion, but it was another false alarm. This time it was an aide who strolled through, asking if anyone wanted something to drink. The other two men showed they still had water. Champion made a bet with himself—the coffee at the White House likely wasn't instant or a Keurig cup.

"I'll take a cup of coffee if it's not too much trouble, thank you."

The silence returned once the aide left. Undaunted, Champion resumed his trip down memory lane. The journey didn't last long, because Champion fixated on the seated, silent partner he didn't know. The more he concentrated, the more he became convinced he'd seen the man before. It was the "where" that wouldn't clear the fog. The man's apparent youth tipped off Champion's brain. Thirty-something? Full blond hair. Not the toned body of a gym rat, probably a jogger. He was a thinker.

Where did he know him from?

Why did Jill enter his mind?

There had to be an association. Champion just wasn't connecting the dots. It was bugging the hell out of him now.

The door opened again and the routine of butts halfway out of seats continued. The aide carried a tray containing a carafe of coffee, cups, and a container of cream and sugar. He placed it on the end table next to Champion.

"Thank you," Champion murmured as the aide left without fanfare. Being bright-eyed and cheerful after 3 a.m. required a lot of practice.

Tending to his coffee gave Champion a task to mask his curiosity. Every day, he read reports and threat assessments, and kept updated with ongoing operations. The workload and pressure that came with it was time consuming, but vital. The only time he read for fun was during vacation, whatever that was anymore, and the Sunday paper with Jill.

That was it. *The Washington Post Magazine.*

He and Jill carved out time together each Sunday morning to relax with coffee, breakfast, and the paper. They enjoyed staying in their lounge wear for hours, getting caught up with each other's week while discussing various articles and opinions in the paper.

He didn't remember the surname, but the man's first name was Jake. The profile piece was months ago, but that much had stuck in Champion's head, because the writer had penned something to the effect of, "You're familiar with Jake from State Farm, but have probably never heard of Jake from State." The article detailed how quickly this wunderkind had endeared himself to the current administration with an uncanny knowledge of what and who made countries tick. He was on a meteoric rise. Even the old guard didn't challenge his effectiveness of assessment. The article further pointed out that he was savvy enough to wait his turn in line. Champion smirked when he realized the irony. Jake from State was just a few feet away, and it was after 3 a.m.

No one got up when the door opened this time. The hesitancy of another false alarm got erased in a hurry as President Hudson strolled through.

"Gentlemen, please sit down," the president said, sauntering to the Resolute desk. He hovered over the distinctive wooden gift from Queen Victoria, sorting through folders until he found the pertinent one.

President Hudson moved with dignified grace, a man comfortable in his surroundings. His slim figure wore the dark slacks and long-sleeved shirt to perfection. For a man who likely hadn't gone to bed yet, the president looked polished. Champion had seen it before, in this very office. The man's resilience to function defied the basic human necessity of sleep. Surely he couldn't keep this routine up throughout his entire term. In the early stages of his presidency, though, he exhibited a surplus of adrenaline.

"I assume you guys didn't introduce yourselves?" The president took a comfortable position on the sofa next to Champion. The lack of responses coupled with sheepish looks provided the answer. "Everything is not a secret around here, except what we're about to discuss." He pointed at Champion. "This is George Champion, head of the National Clandestine Service at the CIA."

The president engaged the two other men, referencing the senior member first. "Tom Stacy, Deputy Secretary of State." The graying, mustached man with an expanded forehead nodded.

"Jake Lancellotti, former Director of Policy Planning at State. He recently moved to the White House as the VP's foreign policy adviser."

Champion speculated that Lancellotti's appointment had everything to do with bolstering the West Wing's inner circle. The administration had done an admirable job of recognizing and utilizing talent.

"Sorry for the timing," President Hudson offered. "Scheduling made it unavoidable, and I want as few eyes on this as possible for the moment. Plus, Tom and Jake pretty much just got off a military plane after spending time in Muscat. Can't have them off the docket for too long. People would start asking questions that we'd have to skirt around. The Associated Press is already snooping."

"Muscat" was one way to stay off the radar, Champion thought. The capital was perched on the Gulf of Oman. In a region of fragile alliances or all-out hatred, the US had an ally in the ruling monarch. The sultan was smart to cultivate decades of good will with America, and the region's two biggest rivals, Sunni-controlled Saudi Arabia and Shia-dominated Iran.

President Hudson passed Champion the folder he'd retrieved, labeled "CAP." On the first page, Champion learned that the acronym stood for Cooperation Action Plan. What followed far exceeded his imagination. Over the years, he'd developed a skill for speed-reading through pages of documents and reports. He took his time with this one, flipping back at select intervals to make sure he'd read correctly. Midway through he looked up, his face an exclamation point.

"This is groundbreaking," said Champion.

"We've swung for the fences on this one," President Hudson confirmed. Reading Champion's face, he added, "It's so sensitive, we haven't given it a security clearance classification yet. Only a tiny circle is in the loop."

Considering nearly one and a half million Americans had Top Secret security clearance from various government agencies, Champion agreed it was wise to keep this contained. One omission of the plan bothered him, though. "Shahroudi's on board with this?"

The president quickly dismissed the question. "Oh, hell no. He'd still like to drop a bomb through the White House roof if he could."

"Then"—Champion closed the folder—"the only way this could proceed is with the blessing of . . ." The stares he received told him all he needed to know.

Hudson gave the room's youngest member permission to fill in the blanks. Lancellotti didn't reference notes. His hard drive of a brain had the specifics stored away.

"As President Hudson mentioned, we just returned from Oman. It was our fourth round of meetings. The delegation was small, to avoid attention. Sandy Flynn, chief U.S. nuclear negotiator, was part of this trip too. It's been a mixed bag of experts from various departments, but Tom and I have been running point."

Lancellotti had a relaxed manner that some might interpret as cockiness, but having been in similar situations, Champion knew it had more to do with preparation. Granted, there had to be an ego in that Harvard body, but he kept it under wraps in this company.

"We haven't had diplomatic relations with Iran since the hostage crisis in '79," Champion pointed out. "Why would they be willing to hash out something so monumental now? Especially with the 'Great Satan?'"

"I thought the same thing," Lancellotti affirmed. "But, when the president asked me to lunch in Denmark, he threw out the 'What if?' I laid out all the reasons I could think of why it wouldn't work. Made even more implausible by recent events."

Lancellotti glanced at the president to make sure he was retelling the story accurately. "Of course," he continued with a smile, "I was tasked with testing the waters anyway. That's when Sultan Azzan bin Said acted as an intermediary on our behalf. Soon after, much to our surprise, we had a meeting with Iranian officials. After a ton of work, and input from the supreme leader, we have the framework of a deal we hope to complete in the coming weeks."

"The other members of the P5+1 are satisfied?" Champion asked, referencing the UN Security Council's group of world powers. The organization was formed to seek diplomatic avenues with Iran to help dissuade it from manufacturing nuclear weapons. Relief from certain imposed economic sanctions was often the dangling carrot, but Natanz had proven how well that had been working.

"Yes, fully committed. Hoping like hell this happens," Lancellotti beamed. "As for Oman, which shares the Strait of Hormuz with Iran, this presents new opportunities in the expanding trade corridor. The deal could translate into nine-figure revenues for them."

Tom Stacy chimed in, his voice hoarse. "Everyone believes this could help to stabilize the region. And I know what you're thinking. Why would the Iranians finally step up to the table? Well, they've got over seven billion dollars in relief from international sanctions as motivation. Also, Natanz proved to be a total embarrassment. This is a path to saving face. It's structured to look like they're not caving under pressure, but that's exactly what's happening. This move helps their economy when there's serious internal pressure. They also won't have to totally dismantle their nuclear program. It will, however, get curtailed, altered, and properly monitored with no military applications for multiple years. That's the short list of conditions."

Champion tried to put it all together, but one piece didn't fit. "Correct me if I'm wrong, but the presidential election is not too far off. Given all that's happened, I don't see how this flies under Shahroudi's rule."

"You're correct," said Stacy, clearing his throat. "But, they have led us to believe this agreement might be a means to an end in terms of the current leadership."

From what he'd heard, there was nothing for Champion to dislike. This was a major undertaking considering the climate of relations. To his surprise, though, there was a name not mentioned— one he couldn't fathom not being involved somehow.

"What about the Israelis?"

"Not part of the process," the president said. "They will benefit, no question, and with the other countries backing it, we hope they'll see the sense of it all. But, if we had brought them in on this, the Iranians wouldn't have agreed to sit down. We realize we're buying time here. Ten years' worth of time before Iran can begin exploring nuclear weapons. Let's not kid ourselves. Intelligence showed that even with the sanctions in place, they were two years away from developing a reliable system capable of striking Israel. Ten years of prosperity, dialogue—who knows? Maybe a long-lasting truce can develop."

Or, we'll have a richer, more powerful, more determined than ever Iran wanting to wipe Israel off the map, Champion considered, but didn't say.

What he did offer was, "This is all very impressive—historic, to some extent. I take it there's something you need from the CIA, sir?"

President Hudson shifted his posture. Finally, a sign he might be getting tired. "I gave Director Doyle a heads up, but this is more in line with your department, I thought, and he agreed. As you heard, in the coming weeks, we hope to complete CAP. We'll dress it up with a fancier name, but appearances are important to the Iranians in relation to the rest of the world. Without question, Tom and Jake have done the heavy lifting, but come signing day, Secretary of State Drake will have to be the official face. Joining him will be fellow foreign ministers. Security will be a nightmare. Each country will bring its own personnel. I can foresee a territorial mess unfolding. Not everyone loves this plan. We've tried to keep a lid on it, but odds are the Israelis know. Shahroudi's blood is probably boiling."

"I doubt the Israelis would risk making a move, considering the parties involved," Champion noted. "Shahroudi, that's a different story."

"I'll worry less about Israel later this week when the prime minister visits. I'll officially inform him then."

"What can I do for you, sir?"

The president appreciated the no-nonsense approach. "DSS branches overseas have been hearing low-level chatter about a potential strike against US and allied interests. Nothing specific, but given what's on the calendar, I want our butts covered. If the signing were to happen on domestic soil, I would have turned this over to Layden at the FBI. Make no mistake, I have absolute faith and trust in the DSS to provide for everyone's safety. They're running point. However, I'll sleep better knowing an extra set of eyes and ears are out there. Nothing too heavy-handed. Doyle says this should be right in your wheelhouse."

The president had a taste of Champion's capability under tense circumstances, believing his work to be thorough and exemplary. He wasn't ready to inform Champion, but this assignment would serve as a final test. If he passed with glowing colors, he'd likely get the offer to replace Director Doyle once he stepped down.

"I'll need all the details, sir. Timetables. The who. The where. Transportation itineraries. The sooner, the better."

The president shook Champion's hand. "You'll get everything you need. Thanks for your cooperation."

Champion didn't have a choice, but he valued the sentiment.

The president ordered Lancellotti and Stacy to get some rest. He walked everyone toward the outer office. Champion was the last to leave, and President Hudson slowed him down.

"George," the president said, producing a playful smile. "Tell Jill, great tie choice."

CHAPTER 40

"I DON'T TRUST him."

The admission carried weight with President Akbar Shahroudi because of the person offering the opinion. Yet, it didn't change his mind. "You must give me more than that. He saved my life."

"And in doing so, it weakened and embarrassed you. Leaving you vulnerable."

Few dared such bluntness with Shahroudi. He still wielded immense power, but Shahbod Gilani had to get his attention.

"Be cautious of your tone," Shahroudi reprimanded.

"My apologies, but I merely speak what others are saying or thinking."

President Shahroudi understood there was a great deal of truth in what Gilani was relaying; he just didn't enjoy hearing it. A less trusted man talking to him in such a manner would chance being sent to waste at Evin prison. Gilani, however, had served him well. His elevated status at the Ministry of Intelligence and Security was well-earned and deserved. He was no "relative of" appointment. His loyalty to country was absolute.

Mid-morning sunlight filled the spacious office at Sa'dabad Palace, providing warmth amid the coolness of topic. Had Natanz been a misfortunate accident, or a grand plan to make him look out of control? Slap upon him the label of a dangerous, unstable man who had no business running a country. If the twelve-member Guardian Council took a vote of support today, the majority would not stand with him. The Majilis, Iran's parliament, were like vultures, waiting to see how much power he maintained. They would lean whichever way the supreme leader considered the best avenue to take. Confidence was waning, and through channels, the secretive talks had gotten back to Shahroudi. Some wanted to salvage him, suggesting he tone down his rhetoric of hatred for all things Western. No matter his fate, they wouldn't deny one final grasp at saving face, and perhaps his presidency. Failure meant falling on the sword. Shahroudi had accepted the challenge. There was nothing to lose in trying to regain one's dignity.

His stature was small, but his bark was loud. Shahroudi had proven he wasn't afraid to bite, either. In the beginning, that bravado had been infectious, inspiring a confidence that Iran was well within its right to demand respect in the region. Shahroudi didn't back down when threatened by talk from stronger nations. The goal of their peacekeeping diplomacy was to portray his defiance as the ramblings of a disturbed man. Openly calling for the destruction of Israel was like walking up to the lion exhibit at the zoo and sticking a pointed finger through its cage. The tough words had sounded good, but they came with a price. There was no talking around reality. Threats didn't erase the vast sanctions that prevented business growth. Too many families struggled to make ends meet. Promises and dreams of a better life had gone unfulfilled.

Once Natanz had literally blown up in his face, the dog on the porch with a big bark suddenly had a leash around his neck. Gilani had heard an earful of concerns from powerful people. Aligning with this president wasn't the best course of action to climb out of the muck he'd created. But, in changing times, making oneself invaluable was important. For now, he had to respect the house he was in.

"Dr. Mueller came through when other options weren't available," Shahroudi reflected, slightly distracted by gardeners making the landscape look as if neatness happened by nature. "He delivered on his end. Our technicians inspected the materials he brought to us. They ran them through rigorous testing. So why the suspicion?"

"I fully understand why you want to believe in him," said Gilani. "It took years to bring Natanz to life. After repeated failures, Dr. Mueller arrives. An unforeseen and timely gift." Gilani wanted to add that since Mueller had been in place before he arrived, the incompetence was at the doorstep of others. That truth, however, remained buttoned up. "I base my suspicions on the overall packaging."

"What do you mean?"

"Throughout the process, as I understand it, Dr. Mueller's one steadfast rule was not to delve into his background. Results would be his resume."

"That is correct. But, we didn't rush into what he was offering."

"When I met with him in London, he was not pleased to hear we had made inquiries."

"Were there any discrepancies? Anything questioning the validity of his credentials?"

Gilani's head dropped. "Not at all. Everything checked out. High marks. There were even some detractors who described him as brilliant. Difficult at times, but brilliant. From our interaction, I can concur on that."

Shahroudi escaped the sun's glare by sitting near Gilani. "You've offered nothing in the way of proof that Dr. Mueller is not who he says he is."

"You're right," Gilani conceded. "We've found nothing that doesn't measure up. But my gut is telling me something is off."

"He could have let me die at Natanz."

"Making sure you survived perhaps served a greater purpose."

An index finger canvased Shahroudi's lips while he contemplated in silence. The horrible image that crossed his mind was one of a far worse tainted legacy. Did he want to make the world take notice so badly that he was blind to manipulation? Steps were being taken behind his back for the nation to resurrect itself. But, until circumstances dictated otherwise, vast resources were at his disposal. One in particular could seal his fate.

"This brings us to our current position, and the trust *you* place in a person to handle a sensitive course of action," Shahroudi pointed out.

Gilani had expected the microscope treatment. Throughout the process, he had documented everything, tucking it away for safekeeping. "I have faith in the recommendations from those who've used his services."

"But you haven't met him?"

"No, it's not how he operates."

Shahroudi angled his head. "The similarity is ironic, isn't it?"

"Yes, except in this case, he didn't materialize out of nowhere."

"Let's pray for all our sakes he's as good as others claim him to be."

"His reputation hinges on success. He was as careful in saying 'yes' to us as we were in choosing him."

The confidence Gilani had in his work was admirable. "Any news on the others?" Shahroudi asked, retrieving a cigarette from a table-top case.

"Not as yet. Most regrettably, the program has not yielded the results we hoped for. Staffing is part of the problem. With nothing concrete to go on, committing high-level personnel and expenditures to so many locations is difficult." Gilani spread his hands in regret. "We have to accept our shortcomings. The people on the job are willing, but too many are not fully qualified for the task."

A long column of smoke flowed from Shahroudi's mouth. "I understand it was Dr. Mueller who made contact."

Gilani masked his disdain for cigarettes. Though he'd grown up around smoke-filled venues, he'd never gotten used to the harsh smell of tobacco. In certain circles, he had to tolerate its existence. When he led an operation, though, the people on his team were prohibited from lighting up in his presence. He turned away to deal with it now.

"Yes, and that reminds me of the other thing I find bothersome about the good doctor."

Shahroudi raised an eyebrow between puffs.

"He's far too polished and skilled in other areas for a scientist."

CHAPTER 41

ALEX HAD THOUGHT he was in the clear over having to tell Nora the whole truth. He'd assumed the secret had died along with the man who held it, buried deep in Iranian sand, next to a mountain, in the middle of nowhere.

He should be so lucky.

Nathan was very much alive, and that put Alex in a terrible spot. Nora could sense there was something on his mind. He'd spent the better part of the train ride into Paris falling in and out of sleep, Nora resting against his chest as she read her novel. He tried to convince himself that he was sparing her feelings. She had achieved closure by hunting and killing the man who gave the order to murder her friend. She'd be downright savage in extracting revenge against the man who'd looked Janway in the eyes, ending her life with a shot through the heart. The longer he put off telling the full story, the worse her reaction would be. She deserved the truth, but he had to be concerned with the fate of a man who'd tried to kill him first. That same man, when faced with the uncertainty of living or dying, had expressed remorse. He'd given Alex directions to escape death, and now he'd taken another step at redemption by warning Nora.

How Nathan had emerged from that graveyard of sand was a miracle. Alex had seen the ground disappear in the rearview mirror as he sped away. They didn't exchange resumes during their first encounter, but Alex was sure Nathan worked for Mossad.

They arrived in Paris late morning to discover their hotel rooms weren't ready. Nora didn't pass up the opportunity to shop at the less crowded stores open on a Sunday. She'd likely do it again to some extent when all the establishments opened tomorrow. Alex filled his time getting a deep tissue massage at the hotel's spa. Duncan, with a few aches and pains of his own, joined him. The masseuse hesitated when she saw the bruises on Alex's body. He used the boxer cover, which made her feel better about proceeding.

Post massage, Alex headed for the whirlpool. He finished his indulgence with a visit to the steam room. Their rooms ready, Alex crawled in bed. Rather than disturb him, Nora persuaded Duncan to join in on her shopping venture.

By the early evening, Nora sported a new outfit, walking in unison with Alex close to the Arc de Triomphe. He was relaxed and looked much better too with a touch of makeup. His pain lingered, but he'd learned long ago how to cope with the annoyance that accompanied movement. They headed down a quiet, one-way street lined mostly by five-story, cream-colored connecting structures. Passing the marker of a travel agency, they stopped at an establishment where the only external signage was a partial face covered in blue, white, and red. The colors ran vertically through the design. The lone eye of the profile commanded the most attention. With it being devoid of any other markings, one could only hazard a guess as to what kind of business existed behind the rustic metal door.

Nora found what she hoped was the buzzer. She pressed it and stepped back, half expecting to get an electric shock. Reminiscent of the speakeasy days, a peephole slid back, exposing two inquisitive eyes. Alex stared back until Nora gently elbowed him.

"Vince Flynn," he uttered in response, feeling a bit sheepish.

After a quick inspection, the peephole closed, and the door unlatched and opened. Alex had second thoughts about leaving Duncan at the hotel once he took in the behemoth standing to the side, welcoming them to enter. Clear of the door, the large man locked it closed. The thickness of the metal made a heavy clunking noise. A desk was wedged in the corner of the enclosed foyer, its only decoration a laptop. Mounted on a wall was a monitor with four different camera feeds. The doorman's head barely cleared an overhead light fixture.

"You must be Alex and Nora," he said in a deep bass. "Welcome. I'm Jumbo. Your party is on the way. In the meantime, I'll give you the quick tour." Jumbo opened another solid door behind them, revealing music and limited conversations that had been entirely inaudible before.

The room had three different dimly lit sections, with a bar serving as the centerpiece. Stacked, backlit shelves held a variety of libations. The Asian bartender took in the newcomers while mixing and pouring.

"That's Min-ji," Jumbo pointed out. "She'll take your order in a moment. The first one is always on the house."

Jumbo showcased the various sitting areas. There weren't many people seated on this Sunday evening. The interior wasn't huge, or cramped with décor, but there were a number of interesting focal points. Jumbo encouraged them to walk around and admire the "classic details."

Legendary spies hung on the walls in either framed photos or posters. Space was carved out for the crafty creator's escapism: Ian Fleming, Robert Ludlum, and John le Carré. Sean Connery as James Bond had a section outlined by his villains and draped by memorable Bond girls. There was Michael Caine of Harry Palmer fame in a scene from *The Ipcress File*. Patrick McGoohan as *Danger Man* shared a corner spot with *The Avengers'* John Steed and Emma Peel. Homage was even paid to the more fanciful of the genre, like Austin

Powers and Hubert Bonisseur de La Bath. And no collection would be complete without the presence of Boris Badenov and Natasha Fatale. They guarded the men's and women's restrooms, respectively.

Finding intrigue everywhere, Nora asked, "What is this place?"

Jumbo had encountered the question many times. "Welcome to I Spy. Entrance is by invitation or recommendation only. No exceptions. For security reasons, it's cash only too. Same principle applies to identification. We only use first names or nicknames. Now, let's get you two a drink."

He led them back to the bar. Min-ji looked to be in her late forties, but soft, lineless skin muddled that observation. Her dark, pinned-back hair gave clear access to attentive hazel eyes.

"Min-ji, this is Nora and Alex." Jumbo let the pleasantries of introduction conclude before continuing with a broad smile. "Let me tell you about this talented lady. If we have the ingredients, there isn't a drink in this world she can't make. Don't know the name of a drink? Provide a description and she'll figure it out." He was beaming with pride. "Now the magic. She can look into your inner drink soul and guess your favorite drink."

Min-ji produced a slightly embarrassed grin. She rested her hands on the bar, waiting to be challenged.

"I'm rather nomadic with my alcohol choices," Nora said. "No clear-cut favorite for me. With that in mind, surprise me with something you think I'd like."

Min-ji shifted her attention to Alex. He played along. "By all means, go for it," he said, expecting a series of well-crafted questions to follow, but none did.

Min-ji grabbed two glasses before selecting the items she needed from the vast choices behind her. She concealed her mixing by doing it underneath the countertop. First, she poured contents from a cocktail shaker into one of the hidden glasses and set it aside. Next, she started working on Alex's drink. She studied his face more, searching for clues. When the answer came, she mixed with a smirk.

Min-ji revealed her handiwork. "For the lady, a Mojo Jojo martini. And for the gentleman, a rum and Coke."

Alex reached for his drink, but Min-ji raised a halting finger. She hovered a hand over a tray containing strawberries, lime slices, lemons, and oranges, glancing at Alex again. Confident, Min-ji selected a lemon, squeezing a slight amount into his drink before garnishing the glass with a slice from it.

Nora responded for him. "Oh, my! That's amazing."

Alex gave Min-ji a thumb up, respecting the trick with no clue how she'd pulled it off. "Right down to the lemon and not a lime. Impressive."

Nora sipped her martini and rolled her eyes. "Wow. You have a serious gift, Min-ji. Thank you."

Jumbo gave Min-ji a soft high five. When Alex produced money from his pocket, Jumbo reminded him that the first drink was always free.

"Sit wherever you want," said the massive man. "We have a waitress, but we only serve pretzels, chips, nuts, cheese, it is Paris, after all, and"—he seemed apologetic—"cereal. Don't ask. Now if you'll excuse me, I'll head back up front. Your party is due any minute."

They looked around for a place to sit. Nora saw where Alex was staring. Before he could suggest, she protested.

"Uh, no. We are not sitting under Pussy Galore."

CHAPTER 42

"BOURBON. TWO ROCKS."

Nathan grabbed his drink and thanked Min-ji. He was in a good mood. Talking to Lauren always balanced his equilibrium. He was late because they had spoken on the phone longer than expected. Knowing he had an appointment to make, he could have let the call go to voicemail, but he tried to be available for her as much as possible. He preferred her in his arms, close enough to smell her perfume, but he'd take what he could get for now. With everything going on, it was too dangerous to have her around. He was working hard to eliminate the multitude of threats. For part of his plan to work, he needed the help of two people who, at one point, he'd thought he would need to kill.

"Dusko Popov. Excellent choice," Nathan observed, referencing the framed, black-and-white photograph on the wall. "Believed to be the real-life inspiration for the James Bond character. World War Two double agent working for MI6. Photographic memory. Spoke multiple languages. A ladies' man. Gained the Germans' trust. Not appreciated by the FBI, though. Alerted them in August of forty-one about a Japanese plan to attack Pearl Harbor. Hoover didn't trust him, so the information never got passed along. History. The back-stories that reveal themselves over time are always fascinating. Quite the gem, this place." Nathan sat down across from Alex and Nora. "Good to see you again, Nora. Excuse my familiarity, but we're only supposed to use first names here. Alex, glad she found you."

"Yes, she can pop up where you least expect her."

"You get around pretty well yourself," Nora noted, sipping from her martini glass. "Speaking of which, what is this place?"

"This"—Nathan scanned the room—"is where spies come to relax. A few hours of freedom. You met Jumbo. Pleasant guy, unless he has reason not to be. Keeps a Vityaz-SN, double-magazine-equipped submachine gun strapped underneath his desk. He calls it 'Tiny.' Jumbo is ex-Hungarian Special Forces. Min-ji used to be NIS, South Korea. Now, along with a few others, they're part owners of this establishment. Enough background, though. I'm sure you want to know why I asked for this meeting. I've got some problems to address. One involves the both of you."

"The Iranians?" said Alex.

"Exactly. They're especially determined to find you. I stumbled upon their operation by accident. They were looking for all of us."

"I was a late party crasher," Alex interrupted. "You were there in the early stages, Dr. Mueller. Considering the outcome, you'd be my top suspect."

"I was, and probably still am," Nathan confirmed. "I had to approach the situation aggressively. The fact I didn't run caught them by surprise. I know they have doubts about my role in all of this. It is, as you pointed out, the logical conclusion."

Bottoming out her martini, Nora questioned, "What's keeping you alive then?"

"I suspect the person who put this plan in motion, President Shahroudi. My job was to gain his trust. When all hell broke out at Natanz, I made sure he got out. I'm sure he's puzzled as to why I'd go to such lengths to save his life if I work for the opposition. The real threat is the person overseeing this operation—a man named Shahbod Gilani. If he had his way, and he might soon, he'd kill us all. He's very astute. Gets the job done and knows how to work the system. He comes from the Ministry of Intelligence and Security. What's also keeping me breathing is that I told him I'd help search for you two."

Nora thought about the logic of what he'd conveyed. "Why did you make that play? Raises more suspicion by suggesting you're not just a scientist."

"Precisely," Nathan agreed. "More for Gilani to think about. But, if there's any possibility I can deliver, he has to let me try. He needs to wrap this up as fast as he can. The operation is putting a strain on their resources, and I suspect there's pressure coming from the Supreme Leader."

"You mentioned you have other problems?" Nora probed.

"From back home."

"More trust issues?" Nora asked.

"Yes."

"The kind that can get you killed?"

"Depending on their conclusion, most definitely."

"You must enjoy living on the edge."

"To a degree in this profession, we all do," Nathan said. "However, I'm trying to reduce my stress level."

"I'm not crazy about having a price on my head," Alex chimed in. "You asked us to meet, so you must have a plan."

"I do. Hopefully, free us from this Iranian threat." Nathan took a moment to feel the bourbon slide down his throat. "The simple answer is, sometime this week, I will have to make sure they kill you two."

CHAPTER 43

NEITHER OF THEM wanted to make the call.

Neril and Sharon at least agreed to be in the same room to frame the story together.

The call went as expected. They got their asses chewed out.

Their only recourse was to silently sit back and take it, because as the Mossad director eloquently said, they had "Fucked up royally."

Neril could tell a fuse had been lit with Sharon when Director Rozen suggested that perhaps the job was "too big" for him to handle. The verbal reprimand was hard to take, but fell short of them tearing into each other for all the miscues that led to Yadin making them look like amateurs. The director reminding that he had expressly warned them didn't help. Fortunate to live another day, Neril and Sharon now had a firsthand understanding of what they were dealing with.

Director Rozen had come down hard on them if for no other reason than to hammer home the seriousness of their predicament. Going over their report, he concluded that another team would likely have produced the same outcome. He kept that to himself.

Because of Yadin's combativeness and reluctance to comply, he gave brief thought to changing the directive. An asset of Yadin's ability, however, was a rare commodity. He had to hold off. They would give Yadin the opportunity to silence the whispers of suspicion. His service to Israel was the deciding factor in affording him some latitude. That grace period wouldn't last forever.

Told that Yadin was working on shredding ties with the Iranians, and that he needed to do it alone, Rozen instructed his agents to monitor the situation. Finding him again wouldn't be easy. Approaching Yadin a second time, against his wishes, one might not have the luxury of conversation.

The way Sharon felt at the moment, he wasn't the least bit interested in talking any more.

CHAPTER 44

NOTHING PRESIDENT SHAHROUDI had said changed Shahbod Gilani's opinion of Dr. Mueller. He remained suspicious. The unfortunate circumstance for Gilani was that he had to follow orders. He dared not jeopardize his rise in the current (or future) leadership by offering his expert opinion too strongly. The winds of change could blow in a different direction without warning.

For weeks on end, countless man-hours in locations around the globe had yielded zero results in the search for Dr. Mueller. Then, out of the blue, he had appeared at one of the stations set up to find him. The staffing was not an experienced group, but Dr. Mueller's reported actions had exceeded what a scientist should be able to handle. His background check hadn't indicated he possessed the training needed to get the drop on two operatives, not even unseasoned ones.

Now, within a short period, he had achieved another amazing feat in supposedly locating the man who called himself Mr. McBride and his female companion. At their meeting in London, Dr. Mueller had said he might have contacts that could assist in the search. *What harm could it do to let him waste his time?* Gilani had thought. He would come up empty-handed, and then convincing Shahroudi to sever the relationship would become an easier sell.

Gilani was surprised to be wrong. Dr. Mueller had explained his discovery by saying that to operate in the world he did, fruitful relationships with unseemly and credentialed characters were a necessity. That was the root of Gilani's problem with Dr. Mueller. Everything fell into place too conveniently. If Dr. Mueller had succeeded in finding the pair, Gilani's mistrust would remain. The search for McBride, the woman, and Dr. Mueller had turned into a sideshow. A swift bullet to the head seemed like a viable conclusion. He'd tell President Shahroudi that Dr. Mueller had gotten caught in the crossfire.

Gilani's first order of business was to assemble a small team of capable professionals, who under his guidance would do what they were told without question. Pleased with his selections, he considered what to pack for Paris and then drifted off to sleep, thinking of Dr. Mueller's death.

CHAPTER 45

THE WIND TOSSED Michelle Orsette's hair in uncontrollable directions, and she loved every face-whipping moment.

For the first time in a long while, she felt so alive. Everywhere she looked was picturesque and serene. The water was clean and pure, the shoreline vegetation lush green. Snowcapped Mont Blanc stole the show in the distance, mingling with the clouds. The warmth of the sun, mixed with intoxicating drinks, conspired to put her in a dreamlike state. Stretched out on the bow in a white two-piece bikini, she didn't have to pinch herself. All she needed for affirmation was to turn her head and smile at the man behind the wheel. There was nothing in her life she could draw upon for a comparison. As a Metro Detroiter, she'd experienced the Detroit River, Anchor Bay, and in her younger, more cavalier days, the wildness of Jobbie Nooner on Gull Island. This was a different life. She had one person to thank for that.

The Azimut Atlantis Yacht could do thirty-two knots, but Erik Snow had no intention of drawing unwanted attention. He eased the fifty-five-foot vessel at idle speed through the calm water of Lake

Geneva. Going faster would send Orsette flying off the sun pad. At select points, he would slow to a crawl to enter notes and measure the distance to shore.

Snow navigated for several miles before turning around to repeat the process. He paused for a lunch break with Orsette, her scantily clad appearance difficult to ignore. He barely carried on a conversation, however, devoting most of his concentration on diagrams and mathematical equations. Snow had been in Geneva for almost a week. Orsette had arrived three days ago. It was her job to sign for the boat and receive the materials that had originated in Kentucky. Minimizing his footprint, Snow had the Iranians rent the boat via a shell company. Orsette had checked into the hotel suite under a fictitious name and unpacked a set of clothes that fit neither of them. They had no intention of staying in the room, but early every morning she would stop by the suite to turn back the bed sheets, run the shower, moisten the towels, and use the soap to wash her hands. In and out in under ten minutes. She was learning a great deal from Snow.

The only drawback to her experience was the guilt she felt concerning her children. She hated to leave them again so soon. The tradeoff was that Mom wouldn't have to travel again for at least five to six months, maybe longer, depending upon the success of this business trip. Snow gave her assurances of that.

She didn't stress over the money anymore. In fact, Snow had convinced her to be flexible by generating multiple accounts at different financial institutions. The balances were generous. Her kids attended private school and wore nice clothes, gifts were abundant at Christmas, and vacations included places like Atlantis, Disney World, and Hawaii. Lasting memories. She owed it all to the handsome man in shorts, his unbuttoned short-sleeved shirt flapping from the breeze. She could love him. Hell, in some bizarre way, she did. Why else would she be here? She had accepted his reluctance to love her back in a committed, defined manner. He exhibited affection in his own way, the only mode his complex psyche could allow. She suspected he didn't care about many people, but he was tender with her. Because of what he did for a living, she'd be foolish to think he'd ever commit to a long-lasting relationship. He wasn't the kind to attend Red Wings games, root for the Lions or coach Little League. She'd already experienced sorrow in her life. The game plan was to not go through that again.

Snow caught her staring at him. She produced an innocent smile and wondered if he knew what she was thinking. He was perceptive that way. A curl on the side of his mouth showed he at least appreciated the attention.

"Having fun?" he asked.

Orsette sucked in a large chunk of fresh air. "Impossible not to."

"You deserve it," he said, like a boss informing a loyal employee of a raise. "And, you look lovely," he added, like a man appreciative of what he had.

She nodded her thanks.

"Tonight, we'll enjoy the evening, have a nice dinner," Snow informed her. "Tomorrow, I'll start testing everything. My Bluegrass associate takes pride in meeting challenges. But if something doesn't work, I'll have time to alter the plan."

CHAPTER 46

ALEX AND NORA had first met in Berlin. Like him, she had been a protégé. Her case officer, Erica Janway, had been on the rise in the ranks of the CIA; he'd been on the job a few months under the tutelage of George Champion. Distinguished careers were on the horizon, with each having shown early aptitude for fieldwork. They'd been part of a joint operation to flush out an upstart terrorist organization trying to expand its European base. The operation intensified, and so did their mutual admiration. A relationship developed that evolved into a much deeper connection. Here they were, years later, together, facing another challenge.

The apartment in the Saint-Denis section of Paris was not worth the rent charged. It embodied the smell of previous tenants from different parts of the world. The kitchen area was all ginger, curry, saffron, garlic, and other herbs and spices that didn't mix well. To get here, they passed prostitutes claiming ownership of select corners or walls. Pickpockets roamed for easy-mark stray tourists. Drug addicts hoped to score. It wasn't the best block of the neighborhood.

Nora was in a corner chair, away from the windows, brooding.

She'd been occupying her time sliding a magazine in and out of the 9mm pistol at least a dozen times.

"Think you have the hang of it yet?" said Alex.

For emphasis, Nora repeated the action a couple more times. Then she took aim at a spot on the far wall, her eyes following the front sight line. Finger on the trigger guard, she exhaled the sound of a round leaving the barrel.

"I've never used a H&K VP9. Just getting acquainted with a new friend." She added a spiteful head jerk and twist of her nose.

To the right of a window, a dusty hanging mirror covered Alex's blind side. "I saw that."

"I don't like this," Nora proclaimed, rearranging two extra magazines on the end table next to her. "You remember Butch Cassidy and the Sundance Kid?"

"This isn't like that."

"Really? Seems to me we're the ones about to stick our asses out to get blown off. All while your friend is down there directing the scene."

"For the last time, he's not my friend."

"Then why do you trust him?"

"Was he wrong about Daniels?"

"Nope, dead on with that one. But did it ever occur to you he wanted Daniels out of the way, and he got us to do his dirty work?"

"Us? You could have let it go."

"Screw you. You know, you can be a real shit sometimes. Erica should still be here. She definitely deserved some payback."

"Look, you did what you needed to do. Honestly, I would have done the same. Happy?"

The shadowed room aided her depression. "I'll be happy when this crap is over. It's interfering with my on-suspension world travel tour. I'm supposed to stay miles away from stuff like this."

"Let's hope it ends tonight then."

Nora rested her head against the wall. "You didn't answer my question. Why do you trust him?"

Alex didn't address her right away. He kept his focus where it was needed for the moment—the street below. He checked his watch. Their expected company should arrive shortly. There'd been no deviation of street activity during the past hour. A prostitute a block over had reclaimed her turf after an appointment. He recognized a teenager who had been on foot earlier, breezing out of view atop his new mode of transportation, a bicycle. This was no place for a kid at this hour, but the street was probably his guardian. Anonymous people of meager means congregated to this section of the city in hopes of staying off the grid. No one came looking for you here unless they had a reason. Out of sight, out of mind.

Nora would not let up, so Alex figured he'd utilize the idle time. "We've been over this. He could have killed me, but he didn't."

"Not that again," Nora exhaled. "He needed you down there for his own survival. He told you about Daniels, but why? He didn't have to offer that up. And months later, out of nowhere, he sits across from me in Monte Carlo, telling me I need to get in touch with you because we're in danger. I'd never met him before. How did he find me so easily? It all makes my skin crawl. Something doesn't add up. This could be a trap—serving us up to maintain his cover. Sacrifices for the larger goal. I wouldn't put it past Mossad. An asset that deep in Iran is worth preserving."

"I get the sense he's trying to save his ass by eradicating the problem. He doesn't believe the Iranians trust him anymore. Look, can we talk about this later?" Alex pleaded.

Nora registered the absurdity of their current situation for the hundredth time. Nathan had provided the weaponry. He had also supplied the explosive charges taped to the walls, set to discharge inward.

"Sure, if we're not dead," Nora chided, sliding the magazine into place.

CHAPTER 47

THE ATMOSPHERE ON the street pulsed with an impending shift from bad to worse. Three prostitutes had been working a corner. They weren't there now, and no prospective clients lingered. A vagrant peeled away from his sidewalk seating, mindful to take his hat bank and today's slogan on a sign with him. The gait of people passing through increased an extra beat. This all happened after three vehicles made a second funeral procession pass of the street.

"I think we got something," Alex uttered. He tapped his ear-attached Bluetooth device. "You seeing this, Duncan?"

"Yeah, some shit is definitely about to go down," an anxious Duncan responded, peering out from beneath a baseball cap from his street-level location down the block. He braced against a car, drinking bottled water from a brown paper bag. "Two SUVs and a sedan coming around the corner now for the third time. The sedan is parking at the end of your block. One of the SUVs just let three guys in jackets out across the street from you. The other one just passed me. Looks to be four more guys inside."

Alex remained hidden while crossing to the other side of the window. He wanted to get a glimpse of the three men huddled across the street. The dullish yellow lighting wasn't the best, but he saw clearly enough to back away from the window when the men looked up toward the apartment. When Alex checked again, there were only two men, and their attention had shifted to an area beyond his viewpoint.

"Duncan, I can't see the third guy. You got eyes on him?"

"Yep. You remember the hooker on the corner with the huge thighs?"

Alex shook his head. "What the hell are you talking about?"

"The hooker from the corner built like . . . never mind. You probably couldn't see from up there."

"Duncan . . . focus."

"Sheesh, I'm getting to it," Duncan exhaled. "Anyway, the third guy just approached a hooker. Not the one with the thighs, but the blonde who's been busy most of the night. They're talking, and he's showing her something. He's pointing up at your building now. There appears to be some bickering going on. Finger pointing. Some money just changed hands."

One of the other men waited for a car to pass before crossing the street, exiting Alex's view. The final guy stepped back, reached into his jacket, and pulled out a cigarette. He took a long drag after lighting it, using the wall of a closed storefront for support. He dedicated his interest on the draped windows of an apartment on the fourth floor.

Duncan took another hit from the brown paper bag, his sleeve a makeshift napkin to wipe his mouth. "My man, I think you're about to have some visitors. The hooker and two bad guys just entered the building."

CHAPTER 48

"NOW WHAT?"

"Now we wait to see how good your information is," Gilani informed his backseat companion. "If it's solid, we take action."

Dr. Mueller stared back. "It's solid. I'm not one to waste people's time."

The sedan occupied a space at the end of the block, across the street from the target apartment building. Gilani had taken the bait. The pressure to find Mr. McBride and his female companion was too enticing to dismiss. Dr. Mueller had possibly succeeded where others had so far failed. The discovery would also raise the bar on Gilani's suspicion that Mueller was more than what he presented as.

The man in the backseat with Dr. Mueller observed the surroundings, checking for anything unusual, a police vehicle on patrol especially. Because of previous terrorist attacks, this area and its transient inhabitants had received an uptick in police monitoring. Dr. Mueller was counting on that being the case when all hell broke out. He couldn't care less about the conjoined apartments he'd rented under an alias. The landlord was a low-life who rented to anyone, often taking advantage of desperate people by charging outrageous rates.

Yadin thought the plan was solid, but it relied heavily on Alex and Nora being as good as advertised. He looked up at the apartment in question and saw nothing except a faintly lit room. If Alex and Nora failed, he would have to improvise. Not wanting to put the Iranians on edge any further, he hadn't packed a gun, opting instead for a tactical knife strapped to his calf. In this close environment, it had a distinct advantage over a gun, provided he attacked in the right sequence. Gilani would have to go first. He was right-handed, and being in the front passenger seat, he could react by shifting away to get in position to fire. Surprise would allow Yadin to hold back the man next to him, while he slashed Gilani's throat. Then he could pin his backseat companion, preventing him from retrieving his weapon. An easy kill. The driver would need a second to get over the shock of what was happening. His disadvantage was that he too was right-handed. He'd not only have to unbuckle, but reach for his weapon in a tight space and try to turn in a restrictive angle. Yadin's prey would be locked into a perfect kill zone.

He didn't want it to play out that way, but at least he had an exit strategy as two of Gilani's men steered a woman inside the building.

CHAPTER 49

CÉLESTE GIROUX GREW up in a working class family with all the right values to make something of her life. She wound up excelling at being rebellious—pushing the envelope with her parents, and hanging with the wrong crowd out of spite. In no way did her nurturing family life prepare her for the stark reality of bad choices.

At twenty-four years old, the start of a good day for Giroux meant not just waking up, but waking up alone without the stench of the night before. Her body was the commodity responsible for paying the rent and putting food in her mouth. She was street smart, but the internet had become a better, safer, and more lucrative business model with France having a law that punished clients. She'd been told her looks would translate well to the internet, so she embraced it. Now Giroux worked the streets less, but tonight, she needed to supplement her income. She had designs of taking a vacation to the coastal south, maybe even splurging for the high-speed train to Italy.

She had sized up the man who approached her long before he said a word. He represented potential trouble. That would cost him extra if she went along with what he was offering. They'd locked eyes when she noticed him in one of the three vehicles that had buzzed the neighborhood. When he'd confronted her, she'd thought he wanted to hire her for a bachelor party. She'd made it clear group sex was not her thing. But the offer instead had been more than 300 euros for a few minutes of her time. Understanding she wouldn't have to perform her usual services, she jumped at the chance to make easy money.

Walking to the fourth floor with two creepy men in tow, Giroux had doubts about whether she'd made the right decision. Were they going to force her to do what she'd refused? She nearly screamed when one of them grabbed her arm. He held up a finger, reminding her to be silent. He produced the two photographs he'd shown her on the street. Her instructions were to go to the apartment they pointed out and convince the occupant to open the door so she could make a positive identification. If the man or woman in the photographs answered, apologize that she'd gotten the wrong floor. She could then leave as quickly as her long legs could carry her down the stairs and out of the building. She'd planned on doing just that before they changed their mind.

The bulges protruding beneath the men's jackets were unmistakable. Trouble for sure. These were bad men.

But they paid well.

CHAPTER 50

"ALLEZ, BÉBÉ. OUVRE la porte," Giroux said in a sexy, somewhat impatient voice after knocking on the door for the second time. "Le temps, c'est de l'argent."

When no answer came again, she gave the two men hugging the wall a "what now?" look. Their no-nonsense responses convinced her to keep trying.

Giroux was more forceful with her knock this time. She also changed tactics by speaking English. "Look, baby, I know you're in there. I'll stay here knocking all night until you open the door."

Silence.

She didn't bother to consult her gun-toting cohorts. She knocked even harder.

What if no one is inside? Then what? Giroux thought, standing in front of the door with a hand on her hip. She wasn't giving the money back. Not her problem if no one answered. She did her . . .

The sudden turning of the door handle almost made her break a heel. The door opened to the measured length of the safety chain.

"What do you want?" a male voice called out, his face shielded behind the door.

Her heart rate elevated, and heel intact, Giroux regained her composure. She inched closer to the opening, trying to look inside. "I'm here because you called me, sweetheart."

"You must be mistaken. You've got the wrong apartment."

"Okay, I get it. Happens all the time. Wife is away, thought you'd order some strange, but you had time to think, and now you're scared. Listen, I'll take good care of you. Make your fantasy come true, baby, and it'll be our secret."

"Like I said, you've got the wrong person."

Giroux's voice expressed her displeasure. "Look baby, time is money, and you owe me for wasting my time. Coming up here." She wedged a foot in the door to prevent it from closing.

Finally, a face appeared through the crack, eyes frisking her from top to bottom. It was the man in the photograph. That was all she needed to complete her job.

"You're starting to piss me off," Giroux exhaled, buying time to think. "Somebody booked the appointment. They said apartment 3F."

"There's your problem right there. This is 4F. You're on the wrong damn floor. Now get the hell out of here!" The man pushed her foot out of the way and slammed the door shut.

"My mistake, asshole," Giroux called out.

She approached the men in the hall. They retreated from the apartment to conceal their voices.

"Well?" the one who paid her asked.

"It's the guy in the photo."

"You're sure?"

She refrained from explaining how knowing faces was one of her job skills. "I'm sure."

"What about the woman?"

"He was the only person I saw."

The two men stepped away to have a conversation in a language she didn't understand. Though they kept their voices low, they were clearly excited. The man who'd crossed the street to join pulled out his cell phone. The call was brief, filled with headshakes. The men talked after. The moneyman confronted her.

"You can go."

Giroux didn't wait to be told twice.

CHAPTER 51

"YOU READY?" ALEX addressed Nora in the hushed room, having shut the door on the persistent prostitute.

"I'm set," Nora answered. She waved at the explosive charges on the walls like Vanna White, then steadied her weapon. Extra magazines were packed into pouches, ready to be carried. Alex returned to the window while Nora concentrated on the door.

"Five to ten minutes," Nora said.

Alex agreed. "Once they talk it over, get everybody into place. They can't afford to linger out there too long."

He couldn't tell if anyone had exited the sedan parked at the end of the block. For that information and what else was unfolding below, he was counting on his best friend being on top of matters. "Talk to me, Duncan. What numbers are we looking at? Anybody get out of the sedan?"

Duncan had repositioned to where he could maintain surveillance on the street. The location also made for a short sprint to their nearby car, should that become a necessity sooner than planned.

"The hooker just bolted out the building," Duncan reported. "Guess you weren't her type."

Alex half smiled, knowing Duncan was trying to ease the tension. In a few minutes, a lot of things could go wrong.

"One guy who went in with her is now out front too," Duncan relayed, his tone all business now. "He's motioning the guy across the street to come over."

The man disposed of his cigarette and detached from the wall. Alex couldn't follow his movement because he had to stay in the drapes' shadow.

"As for your other question, nobody's gotten out of the sedan. The bad news, however—three more guys just turned the corner to meet up with the others. I'm assuming the drivers stayed with the SUVs."

Alex mouthed to Nora that one guy was probably still in the hallway to make sure they didn't leave.

"You at a safe distance?" Alex followed up with Duncan.

"Don't worry about me. You two just haul ass when the time comes. The guy who came out of the building is on his phone. He's taking a head count and just ended the call. He's talking to the group now. Looks like a bobblehead convention. All right. They're coming your way. When do you want me to make the call?"

Alex gave Nora a thumb up. He turned off the lights, reducing visibility to what illumination filtered in from the street. The darkness highlighted the glow of the hallway through the small slit under the door. Any minute now, an eclipse was about to take place. Alex positioned himself to the side of the window, bending down on one knee, careful to stay hidden. He'd carried the Sig MCX 5.56 rifle around long enough to get used to the weight. It felt like an extension of his arm now. He calculated the distance to his intended target, resting the buttstock against his shoulder. Alex slowed his breathing to a steady, calm pace, compensating for the adrenaline flooding his system.

"Duncan, I'll make it obvious for you."

CHAPTER 52

THREE MONTHS' RENT paid in advance had secured the apartment without any need for references or a credit check. The landlord preferred to maximize his profit by renting the renovated apartment to large families or multiple roommates, but the passionate musician, who mentioned something about good acoustics, had the most redeeming quality—he paid with cash.

To save money, the landlord had decided not to seal off the second entryway during the apartment expansion. The cheaper option had the unintended effect of offering privacy, since the apartment wrapped around the hallway with a door letting out to the back stairwell.

The new tenant had met Alex and Nora at the apartment two days earlier. Yadin couldn't read a line of music if his life depended on it, but he was well versed in all things destructive. He went over the plan and helped them set up a controlled explosive pattern along the walls. Yadin supplied sufficient firepower, and walked through every detail several times, particularly the escape route. If there had been anything they didn't like, they could walk away, regroup and deal with the problem another way. He'd told them to sleep on it.

After a final dry run the next day, all parties were in agreement. Alex hadn't told Nathan about Duncan. He wanted to make sure his friend stayed safe should something go wrong. And if Nora's apprehension about Nathan turned out to be correct, Duncan was the eyes on the street covering their butts.

Alex monitored his target below and watched for an eclipse of light beneath the entry door. By Duncan's account, five men were heading upstairs to join the one already in place. He suspected the drivers of the SUVs had remained behind to facilitate a hurried exit. To the best of Alex's knowledge, no one had gotten out of the sedan. Alex hoped his guess was right that Nathan would be in the back seat, being closely monitored. Chances were they wouldn't have trusted him to drive. Alex was sticking with that assumption as the light under the door blinked into darkness twice.

Balancing the assault rifle in his hands, Alex eased against the window frame for added support. Comfortable, he massaged a foam plug into his right ear. He took a final look at his target and set the fire selector switch to full auto. He acknowledged Nora, who relayed that she was ready. She also saw the light flickering in the hallway.

Alex took a deep breath, steadied his aim, and squeezed the trigger. The noise created by the 220-grain subsonic ammunition echoed in the night air. Everything that could move on the street did so at an accelerated pace, seeking haven from unseen danger. The front lights of the sedan shattered into pieces. Bullets hammered two rows of holes into the hood, followed by a well-placed typing pattern low on the driver's side door, just in case Nathan was behind the wheel.

Inside the vehicle, calmness shifted into survival mode. There was little room for shelter from the sudden onslaught. The driver cried out in Farsi. A stream of hot blood flowed through big holes in his left leg.

From under the dashboard, Gilani reached to turn the ignition keys. Thankfully the car still operated. "Get us out here!"

Motivated by self-preservation, the driver put the car in reverse, despite the searing pain in his leg. He floored the gas pedal so hard he slammed into the parked car behind, sending it crashing into another car, alarms blaring. He shifted into drive and sped up down the street.

The sedan out of the picture, Alex rushed to join Nora near the rear of the room. He folded the buttstock to make the rifle easier to manage for close engagement. Alex fed the Sig a fresh magazine. "Duncan, if you haven't already, you can make that call now."

A block away, Duncan had heard the loud series of *pops* in endless succession. Bystanders ran for shelter and one man narrowly missed being roadkill as the bullet-riddled sedan with blown-out headlights zoomed through an intersection. "Hell, I already called. I suspect the whole neighborhood did, too. You should start hearing sirens real soon."

"See you on the ground," said Alex.

A hail of bullets tore through the entryway door. Nora had anticipated the assault to begin sooner. Six men had taken positions on either side of the apartment door. The man in charge had instructed them to go on the count of three. Bodies tensed as the count had reached two. They then heard the unmistakable sound of heavy fire. They spun away from the door, expecting it to explode from a barrage of bullets. They were face planted on the floor, crawling away before realizing the door had remained intact. Regaining their composure, they picked themselves up. When the firing stopped, they abandoned the count and rushed in through the poorly constructed door.

The first man through the door didn't stand a chance. Shadows mixed with light from the street distracted his immediate search for a target. Nora had become accustomed to the ambient conditions, making her aim that much easier.

Thump. Thump. Instantly she came to trust the H&K V9, the shots landing exactly where she intended.

The second man stumbled over the first. Trying to regain his balance, he shot wildly, his bullets wounding the ceiling. Nora put him down for good with a single shot to the heart area.

The four remaining men changed strategy, firing into the room simultaneously, advancing behind their onslaught. Nora and Alex returned fire to cover their retreat. They took positions inside the opening to the converted apartment, waiting for the men to enter further. The exchange of gunfire didn't drown out the sounds of sirens advancing from the distance. Their closeness caught the attention of the man in charge. He decided to hang back, cowering near the entry door. Having lost two of their associates, the other three became more determined. They had their orders. Failure was not an option. If they continued to press forward, their targets would run out of space and be trapped with nowhere to go. That was exactly what Alex and Nora wanted them to think.

The cross-blast zone was engineered to blow outward and kill everything caught in the room. Nora darted for the entry to the original two-bedroom unit. The moment she made her move, Alex unleashed a zigzag stream of automatic fire, pinning the assailants in place. By the time the magazine emptied, Alex was next to Nora. He ejected the cartridge for a fresh one. Nora grabbed the detonator mechanism hanging from a chain around her neck. She saw an assailant draw a bead on her through the opening. He never got the shot off. Rigged to engage in successive order, the explosives were so closely timed they sounded like one huge detonation. The blast created a giant vacuum, sucking the room outward. The windows and part of the street-side wall blew apart in a screaming fireball of energy.

The Iranian who'd stayed back struggled to regain his senses after being ejected into the hallway. Dizzy, he tried to work through the smoke and dust around him. He didn't see flames, but the heat from fire was close. The muffled sound of blaring sirens washed over him.

His name was Rami. He couldn't remember that a few seconds ago. He had no clue where his weapon was, and it was probably better that he didn't. He had to get out of the building. As he tried to rise, intense pain shot through his right side. He fell back to the floor, horrified to discover a large fragment of wood lodged in his thigh. Smaller splinters dug into his torso. He'd attend to those later. For now, he had to get moving. The police would be here any second. He clenched his teeth, closed his eyes, and yanked the large piece of wood from his leg. His body spasmed, a powerful reinforcement that he was still alive. The rip in his pants flapped back and covered the wound, sticking to blood running down his calf.

Rami managed to get up on his good leg and hop toward the stairs. He took a look back at the smoldering apartment. There was a large hole blown out in the wall—nothing inside could have survived. He braced himself against the banister for support as he headed down in a hop, nearly tumbling down the stairs. He felt his chest buzzing, too caught up in surviving to notice it before. Reaching inside his jacket, he retrieved his cellphone.

"Rami? Rami?" an excited voice called out.

"Mahir! I need you to pick me up. I'll be out soon," Rami responded to one of the SUV drivers, surprised that his voice sounded so guttural. "Meet me at the corner."

"Rami, what the hell happened? I've been calling you and the others. Shahbod is about to lose his mind. No one is answering their phones."

The police sirens prompted Rami to keep moving. "They're dead."

"What?" the SUV driver said in disbelief.

"All of them," Rami confirmed. "The man and woman set off explosives."

"They're dead too?"

"Have to be. The blast was intense. Destroyed everything in the apartment," Rami said hurriedly, speaking Farsi as he reached the first floor to see tenants rushing to escape. He joined them.

"Meet me at the corner. I have to hang up now."

Rami ended the call as police in tactical gear ushered people out the door. Rami winced from the pain. Once outside, he encountered activity in every direction. Flashing police lights from countless vehicles blocked the intersections on both ends of the street. Specialized units of officers carrying heavy armament synchronized their movement forward. They were ready to shoot anyone on the street not in uniform.

Two officers grabbed Rami and led him a short distance away. He stayed calm. The people who'd exited the building before him had received the same treatment. He followed orders to stand against the wall. An officer patted him down under gunpoint. He was more relieved than ever that he'd lost his weapon.

"Do you live in the building?" the officer asked.

"No."

"Why were you here then"

"Visiting friends."

"What floor were you on?"

Rami took a moment to catch his breath. A victim would be a little nervous.

"Second floor."

He was nudged to go see the officers at the end of the block for additional questioning. Rami thanked them and took off in the ordered direction, but he had no intention of talking with anyone beyond this point. His leg hurt like hell, but he only needed to gut it out a few more steps.

The officer who'd questioned Rami was listening to commands on his headset when he noticed what appeared to be droplets of blood on the ground, freshly deposited. His eyes followed the trail on the pavement. When he looked up, he saw the man they'd talked to favoring his right leg. If he'd been two floors below the blast, why was he hurt so badly? The officer readied his rifle as he headed toward the man.

Rami couldn't believe his good fortune. First surviving the bloodbath in the apartment, and now this. Praise Allah. He was nearing the end of the block when commotion across the street flickered in his peripheral vision. Staying in painful stride, he turned his head to get a better look. What he saw got his heart pumping. The prostitute they'd used was pointing him out to the police. The officers followed her accusatory aim. Rami looked away, concentrating on making it to the corner.

Where was Mahir?

The inquisitive officer coming up from the rear noticed the woman across the street throwing finger darts at the bleeding man. The officer increased his approach. The others closed in from across the street. The rhythmic coordination captured the attention of onlookers.

Where are you, Mahir!

Beads of sweat flowed down Rami's face. His right leg was soaked with blood. He ignored shouted orders to stop, opting to continue his escape. A television crew had arrived, their camera light finding him from their position behind a police line. Rami didn't know where to focus; there was too much going on. He had to call Mahir. The police met the move to his chest with resounding choruses of "Non!"

He didn't comply.

The officer behind Rami saw him reach inside his jacket. Rami's arm came forward and the officer fired his weapon without hesitation. The tactical officers encroaching from the street dropped to a knee and joined in.

Rami's body jerked forward, crashing into a storefront wall. Struggling to stay upright, his body slid to the ground. Dying, he stared at his phone.

Where was Mahir?

CHAPTER 53

THE MAN HAD zeroed in on Nora. The shot was almost too easy. Straight on, from about thirty feet. All he had to do was pull the trigger. Unfortunately for him, Nora had been quicker. Her finger had already been on the button to detonate the explosives. She pressed it, and in the blink of an eye, he was vaporized by the blast.

The floor shook, and the walls cracked from the intense pressure. Alex picked up an oversized backpack he'd left by the door and followed Nora into the hall. Smoke billowed into the main hallway, but they had clear access to the back stairway door. Nora kept her weapon hidden. Should they encounter an unfriendly that had discovered the back stairs, she was ready to clear a path. In the stairwell, they heard heavy footfalls reverberating in fast decent. Nora and Alex headed in the opposite direction, taking the stairs two at a time to the roof access door.

Alex canvassed the roof through the partially opened door before sticking his head back in. He handed Nora the backpack to wear, then took her gun and placed it inside. He did the same with his weapon and the remaining magazine clips. They made their way outside, navigating from one rooftop to another.

Alex engaged his Bluetooth device. "On our way," he said, updating Duncan.

"Man, push it. This place is getting crowded with cops in a hurry," Duncan responded.

From the rooftops the sound of sirens seemed omnipresent. Blue and red lights bounced against buildings on all sides. They'd practiced this run several times in the dark. Thanks to adrenalin, they were way ahead of their best time. Nora matched Alex stride for stride, even with the weight of the backpack.

Reaching the final rooftop, the lock they breached days earlier on the entry door hadn't been fixed. Inside, it became a mad dash down the stairs to the first floor. They caught their breath before entering the lobby. There was a collection of people talking and watching the police activity on the street. Nora and Alex blended in, forging to the front. Stepping onto the sidewalk, Nora searched for Duncan. She tugged on Alex's arm when she spotted him down the block outside the rental car, having what appeared to be a candid conversation with an armed police officer. When Duncan saw them, his face lit up. He waved for them to hurry, appealing to the officer that the situation was about to end. Still talking, Duncan began walking around the car to the driver's side. The officer wanted him gone anyway, so he jumped in. Nora appeared and got the officer's attention. She distracted him while handing Alex the backpack to take with him into the car.

"I'm so sorry, officer." The French accent was perfectly executed. "Our friend was waiting for us when we heard all the commotion. Oh my goodness, I'm trying to catch my breath. It's so frightening. We didn't know if it was safe to come out. Thank goodness you're here. We just want to get out of the area, if that's okay."

He made a quick inspection. "Yes, you can go. Make it quick," he demanded, eager to go help in a more meaningful way.

Duncan followed the direction of officers who controlled the intersections for blocks. Waiting in traffic for his lane to get the right of way, Duncan spoke to Alex over his shoulder.

"What the hell? You didn't mention blowing up a building!"

Alex cringed. "It was actually just an apartment. And only the bad guys got hurt."

Duncan shook his head. "Unbelievable. Fricking unbelievable."

CHAPTER 54

THE DOCTOR WORKED minus a surgical team or high-tech equipment. Trying to save a man's life in an automobile repair shop offered a less-than-stellar prognosis. It was the only emergency room the wounded man would see, however. The doctor had removed three bullets from his left leg, but the one in his abdomen was tricky. Considering the blood loss, time wasn't on his side.

Shahbod Gilani could ill afford to lose another man. The night had proven to be costly. Six damn good men dead. One shot to death by police on the street, part of a *Breaking News* video montage served to the world by the likes of CNN and Al-Jazeera. The incident was being branded as the takedown of a possible violent terrorist cell.

The mission had been successful, but at a heavy price. The blame would surely fall on his shoulders. The ruling powers were on board with punishing those responsible for the Natanz disaster, as long as it didn't exact too great a toll or bring about further embarrassment. Tonight would be hard to explain. Gilani had to mitigate the situation as best he could. Once he'd received the frantic phone call from Mahir, he'd instructed the man to not say another word, dispose of the burner phone, and return to the rendezvous location immediately. The authorities would collect Rami's phone. It too was a burner, paid for in cash like the others. The men who sacrificed their lives didn't carry any form of identification. Rami's body was the only intact one left behind. His face and fingerprints would be run through sophisticated databases. They were likely to come up empty, but that sophistication would signal a level of expertise and funding not available to upstart terrorist groups. Once they'd arrived at the shop, Mahir and the other driver were at the beck and call of the doctor should he need anything. It gave them something to do beyond focusing on their anger.

And then there was the matter of Dr. Mueller. Gilani couldn't kill him now. Six men dead was enough for one night. Besides, the doctor's information had been correct. Gilani remained puzzled, though, that Mueller's connections could harvest such intelligence. For the moment, he accepted the unknown, because when the bullets started ripping the car apart, Mueller's life had been in just as much danger. If he'd been playing them, the shooter wouldn't have taken such a risk in the dark, not knowing whether Mueller was behind the wheel.

Gilani's men were still riding a wave of adrenalin, but Dr. Mueller was calm, resting in a chair. The man's eyes were closed, his breathing barely noticeable. He might have fallen asleep. The reports Gilani had received about him from surviving workers at Natanz were true. He was very cool under pressure.

Exhaustion tipped the scales, requiring Gilani to sit down. He hoped to steal a few minutes of rest. The TV served as background white noise, the news regurgitating the same information that amounted to nothing more than speculation, and interviews with neighborhood "eyewitnesses." The medical doctor had given his patient sufficient painkillers to stop the incessant moaning.

The automobile repair shop was a profitable front. Parisians drove like shit, and when their cars got dinged and dented to the point of ridicule, they needed patching up. Set up to be a low-key, low-traffic business, the shop did such good work it became a legitimate enterprise that doubled as a safe house. More functional than comfortable, the two-room office where Mueller and Gilani were, greeted legitimate customers during normal business hours. Off to the side was a doorless break room, equipped with a refrigerator and sink. The smaller room directly across from the office was now the temporary medical facility. The doctor tended to his patient on an oversized desk ill-suited for the room chosen because it provided the best lighting. One flight up was a dorm-room-sized box with two twin beds. A full bathroom with weak water pressure was back downstairs, along with a half bath accessible via the garage. The office smelled like a hospital operating room, which came as a welcome departure from the usual overflow smell of paint, glue, grease, and oil from the garage.

The first order of business had been to get the bullet-riddled sedan off the street. The wounded driver miraculously drove three blocks before pulling over. Gilani had rushed out of the passenger side, oblivious to his bloodstained clothes. Aided by his backseat countryman, they slid the barely conscious driver to the front passenger seat. They took mostly backstreets to make it to the garage without incident. The lateness of the hour had prohibited seeing the doctor at his clinic. It opened to the public at 8 a.m., making the risk of exposure too great. The doctor had done his best to coach Gilani over the phone on what preparations he needed, emphasizing not to expect a miracle without the proper resources.

With the time adjustment, it was just after 6 a.m. in Tehran. Gilani remained undecided on how to proceed. Being emotionally drained clouded his thinking even more. He wasn't aware he had drifted off until Mahir shook his shoulder, interrupting his twenty-minute escape. The doctor wanted to see him. A bit of good news—the patient was still breathing. The doctor had managed to remove the bullet from his abdomen and was transfusing a second bag of O-positive blood into the injured man's depleted system. He needed more, but had a sufficient amount to get him through the danger zone. Since transporting him was out of the question, what the patient needed most was rest. Monitor his condition and hope for the best. The doctor promised to check in periodically, and after his clinic closed for the day, he'd return with a fresh supply of everything. Gilani thanked and dismissed him, along with Mahir and the other driver. Gilani further instructed his men to inform the garage staff that the business would be closed today. He'd stay to watch over the wounded driver.

To stay awake, Gilani paced back and forth with a cold bottle of water from the refrigerator. He alternated between taking sips and splashing water in his face. This was unfamiliar territory. He was worried, and that wasn't like him. Though successful, this operation had spiraled out of control. The TV reports highlighted one aspect that was true. The loss of lives was sloppy and careless. Gilani had never truly put his heart into the project. In fact, showing proper respect politically, he'd suggested to Shahroudi that he might want to concentrate his efforts on far more pressing matters, such as safeguarding his presidency. But, it was difficult to reason with a delusional mind.

Speaking of mindset, there sat Dr. Mueller. Motionless, his head angled back, his body comfortably slumped in the chair. Gilani conceded he was just one of those people. Somehow, they always survived, even through the worst of circumstances.

"If I were you, I'd get ahead of all this."

In the stillness, the words so startled Gilani that he almost dropped the water bottle. "I thought you were sleeping," he said, addressing a comatose Dr. Mueller.

"Just resting my eyes."

"And I am on top of this," Gilani shot back.

"If pacing helps you think, sorry to interrupt. But, you don't want to be the second version Tehran hears," Mueller offered. Even with his eyes closed, he could feel Gilani's intense glare.

"What are you talking about?" Gilani's voice was edgy but inquisitive.

"You'll be going home minus six men. Possibly seven." Mueller stirred to an upright position, his eyes offering trust. "The two guys you sent away, are they friends with the others?"

Gilani reflected. "Mahir and Rami attended school together and played on the same football team. The families know each other."

"So you think Mahir will wait to deliver the bad news? What if he feels compelled to reach out?"

"He wouldn't."

"You're sure about that? You know him that well?"

"They know and respect the chain of command. There's a reason I chose them for this mission," Gilani emphasized. He saw no reason to give the man he wanted to kill the satisfaction of knowing his argument held merit. Gilani had only specific knowledge about three of the men. The rest, including Mahir, he had learned about from reading their dossiers when mapping out strategy. They'd assigned Mahir and Rami to him because of their familiarity with the region.

Mueller spread his hands. "Okay, you're the man in charge. The mission was successful. Offering my advice for what it's worth, I'd be proactive. Inform Tehran. Make Shahroudi happy. Be assertive in shutting down this global operation of searching for Mr. McBride and his female companion. You found them." Dr. Mueller stretched out to get comfortable again. Shutting his eyes, he added, "You march home a little scarred, but further your reputation as a man who gets things done."

Gilani recognized he was being seduced, but much of what the German said made sense. He wanted to return home, to be done monitoring this costly endeavor staffed by too much incompetence, like those idiots Jafar and Navid in London.

"I need to go make a call," said Gilani, exiting to find solitude and privacy.

Satisfied, Dr. Mueller called out, "I'll be right here."

Yadin folded one foot over the other and, in doing so, brushed against the sheath wrapped around his calf. He could feel the handle of the knife he would use to kill Gilani.

CHAPTER 55

GEORGE CHAMPION HAD built a career around secrets. They were power in Washington, DC. Lobbyists paid good money for them. Careers on the Hill were advanced or destroyed by them. Foreign governments, friend or foe, were always in the market for information. People and organizations were sometimes willing to make ethical and moral compromises rather than have their deepest secrets emerge from the dark.

Champion found himself in the dark at the moment. Only a chosen few knew of the secret he guarded, and that fragile bubble had a fast-approaching expiration date. In a world of leaks, the information would garner huge headlines when revealed.

A notification woke Champion's cell phone. There was a mandatory security briefing in five hours. He'd crawled into bed two hours ago after getting status updates, shaking hands, and committing faces to memory. During the nearly eight-hour flight from suburban DC to Geneva, he'd gone over pages of notes, bios, and background information. He'd shared the flight with Stacy and Lancellotti, reuniting for the first time since meeting at the White House. Their sporadic interaction had centered on the basics of the mission. Midway through the flight, whiskey, for relaxation purposes, had knocked Stacy into a nap. He provided amusement by waking up during bouts of turbulence to chime in on whatever discussion was taking place. They killed time by filling in the blanks of hometown, schooling, and family status. The benefits of the forced grouping were paying off. They walked different paths, operated differently, but served the same ideology.

The ride to the hotel showcased Geneva's impressive shoreline. The Jet d'Eau fountain lived up to its hype, serving as the focal point against the darkening sky, bathed in light as water spouted skyward. The DSS advance team had taken care of the hotel check-in. The trio had an hour to unpack and freshen up before the initial briefing was to take place. Champion stored his belongings away and spent the rest of the allotted time touching base with Jill. In the middle of the afternoon DC time, he caught up with her at work. Talking with her reminded him why he needed to stay focused. His intention was to always make it back home to her. Overseeing operations from Langley made that a lot easier.

Champion knew most of the names at the meeting, but he didn't let that spoil the freshness of every encounter. There was no sense in coming off like a know-it-all Washington insider. The DSS had established itself as more than capable of handling the kinds of dicey situations the diplomatic core faced in hot spots around the world. Champion suspected some resented his presence at the president's request. He hung back, observed, and offered an opinion only when asked. He'd share information if Langley unearthed chatter pertinent to the proceedings.

Secretary Drake was scheduled to arrive fashionably later. His overemphasized role called for him to put the deal to bed. Negotiators like Lancellotti and Stacy had done the lion's share of work. The disputes and clarifications that remained were minor. Drake's presence and deliberate personality would help iron out such wrinkles.

Champion hoped to stay clear once the secretary was in the mix. He didn't want Secretary Drake bringing up the firestorm created during their initial get-together. Ironically, that night had probably contributed to this landmark undertaking.

An hour earlier, Champion had taken the bait to rise out of bed and sit by the window. He was restless. The prism of colors from the shore that danced on the darkened waters of Lake Geneva was hypnotic. He'd thought the backdrop might soothe him back to sleep. Instead, he wondered who else was up like him? What were they up to behind their windows? Was there someone or some group out there plotting to make this undertaking a disaster?

Back in bed, Champion stayed put this time. He pulled the bedspread over his shoulder, buried his head into the pillow, and closed his eyes. He thought about the woman across the Atlantic who loved him as he drifted off to sleep.

CHAPTER 56

GILANI STEPPED BACK into the room like he was navigating a sheet of ice. His face held the look of a man who'd seen others lose their footing and hit the ground hard.

"Everything all right?"

Once again, Dr. Mueller's words were unexpected. "Tehran is pleased to hear the job is done. But as you can expect, they're not thrilled by the mess left behind."

"You've covered your tracks well. Completing the mission has to count for something." Dr. Mueller worked to loosen the stiffness caused by lounging in an uncomfortable chair. He bent over to stretch, his hands grabbing the front of his shoes for resistance. The pose shielded the retrieval of the knife strapped to his ankle. He was that much closer to seeking what he'd previously considered unthinkable—living a meaningful, normal life with a woman who had unearthed his capacity to love. First, he had to rid himself of the obstacles that stood in the way. Getting off the Iranian's radar was a good start.

"I suppose you'll be heading back to Tehran then?" The knife was now tucked inside Dr. Mueller's right shirtsleeve. Before he could strike, he needed to know if the Iranians remained a threat. "Yes, but not before I tie up some loose ends."

"Can I be of any help?" Dr. Mueller rose, then sank back into the chair. Gilani had a 9mm handgun pointed at his head.

"Your participation is mandatory, since you've become one of those loose ends."

Dr. Mueller did the most sensible thing in yielding control to the person who could handle this situation. Nathan Yadin calculated his options. On the outside, as Dr. Mueller, the response required a sense of dread. He swallowed hard, his eyes darting back and forth from the gun to Gilani. Dr. Mueller spat out, "What is this?"

"*This* is the end, Dr. Mueller. Thank you for urging me to make that phone call. As it turns out, tonight's untidiness has called for your demise. Tehran can't afford to have you running around. Not with what's at stake."

"What's at *stake*? The mission is over. McBride and the woman are dead."

Gilani nodded in agreement. "True, and if that's all Shahroudi had required, you more than likely would have walked out of here."

"After everything I've done for Tehran?" the doctor pleaded, cupping the knife in his hand, the transfer hidden by his knee.

Gilani let go a slight laugh. "All you've done is make yourself a very rich man. Natanz was a monumental failure, Dr. Mueller. A win, if you will, for the West. And the Zionist regime will benefit under the umbrella of a nuclear treaty!"

Yadin came to the surface, puzzled. An agreement? Was Gilani testing him? "What are you talking about?"

"Things are way more complicated than getting rid of two spies from the West," Gilani went on, resting his back against a counter, holding the weapon with less authority. "Shahroudi has engineered his own demise. He's too blind, too stubborn to see that. He thinks this crazy plan he's sanctioned will return him to political prominence. He fails to recognize the supreme leader, and

Parliament's desire for growth and prosperity. Facilitated by, of all places, the West. They'll let Shahroudi have his moment because it will strengthen their position."

Yadin was ready to go on the offensive at the slightest hint Gilani might pull the trigger. But getting more information was worth holding back. Yadin stared Gilani directly in the eyes. Then he laughed.

Gilani bristled. "You find this amusing?"

"I find it odd you feel a need to lie at this moment," Yadin replied. Gilani failed to notice the subtle shift in personality.

"Lie to you? For what purpose? A dead man has no voice."

"This story of yours is bullshit. Spending years dodging the Israelis—mostly for Tehran, I might add—there's no way Israel would sit down at the negotiating table so easily."

A Cheshire cat-like grin formed on Gilani's face. "This should make it palatable for you then. Call it punishment for Natanz without worldwide admission of guilt, but the P5+1 nations felt it was best to exclude the Zionists from the process. However, they will play a part. One that will jeopardize powerful relationships."

"Forgive my skepticism. When is this treaty supposed to happen?"

Gilani considered pulling the trigger, but toying with the overly confident Dr. Mueller while he attempted to extend his life was enjoyable. Gilani shrugged. "What the hell. You won't be around to see the outcome. The treaty gets signed this week in Geneva."

The confusion Yadin displayed was real. He fidgeted in the chair, trying to find a balanced position to spring from. "If the Israelis aren't at the table, how can they, as you say, 'Play a part?'"

"Once Shahroudi caught wind of the proposed treaty, and its growing support, he hatched a plan of his own. Its cleverness impressed the supreme leader. A lone assassin, with undeniable ties to Mossad, will lay blame on Israel's doorstep for what happens."

"Mossad goes to great lengths to protect its operatives identities. What makes you think this plan will have any credibility?"

"This assassin is special. Mossad takes great pride in his notoriety. They call him The Devil."

Hearing the name froze Yadin. He knew it all too well. A moniker painstakingly built over the years with the blood of those who made the fatal mistake of challenging Israel's resolve.

"The Devil," Yadin whispered.

"Yes. I can see by the look on your face it's not the first time you've heard the name."

"No," Yadin responded with glassy eyes. "But surely, he's a myth."

"Tell that to the countless number of Arabs he's killed."

In disbelief, Yadin said, "It'll never work."

Beyond tired, Gilani was near the end of his patience. There was a full agenda of things to tidy up before he could return to his homeland. "I assure you. The man we hired is up to the task."

Yadin gave his approval. "It's good to have faith. But, I can tell you, The Devil will probably mess everything up."

"I highly doubt that. There's no way he could know. It's been a well-guarded secret."

"He does now."

Gilani didn't grasp what Dr. Mueller was getting at until the knife was hurtling through the air. Gilani tried to aim his firearm in defense, but his arm fell to the side when the knife penetrated just below the rib cage. Gilani switched into survival mode, but Yadin was all over him. Pinning Gilani against the counter, Yadin restrained the Iranian's gun hand as he grabbed the knife. He worked it upward and inward.

Yadin heard the gun hit the floor. Gilani took fewer, more labored breaths. Embraced in an intimate slow dance, Yadin could feel the warmth of his own breath against Gilani's neck.

"Yes, Gilani, you were right to have your suspicions. Now go join the others. Tell them The Devil says hello."

Yadin let Gilani drop. He backed away and retrieved his phone, checking to make sure technology had not failed him. He'd programmed the phone to record if he tapped the volume button four times. He exhaled when he heard with clarity.

"If the Israelis aren't at the table, how can they, as you say, Play a part?"

"Once Shahroudi caught wind of the proposed treaty, and its growing support, he hatched out a plan of his own. Its cleverness impressed the supreme leader. A lone assassin, with undeniable ties to Mossad, will lay blame on Israel's doorstep for what happens."

The recording gave him the framework of a plan for survival. He gave his current situation some thought. In the next room, the wounded driver was recuperating, knocked out. Yadin bent over Gilani's body to get his cell phone. He'd seen him enter the passcode from the sedan's backseat, and again in the garage before a call to Mahir. Yadin gained access and searched the call log for the most recent activity. He found the time line he was looking for and sent a text to the corresponding number.

I need you back at the garage. Change of plans. We need to move the patient. Hurry!

Mahir responded that he'd be there as soon as he could. Yadin wiped clean the places his fingerprints might be, not that they'd show up on anyone's database. However, he preferred to be thorough. Searching the garage, he found the flammable and combustible liquids he was looking for on a shelf. He poured a hefty amount on the floor and covered a portion of the walls. Lighting a rag, he tossed it to the ground. It ignited with a loud whoosh. Yadin exited the building through a door that led into the poorly lit alley. He kept his head low, his feet guiding him. Two blocks away, he unlocked Gilani's phone again. He punched the number for the Police Nationale. Using perfect French, Yadin altered his voice to sound winded and anxious.

"I think I have information related to what's going on in Saint-Denis. This car with a lot of bullet holes sped by me and pulled into a garage at the end of the block. It's supposed to be closed right now. It could be nothing, but they were driving crazy."

The police took down the name of the garage. They promised to get right on it. Yadin hung up before they could ask any more questions. With his own phone, he took pictures of all the numbers listed in Gilani's call log. He then slammed the phone into the ground, crushing it into pieces with his foot.

As he walked away, there was a smile on his face.

One step closer to freedom.

CHAPTER 57

"LOOKS LIKE YOU can use this." Alex handed his guest a glass of bourbon. "Until you called, I wasn't sure you made it."

"There were some tense moments." Nathan gave the glass a swirl, mindful that the clock had just clicked over to 9 a.m.

Alex recognized the apprehension. "It's five o'clock somewhere."

Nathan raised the glass in salute. "Well, when you apply that logic. To Beijing, then." The burn ran down his throat as he emptied the glass. Declining another, Nathan heard the hustle of Paris encroaching through an open patio door. The Eiffel Tower was in plain view. He looked around the accommodations of the one-bedroom suite.

"She's still asleep," Alex said. "Last night was tense for us too."

"No civilian casualties, though."

"Amazing, considering."

"One thing has been bothering me," Yadin stated, joining Alex on the sofa. "How did you know I wasn't behind the wheel of the sedan?"

Alex smirked. "I'll admit I wasn't working with the best lighting down on the street, but I thought I made out it wasn't you driving."

"So you guessed?"

"Yeah, pretty much. An educated guess, though. I figured they wouldn't risk letting you drive or ride in the front."

Nathan wanted to smile at the brashness of the confession. Alex's abilities and intellect were growing on him. A lone wolf for most of his career, Yadin had not embraced the concept of teamwork. The last several days, however, had given him a sense of comfort. Unusual circumstances had tied them together. If he stayed true to the norm, now was the right time for everyone to go their separate ways.

"Fortunately for me then, everything turned out okay." Nathan punctuated the sentence with a yawn. An hour's worth of sleep had been his only rest since the activity at the garage. "I just stopped by to thank you for your help. Also, you and Nora shouldn't have to look over your shoulder anymore. The Iranians believe you're dead."

Alex sensed it wasn't just weariness at work. "You could have saved yourself a trip and told me that over the phone."

"Very perceptive."

"We're in the clear. What about you?"

"Complicated. From the Iranians, yes. A larger problem, not quite. I'm hoping I can mitigate the severity of the situation."

"You have a plan then?"

"If flying by the seat of your pants is a plan, then it's a great one. Starts off with me going to Geneva. I'm booked on the 6:11 express train leaving Gare de Lyon."

"No shortage of drama in your life."

"Tell me about it."

Alex opened his mouth to speak. He dismissed what surfaced in his mind, only to come back to the question he felt compelled to ask. "If I may, what's going on in Geneva?"

Nathan waved him off. "Don't concern yourself with it. I'm sure your people have their bases adequately covered."

"Hard not to be inquisitive after that statement."

Considering what they'd been through, Nathan trusted the American. But he could only be forthcoming to a point. There was no way he'd tell the truth concerning his former Mossad handler.

That secret he'd take to his grave. If he didn't stop the assassin the Iranians hired, or failed to convince Tel Aviv of his storyline, he'd be in that grave sooner rather than later.

Yadin detailed what he'd learned from Gilani. He addressed Alex's initial skepticism, filling him in as much as possible. He stressed why the Iranians, or more accurately, President Shahroudi's deadly addendum, could work. It got tricky when Alex pressed on why Mossad didn't just produce their operative prior to the planned attack as proof of non-involvement. Yadin danced around the truth, providing enough ambiguous responses that weren't outright lies.

"The office," Yadin continued, "is reluctant to acknowledge his existence. He lives and operates in the shadows. In fact, few in the Kidon have ever met him."

"Under the circumstances, this seems like an exception," said Alex.

Yadin looked away with a sigh. "There's another issue that doesn't make it so simple. He'd gone dark for a lengthy period. Not on assignment to anyone's knowledge."

"You think he's been compromised?"

"Doubtful, but Tel Aviv has questions, and he's reportedly reluctant to come in."

"Sounds similar to Nora's situation a few months ago."

Yadin's jaw dropped into his chest. "I still bear the emotional weight of that," he sincerely said. "When I approached her in Monte Carlo, I wasn't sure I'd walk out alive. She's been tepid toward me, but nowhere near what I expected. Which leads me to one conclusion. You haven't told her, have you?"

Alex's initial silence answered Yadin's question. "That's a wound you don't want to pick at," he said. "She found some closure with the name you provided. Trust me, it's best to leave it at that."

Yadin agreed without protest. "You know her better than I do."

Alex glanced at the bedroom door, listening for activity behind it. He changed the subject. "Geneva sounds like a big job for one man, or is the office sending a team?"

"No time to put anything of substance into play. Plus, since

Israel is shut out from the proceedings, a clandestine show of force could backfire if this imposter should succeed. Best if I try to resolve it my way." Yadin pursed his lips. "Though, I suppose something bilateral might work."

Alex's face was full of regret. "I'm flattered, but I've had enough excitement lately. Besides, I'm not on the government's payroll."

"Totally understand. Can you or Nora make someone on your side aware of the threat?"

Nora's suspension precluded any involvement from her. A grin crossed Alex's lips. "I know a guy. He'll get right on it."

"Perfect," Yadin replied. Rising from the sofa, he extended a hand. "I'll get out of your lives now."

Alex was about to offer a friendly departing salutation when the door to the bedroom opened. Draped in a hotel robe, Nora stepped through. She examined both of them without saying a word. Her hands bore deep into the robe's pockets as if seeking warmth.

"Good morning," Yadin greeted. "I was just on my way out."

She heard him, but didn't respond. She reserved her focus for Alex. "What exactly haven't you told me, Alex?"

Nora's right hand was now exposed at her side. She had a firm grip on the suppressed H&K VP9.

CHAPTER 58

STANDING NEXT TO Alex, Yadin took a cautious step forward. Nora's response to the ill-advised movement was a no-look shot that vaporized the bottle of bourbon.

"Move again," Nora dared Nathan.

"Your question is better directed at me," he replied.

"Oh, I'll get to you," Nora answered. "For now, do yourself a favor and shut up. Answer the question, Alex. What haven't you told me?"

This was precisely the situation Alex had hoped to avoid. He should have told her, but for months he'd rationalized that withholding the whole truth was in her best interest. She was healing from the death of her friend, having found some closure in putting down the man responsible for giving the order. The identifying information had come from Erica Janway's executioner. There damn sure was no comfortable way for the truth to come out now.

"Nathan gave me the name of the person who ordered Erica's death. I passed it along. You used that information. It gave you some closure." Alex didn't risk moving either.

"Yes, but you didn't tell me everything. Who is this man, really? How did he specifically know Roger Daniels was responsible?"

Nathan took the initiative. "I did, because I'm the one who acted on that order. I killed your friend."

Alex gave Nathan an incredulous "what the hell are you thinking" look.

Nora's eyes turned demon–possessed dark. She tried to swallow, but couldn't. Hearing the revelation reopened a gaping wound.

"You knew all along?" she demanded of Alex. He didn't have to respond. She knew it was true.

Alex wasn't the best at expressing matters of the heart, but he loved the woman that stood just a few feet away. He wanted to protect her like she had often done for him. In the back of his mind, he thought he'd done that by not telling her the whole truth. Ridding the world of a misguided, dangerous billionaire like Roger Daniels was one thing. Hunting down and trying to kill someone like Nathan carried perilous risks. Then there was the other troubling factor. The man from Mossad could have ended Alex's life, but didn't. Instead, he had helped Alex escape a crumbling installation deep underground. In that moment, when getting out alive was uncertain, Nathan, it seemed, had been remorseful about killing Janway.

Nora's rage was real and unpredictable. Janway had become her moral and ethical barometer, the definition of a true friend. Nora adjusted her aim. If she pulled the trigger at this range, Nathan would have a sizable hole in his forehead.

"Is this how you did it? Close enough to hear her breathe? See the final look in her eyes?"

Nathan planted his feet and kept his mouth shut.

Nora flinched, prompting Alex to step in front of Nathan. "Put the gun down, Nora," Alex pleaded, hoping a part of her rational side was present to listen.

"Get out of the way, Alex."

"Nora, lower the gun."

"I swear, if you don't move."

"You going to shoot me?"

"Somewhere that will really hurt, but you'll survive."

"Nora, you can't."

"He killed Erica, so I damn well can!"

Alex raised his head toward the ceiling, seeking guidance. Frustrated, he exhaled. "You can't kill him right now."

"Sure I can. Just get out of the way and watch me."

Alex held his arm out. "You have to let him go. There's something happening in Geneva that involves the U.S. in a big way. If he's right about what might happen, global relationships might suffer."

The gun didn't waver an inch, but Nora was listening. That was a good sign.

"I heard some of it," Nora said, "Sounds like a lot of bullshit." Visible pain washed over her face, followed by disappointment. "I can't believe you're protecting him. We don't even know his full name. Hell, Nathan might even be an alias. You know what Erica meant to me!"

"I know. I also know he was just following orders, trusting people and institutions that claim to be on the right side of an issue. I've done it. You have too."

"Alex . . . move. I swear—"

"He's no Nevsky, Nora."

Nora breathed deep, her nostrils flared. Her hurt eyes locked on Alex's sorrowful face. She maintained her gaze as she lowered the weapon and tossed it on the sofa. She stood motionless, wounded by the betrayal. Without saying a word, she headed toward the bedroom.

"I'm sorry," Nathan called out.

Nora stopped, but didn't turn around. She dropped her head and balled her fists, summoning the strength to keep moving. She didn't slam the heavy bedroom door shut. Instead, she let it close with a simple, unsettling click.

Unsure if the door would suddenly reopen, Alex said to Nathan, "If I were you . . ."

"Yeah, I'll be on my way."

Nathan exited while Alex remained paralyzed, not sure what to do next.

***

There was a moment at the hotel when Yadin doubted he'd make the train to Geneva. Nora Mossa's rage-filled eyes wanted retribution. He didn't blame her. He'd never been confronted so directly by someone personally affected by his work. His modus operandi was to strike and disappear like a well-performed magic trick. The carnage left behind was proof of his existence. Today, he'd felt empathy.

Boarding the train early gave Yadin the luxury of getting a solo seat. He hoped it stayed that way for the entire trip. The last thing he wanted was idle chitchat with a stranger. He needed to hash out a plan, and there wasn't much to work with. Tehran had kept Gilani in the dark regarding specifics. He didn't know the identification of this unknown assassin, nor did he have any means of contacting him. Since this person was mimicking him, Yadin questioned how much he had studied and prepared. He was well financed, but given the high level of security, how would he try to pull off the assigned task? Lots to ponder as Yadin sank his head into the padded headrest of his seat. He closed his eyes and felt the train pull away from the station. Maybe he could shut out the world, at least for an hour.

"Excuse me, sir?"

Yadin thought he was dreaming when the voice interrupted. He kept his eyes closed. Hopefully the man would get the message. The do not disturb sign is on. Stop being a rude ass, go away.

"Excuse me, sir?" A level hand accompanied the query, shaking Yadin's arm.

Yadin prepared for an unpleasant confrontation. He opened his eyes. The hand belonged to the seated man leaning across the aisle. Yadin's frustration lifted, replaced with what passed for a smile.

"This is the train to Geneva? A little over three hours?"

Yadin nodded.

"My girlfriend abruptly cut her vacation short, so I have some free time now."

Alex said nothing further, opting to plug in his Bluetooth earbuds. He loaded his music playlist. He'd be out before John Klemmer's *Touch* album was halfway through its track list.

CHAPTER 59

FOR THE MISSION to have a chance of succeeding, Daniel Sharon and Lisa Neril had to accept being paired together. Too often, singularity of mind and purpose guided them. It was partly why they excelled, but there was room for improvement. Their cooperative conclusion also had to do with the unpleasant experience of getting chewed out by Director Rozen.

Field operatives often used hunches and gut feelings to guide them through treacherous waters. Last night, Sharon had listened to his inner voice that compelled him to forgo sleep. He got out of bed and made his way to the Strasbourg Saint-Denis neighborhood, where an explosion had blown open part of a building. By the time he arrived, the streets were heavily secured, and remained so long into the morning hours. Sharon had pushed his way forward to get a glimpse of a tarp-covered body on the sidewalk. From news reports and chatter around him, he'd gathered there were more fatalities. He also overheard that police had found body parts on the street. Judging by the size of the hole, the occupants of the building, aside from those blown up, had been very lucky to survive. Or, perhaps, they had never been in real danger to begin with.

Sharon didn't linger. He concluded it was all too surgical. The dead man on the street would probably have false identification documents on him. He'd bet any other bodies found would present the same discovery problem. In this ethnically diverse section of Paris, the deceased's birthplace could anywhere, but Sharon had a feeling he was Iranian.

Iranian.

He'd recently had a conversation with a man who had an Iranian problem. A man talented in getting rid of problems. If this was Nathan Yadin's work, were his troubles over, or was more bloodshed ahead? The uneasiness prompted Sharon to contact Director Rozen at dawn. He asked the director if he could disclose the location of the treaty deal.

Feeling Sharon had learned his lesson and deserved another chance, Rozen caved, agreeing to let Sharon act on his assumption. He also made it clear that Sharon must include Neril in his plans. Eager to get started, Sharon had gathered his travel belongings and caught the midday train to Geneva.

Sharon topped off his good tidings with a glass of Cabernet Sauvignon, reading the local newspaper in the lounge area of the hotel where the historic treaty signing was to take place. The activity level was high. Security milled about, purposely easy to spot. Men and women dressed in dark suits with their jackets buttoned gave off the right amount of intimidation. Security knew the drill of showing force without revealing procedure. Sharon had seen enough. He left a tip on the table and exited the hotel. The daylight left provided the perfect opportunity to survey the building's exterior. He'd check out the surrounding neighborhood too.

Conscious of the time, and Director Rozen's order, he gave Neril a call. If she hurried, she could make the last train of the night out of Paris.

CHAPTER 60

MICHELLE ORSETTE SHOOK off the goose bumps created by a blast of passing air. She struggled with which was more interesting, the scenery or her dinner companion. How Erik Snow powered through a day with little fatigue dumbfounded her. Back in Michigan, she'd be down for the count after chauffeuring the kids to their various after-school activities, feeding them, helping with homework, and putting them to bed. Her end-of-the-day reward was an occasional sleep-inducing glass of wine.

Snow had kept her busy the last couple of days in Geneva. Rising early, she either accompanied him on the boat or stayed behind on land at designated points. Snow didn't miss a day of testing the equipment from Kentucky. Run-throughs were conducted during non-busy hours, in peak traffic, and at night. The most daunting test was when "Buckeye," the nearly six-foot mannequin, had to die twice or three times a day. Snow didn't catch on at first as to why Orsette had nicknamed it "Buckeye." She explained it to him from a Michigan perspective. He'd merely looked at her like a dog angling its head, more confused or less interested than when he didn't know.

During Buckeye's initial setup, Snow reinforced the backdrop with thick pillows taped together to avoid leaving any damage to the hotel room. Buckeye was placed in a central location, its feet weighed down with sand bags. Snow opened line-of-sight windows before heading down to take the boat out on Lake Geneva. Once positioned at optimal range, he'd called Orsette, instructing her to follow directions exactly.

"Lie flat on the floor, and don't hang up the phone."

Minutes later a swoosh noise had cut through the air, followed by a soft puff. From the corner of her eye, Orsette had seen Buckeye wobble, but remain upright. Snow had wanted a status report.

She stared at the mannequin before casting a disbelieving glance out the window in search of the boat. "He's fine, except for the hole in his chest."

This test was repeated under varying wind and light conditions. Snow's accuracy had improved on each round. All the equipment had checked out just fine. Orsette didn't know precisely what he was planning. Her job was to assist when asked. Considering what he did for a living, it was a logical guess there'd be a human substitute for Buckeye soon enough.

Daily exposure to the sun had given them both a perfect golden hue. Now, the cool night air at the outdoor café was refreshing, despite the goose bumps.

"Do you want my jacket?" Snow offered, raising his glass for a post-dinner toast.

She appreciated him noticing. "No, but thank you." She grabbed her wrap from the armrest. "I've got this if I need it. The air feels good."

Snow smiled and continued his toast. "Here's to this being over soon. And then, months of R&R."

They clinked glasses, but Orsette couldn't contain a giggle.

"What?"

She bit her lip and then pleaded with her eyes. "You, take months off?"

"You doubt my sincerity?"

"I doubt you can give up the adrenaline. Plus, you like money."

He leaned closer to the table. The candlelight bounced over his animated face. "Think you know me, huh? Yes, I like the action, and yes, the money is comforting. But this job is paying me very well, and I need a little rest."

Orsette wasn't buying it.

"Who knows," Snow added, leaning back, "I might even find time to take in one of those Red Flyers games you've talked about."

Orsette burst out laughing, drawing momentary looks from nearby tables. "It's the Red Wings. How do you not know this?"

Snow laughed with her. "Close enough. And soccer is my sport."

Like most places her changed life exposed her to, Orsette savored the surroundings. She wanted to commit as much as possible to memory. Geneva was a landscape of tranquil beauty. The majestic mountains, the mesmerizing Jet d'Eau fountain, the fresh air, and heavens, the chocolate.

Snow liked that she could indulge so freely in small things and find joy. His guilt was that he couldn't afford such luxury. Not while working, at least. He'd trained hard to stay focused. The playful time at dinner was for her. But he could never drift too far away, not with the job unfinished.

"Tomorrow we'll rehearse again," Snow said, bringing Orsette back into the moment. "This time, I'll need you to take the boat out. We'll also go over the final preparations."

Orsette's participation was coming to an end. From the beginning, Snow had been adamant about sending her home to family. She read it as another expression of his concern.

He paid the bill and saw her back to the hotel. Each night, the routine was the same. He never went up to the room with her, excusing himself at the hotel entrance to disappear into the night. She was clueless as to where he went, sometimes for hours.

Tonight, Snow turned the corner of the hotel and strolled down the block, looking every bit a man walking off a meal, trying to hit his daily step goal. Everything looked to be the same as it was on prior nights. He entertained the thought that maybe he was being a bit too cautious.

Another block. Nothing.

Another block. Couples. Couples with children, joggers, and an elderly man he envisioned one day would be his future. Otherwise, nothing.

Another block . . . he spotted something that gave him pause. Instinct made him slow his pace. To most people, it would have only been another man out for a walk. The man was dressed conservatively, his outfit topped off with a sport coat. It was the way the man walked that drew Snow's attention. He seemed to take particular interest in the hotel where the treaty signing was to occur. The man also inspected adjacent buildings, going back and forth, as if measuring. It could be nothing. He might be an architect or builder, sizing up future business opportunities. He could be a tourist admiring the symmetry and contrast from one building to the next. But with mere days to go before Snow completed his contract, he had to be sure.

Daniel Sharon's preoccupation blinded him from noticing he'd picked up a tail. The thought never crossed his mind. He was fresh to Geneva. And already, he'd let his guard down.

CHAPTER 61

ANOTHER LONG DAY was mercifully close to wrapping up. Champion tried to avoid drinking coffee this late in the evening, but the aroma of a freshly brewed pot, coupled with boredom, drew him to the beverage setup in the back of the conference room. He also made room for a cinnamon stars cookie.

Nothing slowed progress like a room full of bureaucrats. The necessary officials from each country were now on site. That included Secretary of State Drake, who surprisingly was cordial to Champion during their brief interaction. Perhaps the White House had instructed him to play nice. Whatever the reason for the personality adjustment, Champion didn't press his luck. He excused himself without appearing rude.

There was not much to iron out, and yet, the diplomats didn't disperse until early evening. Dinner ranked high on the priority list. For some, the work didn't stop there. Following a short break, the security services again gathered to discuss the precise details for maintaining a safe environment.

The Germans, Chinese, and Iranians reviewed, of all things,

seating arrangements, and last-minute changes to the security ros-
ter. This was as good a time as any to duck out. Champion grabbed
a to-go cup of coffee, and exited, cell phone in hand. There were
two messages waiting for him. It was nearly four o'clock in Langley,
and true to form, when his administrative assistant, Mrs. Prescot,
answered his call, she sounded fresh, like it was the start of the day.

"Mr. Champion, good evening. How's Geneva?"

"Haven't really seen much of it, Mrs. Prescot. They have a nice
fountain, though. Oh, I've got a box of chocolates for you."

"That's very nice of you, thank you."

Champion realized he should have kept that nugget to himself.
Surprises were much better. Maybe next time. "I've been in meetings
most of the day, noticed you've left a couple of messages. What's up?"

"Yes, sorry to trouble you with this, sir, but he said it was urgent.
Since you took Mr. Koves's call a few months ago, I thought you'd
want to know. He left a number for you."

Champion found a wall to lean on. "Not now," he said under his
breath. "How long ago did he call?"

"Within the past hour."

"Did he mention what this was concerning?"

"No, he just said he had urgent information you'd might want to
know, and needed to get in touch."

"I'll take the number when you're ready." Champion jotted down
the information on a notepad from the meeting. "Please transfer me
to a secure line. Anything else pressing?"

"Nothing that can't wait until you return."

"Thank you, Mrs. Prescot."

"You're welcome, sir. Safe travels. Switching you over now."

A series of clicks started, and then a dial tone came online.
Champion debated whether to call right away, or put it off until
morning. The more sensible course of action was to call after the
Iran deal was over. It could be Alex finally getting back to him on

the last conversation they'd had in the Virgin Islands. If that were the case, though, he wouldn't have told Mrs. Prescot it was urgent.

Damn it.

He dialed the number, tapping a foot while he waited for someone to answer. He didn't know what time it was on the other end and didn't care.

"Hello?"

"Alex?" Champion questioned, wanting to be sure.

"George!" The animated, playful response left no doubt.

"What's up, Alex? I'm in the middle of something. Mrs. Prescot passed along that you said it was urgent?"

"George, all business. No, how have you been? Haven't heard from you in a while."

Frustrated, Champion sought a more isolated corner. "I don't have time for this Alex. What do you have?" Before Alex responded, Champion lowered his voice. "Ms. Mossa better not be with you."

Alex considered the wording of the threat. "Nora? Nope. She's not with me."

"For her sake, that's a damn good thing. Now excuse my lack of patience, but what do you need to tell me?"

"You know, your bedside manner needs some work."

"Alex," Champion said, deepening his tone.

"All right. All right. I'm assuming this is a secure line."

"Go ahead."

"Is something big going on in Geneva?"

No way was the question a coincidence. "Why are you asking about Geneva?"

"Potentially, some bad shit is about to go down. Considering the schedule, there isn't a lot of time to screw around."

Champion couldn't believe his bad luck. He didn't like it, but he'd have to hear Alex out, because the man's intel had a way of panning out.

"Okay, let me get to my room, and I'll call you back," Champion said. Thinking ahead, he was already regretting that he might have to insert himself more by alerting the DSS officer in charge. Depending on what Alex had to say, that could lead to a lengthy conversation. And to think he'd done such a good job of staying in the background. Wondering about the difference in time again, Champion had to ask.

Entering the elevator, he pushed the button to his floor. "Where are you?"

"About to check into my hotel in Geneva. Where are you?"

The closing elevator doors muted Champion's agitation.

"Shit."

The long day just got longer.

CHAPTER 62

THE FONDNESS GEORGE Champion had for Alex Koves afforded his former protégé a degree of access. Recent events had Champion thinking the privilege might have to undergo a careful review. He had taken a leap of faith in recruiting Alex into the CIA. That seemed like a long time ago. Much had changed since then, and only one of them remained on the government's payroll. They had unexpectedly reunited months ago to work on avoiding a Middle East firestorm, and here they were again, meeting in a Geneva hotel room. Champion sat at the desk so he could write down notes more quickly. He reeled in his opening question, wanting to string together the right approach to garner direct answers.

"You're a civilian. You don't have security clearances for anything anymore. So how in the hell do you know about Geneva? Let's start with that."

Alex hesitated. He had to get the sequence of events correct without involving Nora too much. The truth, but not the whole truth. He recently was made aware that he was good at that. Nora was very much on his mind. The only reason he accompanied Nathan was to help ease his misery. He should have been forthcoming about who

Nathan was long ago. Keeping it from her was an act of betrayal. The situation reminded him how stupid he'd been years ago to turn his back on her when she'd had his best interests at heart. He'd held it against her, and their relationship ended. Fortunately, she'd come back into his life, but now he didn't know if he'd lost her again. It hurt and confused Nora that he'd come to Nathan's aid, knowing he was the person who'd put a bullet through her friend's heart. After Nathan left, Nora had packed. She just wanted to get away from him, no matter how hard he tried to explain himself. Her words looped in his head. "You made your choice." She then lowered the guillotine. "I'm not sure you're capable of loving someone."

Accepting there was no getting through to her, Alex had called Duncan to the room. He'd explained what was happening and asked Duncan to leave with her. She could use a friend. Someone she could depend on. Trying not to be judgmental, Duncan had agreed in thinking it was probably for the best.

"I just learned about Geneva this morning," Alex responded.

"And you're already here?"

"I happened to be in the neighborhood. Took a train from Paris."

Besides brief check-ins with the office at Langley, the summit consumed Champion's time. He didn't have the luxury of paying much attention to anything else, but he remembered seeing a "Breaking News" blurb concerning Paris on television. He picked up the day's unread newspaper. The headline and corresponding story were above the fold on the front page. He held it up for Alex.

"You involved with this?"

Alex spread his hands in guilt.

"Unbelievable," Champion exhaled.

"Since you're pressed for time, I'll give you the condensed version," Alex said, trying to stave off a tidal wave of backlash. "Because of what went down at Natanz, the Iranians, pissed as hell, started a global search for Nora, me, and the guy from Mossad I mentioned in my briefing. They weren't out to have a conversation. A guy named

Shahbod Gilani headed the operation. He worked with the Ministry of Intelligence and Security. Should be easy to confirm that."

Champion raised a finger. "When we spoke earlier, you said Nora was not with you."

"You don't see her, do you?" Alex shot back. "For her safety, and as a precaution, I told her I'd try to handle it, with help from the Mossad operative."

"The same guy that tried to kill you?"

"Yeah, we had a misunderstanding, but he made amends for it. He got me out of that place before it pancaked, and he gave me a heads up about the Iranians."

"Now you're like BFFs, running around the world blowing shit up."

Alex chuckled at Champion's use of the acronym. "Allow me to continue. The Iranians were on the fence concerning Nathan's complicity, so he set up a meeting. It gave him an opportunity to avoid suspicion by offering me up. They thought Nora would be with me. We laid a trap, and things went boom in Paris. They think we're dead. End of the witch-hunt. This Gilani then lays out this plan to disrupt a nuclear agreement brokered by the US. Said it was the brainchild of President Shahroudi. The idea is to frame the Israelis because they don't want the deal or trust Iran will abide by the rules."

"Why do they think everyone will point the finger at Israel?"

"Nathan says Mossad has this folklore of an assassin the Arabs call 'The Devil.' Shahroudi apparently contracted a freelancer who will make it look like Mossad's guy took action."

Champion stopped taking notes. "This place is crawling with security. Every diplomatic core brought its own team. The signing you're not supposed to know about, the hotel, the room where it'll take place, gets checked and re-checked all day."

"If you think you've got this covered, fine. Not my headache."

Champion scratched his head. "What's this Nathan's last name? And where is he? I'd like to ask him some questions."

"I only know him as Nathan. He's never provided a last name. And he definitely does not want a face-to-face."

"I don't like it, but I'll at least make some calls," Champion conceded. He walked Alex to the door. "I need you to stay around until I check all this out. Maybe my judgment was off when you worked at the Agency, but were you always this much of a pain in the ass?"

"You saying I wasn't as charming back then?"

The sound of the door locking signaled there was a lot more work to do before the day concluded. There was no need for Champion to contact 1600 Pennsylvania Avenue until he could investigate the threat. He'd also hold off alerting the DSS Agent In Charge. Champion's first call needed to be to his counterpart in Israeli intelligence. He wanted to establish the worthiness of a Mossad agent named Nathan. He'd even inquire about the fairy tale of someone called "The Devil."

CHAPTER 63

SHARON WAS IN good spirits at his second bar of the night. He carried on a promising conversation with the brunette next to him. He displayed a sense of humor without being overbearing, and it seemed to work in his favor. That made the interaction even more enticing. Sharon had no intention of seeing this through. It was harmless fun, a way to pass time while he waited to see if his intuition proved correct.

For a man of his talent, getting caught off guard was hard to swallow. By the fifth block of his walk, he sensed he wasn't alone. Whoever it was, they were good. No one seemed suspicious or out of place during checks over his shoulder. He had navigated low-traffic streets, trying to isolate a figure. He'd come up empty. The only recourse left was to narrow the playing field. They'd eventually have to reveal themselves. He'd entered the first lively bar he'd encountered, finding a position to monitor the entrance. People came and people left while he nursed a couple of drinks. Sharon committed faces to memory for nearly an hour before leaving. His plan landed him at his present location, bar number two.

"Wife checking up on you?"

Distracted by responding to a phone message, Sharon re-engaged the brunette. "I'm sorry, what did you ask?"

The brunette pointed at his phone. "The wife?"

Sharon laughed. "No. I'm not married. This is a business associate who's on this trip. She's disappointed I didn't tell her I was going bar hopping. She can be a pain sometimes."

That was how he perceived Neril on this assignment. He was messaging her back after being informed she was climbing into a taxi, having arrived at the Geneva train station. She demanded to know where he was. His text of, *I think I've gained a tail,* drew an immediate response.

Even more reason to tell me where you are.

Before he provided the location, a man he recognized from the previous bar entered. The man scanned the crowd with purpose. Sharon leaned behind the brunette for partial concealment.

"So are you going to tell her where you are?" the brunette wanted to know.

Sharon peered around her shoulder. "She's hopeless. This is her first big road trip. She's nervous about going out alone in a strange city." The brunette didn't catch on that he was looking through her. "I'm sorry to say I have to play the good guy and go get her. We work in the same department. Let me buy you another drink before I leave."

The brunette accepted. At least she'd get something for wasting her time.

"I hope you're still here when I get back," said Sharon, knowing he wasn't returning.

The drink arrived, they toasted, and Sharon gave a promising goodbye look. On his way out, he sent Neril another text. *I think it's Nathan. He must have followed me. This time he'll play by my rules.*

Don't do anything stupid. Wait for me!

I got this, Sharon replied, pleased to have the upper hand for once.

CHAPTER 64

THE TRAIN RIDE gave Yadin the chance to expunge past events from his mind so he could think with a fresh perspective. There probably was no way he'd gain access to the actual room where the agreement signing was to take place. By now, security would have the location on lockdown, entry granted only to those with pre-approved clearance. Israel didn't have an invitation.

The prevailing questions swirling in his head centered on the assassin the Iranians contracted. How good was he? Working solo or with help? Gilani had said the plan was to make it look like The Devil was responsible. For that to happen, he'd have to have some familiarity with Yadin's past successes. Undoubtedly, the Arab world had compiled a file on him by now. His identity a mystery, the dossier would make an interesting read. He'd get credit for kills he'd played no part in carrying out. From the beginning, that had been Mossad's plan. Create a legend that stoked fear and confusion.

The pressure of figuring out the assassin's plan intensified by the minute. With that in mind, Yadin questioned the wisdom of wasting time wondering what the hell Daniel Sharon was up to.

Learning from Gilani what was at stake, Yadin thought there might be a way to deflect the growing suspicion over his involvement in the death of his former handler. To create a scapegoat, he'd have to put the Iranian's assassin in the limelight, and that required being in Geneva. The decision proved to be the right call when he'd discovered Sharon had gone ahead of him. While running Sharon around Paris, Yadin had the forethought to keep tabs on him by cloning the Mossad agent's phone. Sharon didn't discard his phone when he'd gotten it back. Like most people, he'd grown attached to his personal mobile device, and probably believed there was sufficient anti-intrusion software installed. Yadin monitored the phone's GPS signal and was delighted to see Sharon had taken off for Geneva. Hours later, Yadin's intention was to take quick stock of Sharon's footprint before moving on to figuring how the assassin might strike if the mission were his.

The oddity of what Yadin encountered forced him to stay on Sharon's rear longer. He couldn't put his finger on it, but from studying Sharon in Paris, his mannerisms seemed off. Keeping a comfortable distance, Yadin had caught up with Sharon at the first bar. The whole time he'd been inside, a waitress had been the only person Sharon encountered. He'd left without fanfare.

GPS had Sharon at a second bar accessible by foot. Rather than go inside, Yadin observed as best he could from the street. With the crowd lively and thick, Yadin had captured glimpses of Sharon talking to a woman at the bar. The exchange appeared flirty, but casual.

Sharon lingered longer than he had at the previous bar. Maybe he was hitting it off with the woman. Perhaps this was about addressing a need, in which case Yadin was really wasting his time. A closer look wouldn't hurt to be sure. Sharon couldn't identify him, so it wasn't much of a gamble. From inside, Yadin understood what Sharon was up to. Twice, he'd responded to someone on his cell phone when he should have been paying attention to his female companion.

This wasn't about sex. Talking to her was a cover that allowed him to sneak a look every time the entrance door opened. Sharon was conducting a facial recognition scan, searching for a match from the first bar.

After a fresh drink arrived, Sharon and the woman toasted. He took a large swig of his drink, set the glass on the table, said something that made her smile, and then headed for the door, texting again as he did so.

CHAPTER 65

SHARON'S ANXIOUSNESS WAS reminiscent of his first solo assignment. The moisture on his hands and the raised hairs on his neck were direct results of the adrenaline pumping through his body.

He didn't know Geneva. He tried to educate himself during the train ride, studying street maps, transportation options, and some general history. When he arrived, his job of capturing Yadin was missing one essential element—a clear-cut plan on how to do it. But now, at last, he had a face. Yadin no longer had the luxury of hiding in plain sight.

Darn near floating on the pavement, Sharon slowed to a snail's pace to respond to Neril's onslaught of texts. He at least muted the sound of the annoying notifications. Trying to catch up to his changing locations drove her driver crazy, but she was paying for the inconvenience. Sharon expressed she could blow the whole thing by spooking Yadin into believing he was walking into a trap. He provided Neril a meticulous description of Yadin, down to the clothes he was wearing.

Sharon refocused on developing a plan. He turned down a street, making sure the man from the first and second bar was still with him. Sharon tried to gain a sense of the neighborhood. Aromas from several foreign cuisines filled the air. A smattering of people congregated outside café doors, smoking shisha tobacco, content with blending into the street scene. After a second prostitute offered him the promise of a memorable time, at a discount price no less, Sharon recalled that the practice was legal in Switzerland. Interpreting what he'd read, this must be the Pâquis district, a melting pot of people, food, sex offerings, and drugs.

Two and a half blocks later on Rue de Monthoux, the light bulb of a plan clicked on in his head. He sent his location to Neril, adding, *Les Cygnes garage.* There wasn't time to be more informative. She'd understand when she got here. He didn't check whether he was still being followed. He knew Yadin was there.

Sharon's knees stiffened down the ramp to the underground parking garage. Visibility turned poor in a hurry despite the fluorescent lights illuminating the dark entrance. The garage had closed hours ago, but the cars that remained would serve Sharon's purpose. In this sparse environment, his footsteps stood out among the occasional crackling of cars settling and the hum from overworked light bulbs.

The goal in seeking a hiding place was to draw Yadin in and keep him guessing while outmaneuvering him. Sharon had to find a spot that offered a clear line of sight because in the stillness, even the ruffle of clothing could betray his position. He spotted what he thought gave him the best option. He crossed to the other side, reaching his destination as footsteps echoed from the ramp.

Sharon took off his shoes and placed them behind a pillar, positioning the left one so that a small part was visible. He then hurried back to hide behind another pillar fortified by the front end of a van. Pistol in hand, Sharon attached the silencer in slow, half-inch turns until it locked into place.

He had to rely on hearing. Sticking his head out to look was out of the question. Cautious footsteps headed his way. They stopped, resumed, and shifted from one side of parking to the other. If Neril arrived soon, they'd have him boxed in. Sharon's confidence grew with each advancing step.

Keep coming.

That's it.

Almost there.

Sharon steadied his weapon with his moist hands. He calculated Yadin was about fifteen feet away when the footsteps came to an abrupt halt. Sharon figured the decoy he'd set up was cause for concern. All Yadin had to do was take the bait, leaving him at a vulnerable angle. Sharon waited for movement. None came. Of course. One of the deadliest men in the world was exercising extreme caution. The uncertainty of what Sharon couldn't see was maddening. Yadin had to just be standing there! Did the illusion fail? Something wasn't right. Sharon had no choice. He had to look. He inched his right eye around the pillar. What he saw made him return behind cover.

Impossible!

Sharon's brain tried to accept what his eye had registered. Instead of Yadin standing where the footsteps ended, there was only a pair of shoes, not his, neatly placed next to each other.

How could he have done that without making a sound?

Muffled gunfire made it a non-issue. Light fixtures on both sides of the garage shattered in no particular sequence, making the origin of fire difficult to pinpoint. The shots were rapid and accurate. The result left the garage in shadows and darkness.

Sharon crouched to become less of a target. He listened, but heard nothing except faint sounds coming from the street at the garage's entrance. He thought about making a run for it, but the precision exhibited in shooting the lights out convinced him that was a bad idea. Plus, he'd boxed himself in. There was no choice but to play this out now. He may not have achieved legendary status, but he was still one of the Kidon's best. The difficulty was the directive to apprehend, not kill.

Staying in place offered zero strategic value. He had to move. Squatting, Sharon redeployed toward the rear of the van. There was enough room behind a compact car to slide through. To his chagrin, the next vehicle was two spaces away. The openness would expose him too much. Improvising, he crawled along the side of the compact and crossed to the next pillar. He held his ground to listen, but received no clues. Was Yadin ahead, behind, or across from him? Sharon thought he had this handled, but nothing would please him more than to hear Neril marching down the garage ramp in a fit of rage. A glance that way dashed his hopes.

Time to move again. The next car over was his destination. He hunched over, gun at the ready. In this darkness, landing a shot would be more luck than skill. Taking a deep breath, he took a measured step, then another. He tried to line his route up with the pillar he'd just vacated, using it for cover.

"You can stop right there," announced a voice from the darkness.

Left foot firmly planted, Sharon was in the awkward position of not being able to turn left or right with authority.

"Bend down further and leave your weapon on the ground."

Disgusted at being outmaneuvered, Sharon complied.

"Now kick it to the right."

The unseen figure approached from behind on Sharon's right. "I'll give you the credit you deserve for getting the drop on me. But, it changes nothing," Sharon said. "Like I told you, my orders are to bring you back."

"You must have me mistaken with someone else."

Sharon chuckled. "No need to play games, Nathan. I know what you look like now. I had a hunch the Iran deal was on your radar. I don't know to what end, but I assume Paris was your handiwork?"

"Who are you?"

"Really? We're doing this?" Sharon turned around, relaxed that the tension was over. The gun leveled at his chest kept him in place.

"Easy," the voice from the shadows cautioned.

"You can lower that. You won't shoot. Not if you're as innocent as you claim. You may have the luxury of operating outside the norm, but we're still on the same team."

"I don't belong to any team."

"I forgot. You're The Devil. I get it," said Sharon with a dismissive hand.

The man stepped forward. "Are you supposed to be a backup plan? I was crystal clear about not needing support."

"What are you talking about?" Sharon shook his head. "Look, I tolerated this foolishness in Paris, but enough is enough. Make this easy on yourself and come back to Tel Aviv with me."

Sharon moved to retrieve the gun he'd kicked away. He abandoned the thought when a bullet tore into his right arm. "Son of a bitch!" Sharon hissed. He grabbed his arm as he did an about-face to lurch at Yadin. He stopped, because this time the gun targeted his head.

"Now that we have an understanding, what are you doing here?"

The initial sting of the gunshot subsided into manageable pain. Sharon's inspection indicated it was a flesh wound. "What am I doing here? Turn that question on yourself."

"You mentioned Tel Aviv. You must be Mossad."

This continued bizarre behavior troubled Sharon. If this wasn't Nathan Yadin, then who the hell . . .

"You aren't Nathan, are you?"

The man's eyes were unyielding, cold. "I don't know who that is. However, I am Mossad's top assassin, but just for this contract."

"Contract? Who hired you to do what?"

"I'm being well paid to keep that a secret."

Sharon measured the distance. He didn't know what this was, but the time was now or never. His left leg swung out, a roundhouse kick shifting the gun away from his center. The move wasn't quick enough to thwart another shot. Once again, the bullet grazed Sharon's right arm. He further deflected the gun with his right hand, using his left to chop at his assailant's throat. Sharon gained leverage and twisted the gun away, letting it drop to the ground. A follow-up knee to the groin was blocked. Undeterred, Sharon unleashed a series of hand attacks. None landed to inflict serious damage. A return blow to the solar plexus backed Sharon up. He gathered himself and used space to pile drive the man against a car. Sharon tried to keep his adversary under control, but he was difficult to restrain. The smaller man attempted to slow Sharon down by attacking his ankles. Sharon maintained the upper hand by sidestepping the kicks. After another kick missed, Sharon reverse pivoted to apply a chokehold. His bulky forearms squeezed tighter. The man was strong, but he couldn't last much longer.

The prognosis changed when a knife dug into Sharon's meaty thigh, forcing his grip to weaken. He reacted by trying to bring the man down to the ground. Sharon jerked the man back and forth, trying to re-establish control. The assailant didn't offer much resistance, because that was exactly what he wanted. He was no longer in an overpowered stationary position with little room to maneuver. Now, he swung his arm back freely, connecting with expanding areas of flesh. Sharon abandoned his hold. He tried to protect himself like a boxer in the ring against the ropes as the stabbing climbed higher and higher. The round was over when the blade delivered a final, twisting blow to Sharon's midsection. He gripped the man's hands, but his fingers slipped away. Sharon fell to his knees.

Erik Snow staggered back. There was no need to do anything more. This could have ended differently. For an uncomfortable moment, it had appeared to be heading that way.

Getting his gun, Snow let the man bleed out in peace. On his way to the exit, he stopped to pick up and put on his shoes.

CHAPTER 66

YADIN HAD NO intention of venturing into a dimly lit garage, knowing that at least one of the two men down there was, like him, a trained killer. It could be a trap. Sharon was that smart.

From his vantage point up the street, Yadin had the garage ramp covered. Anything going in or out was within view. He pressed up against a cheap plastic standup table outside an English-named pub. A decorative sign on the building advertised fish and chips and ale. Interesting advertising, since the establishment was a Thai restaurant that served up a vibrant karaoke experience with some acts performing in full costume. He heard a sample of the talent every time a patron opened the door.

The two men had been in the garage for a while. If there was another exit on the other side, he might as well call it a night. Sitting on his hands and waiting wasn't getting him anywhere. He moved to do something against his better judgment when the second man to enter the garage came up the ramp. The man paused, then headed off to his immediate right, which led to a collection of closed shops and presumably a different way out. Overhead lights did nothing to reduce the shadows that concealed his face. The emergence made Yadin hold tight, waiting for Sharon to appear. He did minutes later, and Yadin broke into a sprint. The closer he got, the worse Sharon looked. Struggling to stay upright, he had a tight grip on his midsection. From a distance, one might have assumed he had too much to drink—if it weren't for the roadmap of crimson leading back to the garage. Yadin reached Sharon as he collapsed on the pavement. Blood oozed from his body in several locations. Of all things, Yadin noticed he wasn't wearing shoes.

"Daniel," Yadin called out on his knees. He bent over to get closer. Yadin shielded his movements by lowering his body even more. He reached into Sharon's pocket for his cell phone, placing it in one of his own. Yadin also found a passport. Confirming the identity was an alias, he put the passport back.

"Daniel," he tried again. "It's Nathan."

Sharon battled with the closing darkness. "Nathan," he responded with the little air he had left. "I thought it was you. He's good." A jolt of pain interrupted. "He's pretending to be you."

"Yes, I know."

Onlookers slowly began to gather, inching forward upon recognizing a person was seriously hurt. Yadin couldn't stay any longer. He brushed hair away from Sharon's sweaty face. "Rest easy, Daniel."

Sharon's eyes narrowed while he tried to find strength. His voice was a mere whisper. "Get him, Nathan. Get him for me."

Yadin nodded, got to his feet, and backed away, avoiding eye contact with the crowd, who had sickened looks on their faces. Yadin spotted Lisa Neril before disappearing into the growing throng. He wasn't sure if she had seen him. Her movements were curtailed by arriving police officers pushing through to the front.

Neril cursed under her breath. She'd tried to get here sooner, but there were too many variables to overcome. Traffic. A strange city. Sharon's constantly changing location. All she could do was watch Sharon take his final breaths.

**

Snow slid into bed after a long, hot shower. Orsette didn't ask where he'd been. She didn't even acknowledge his presence, pretending to be asleep. She had to stop worrying about this man. He wasn't really hers. That was a fantasy she allowed to seep into her thoughts on occasion. Her reality was back in Michigan.

Didn't hurt to dream, though.

CHAPTER 67

SNOW'S ACCURACY PROMPTED a necessary switch. Badly damaged Buckeye got substituted for "Sparty." Snow was finally beginning to catch on, remarking to Orsette, "Because you and your father went to the University of Michigan and Michigan State is your little brother."

Orsette applauded his growing knowledge. "You've done some research."

From the moment Snow woke up, he was on top of every detail, mapping out in his mind how the day would transpire. Breakfast, which they always ate in the room, was part quiz session for Orsette. He accompanied her to the docks, double-checking the equipment on the boat. He made sure there were no jitters before letting her take off solo. Orsette's position on the lake had to be within a precise range, and beyond harbor security that patrolled the shoreline. Any adjustments had to get done today. There could be no screwups tomorrow.

Through binoculars in Sparty's room, Snow monitored Orsette's progress. She dropped anchor when positioned in the right area and then called to confirm everything was ready. She went on deck to keep a lookout for harbor security or anyone who might seem to take an interest. This was all Snow required of her tomorrow. She would pack her bags tonight and check out in the morning. Her final responsibility would be to take the boat out on Lake Geneva and put the equipment in standby mode. She'd then take the dingy to shore and head straight for the airport. They would not see each other again or converse in any manner until he got in touch.

Snow gave Sparty a sympathetic pat on the head. He lowered to the floor, opened an application on his cell phone and toyed with the flexibility of the guidance mechanism, bringing a target to rest on Sparty's head. The software calculated the distance, measured the airflow, and corrected leveling issues caused by the bounce of the boat. Snow locked in and sent a command. Seconds later, a bullet ripped a hole in Sparty's head. The reinforced pillows behind the mannequin stopped the bullet from advancing. When Snow finished, he admired the ingenuity of design. Its Kentucky architect was worth every penny. Running a field test on the other included ordinance was out of the question. There was no way to minimize the noise level or the damage it would cause. He had confidence that when the time came, it would work as specified. He had a crucial, final test to run that would reduce having to rely so heavily on his smartphone. Truly, a work of genius.

At dusk, Snow would venture down to the boat to reload and make a final inspection. An early dinner was in order. He intended to get a good night's sleep. The one thing he tried to not overthink was what had happened last night. The Mossad operative had brought up the moniker of the man he was impersonating. He'd called him "Nathan." If the infamous "Devil" were really here, taking him down would bring a king's ransom from the Arab world.

CHAPTER 68

"CHOCOLATE, THE BREAKFAST of champions," Alex scolded, watching his former boss top off the room service meal. "I hope you're taking some back for the Missus."

"There's fruit on the table," Champion responded between a sip of coffee.

"By all means, have another bar then."

"Thanks to you, I need all the energy I can get. I'm guessing you got a good night's sleep?"

"Like a baby," Alex lied. The complexity of the Nora situation had weighed on his mind most of the night.

From all indications, Champion had adjusted to the time difference. Burning the candle at both ends came with the job— trouble doesn't punch a time card. Champion was fully functional now. "I didn't notice last night, but you get into an accident? That from Paris?"

"No. It's from Moscow. I ran into a fist several times."

"Moscow. Do I want to know?"

The bruises were nothing like they'd been a few days ago. Alex didn't have Nora around to remind him to use a touch of makeup. "Remember in St. Thomas I told you there was something I had to take care of? I took care of it."

"Glad that worked out for you—I think." Champion placed his napkin on the table, stretched out, and strode over to the window. There was plenty of harbor activity on this sunny day. "This Nathan guy, something's not right."

"How so?"

"Phone conversation with the Israelis last night. It's what they didn't say, and how they worded other things. Standard back and forth until I brought up Nathan. There was a cautious pause, followed by a denial. Then I mentioned this "Devil" business. Didn't have to be face-to-face to feel the tension."

"So they're hiding something?"

"About Nathan? Definitely. Makes me a little uneasy. After dismissing him, they came back around to ask why I wanted to know. What was the source of my intel? You've been around this guy. How good is he?"

"Highly capable," exclaimed Alex.

"Trust him?"

The answer required some thought. Taking everything into account, Alex answered, "Yes, I do."

"Good to know. However, I can't take the chance on this one. You pack a suit?"

Alex didn't grasp where Champion was going. "Not on this trip. You taking me someplace nice for dinner?"

"Hardly." Champion reached for his suit jacket. "Dinner should be on you for all the hoops I've had to jump through to get you clearance."

"Clearance?"

"Yep. I need you to keep an eye out. I'm not comfortable with how the Israelis responded. Trouble seems to follow this Nathan." Champion headed for the door. "I've got a meeting to attend, and you've got a suit to buy. You know the drill—basic black, white shirt, dress shoes." Champion pulled out a piece of paper from his jacket and handed it over. "I did the groundwork for you. There's a Hugo Boss on the other side of the Rhône. That's the address. Congratulations."

"Why congratulations?"

"For the next forty-eight hours, you're back on the government's payroll."

CHAPTER 69

THE BLACKNESS HAD turned into a movie screen that kept showing the same horrific scene in vivid color. Repeatedly, Neril witnessed her colleague dying—alone. The only way to stop seeing the images had been to open her eyes. Raiding the hotel room mini bar had helped, but it was far from a solution. The night had seemed never-ending. She held out hope that at some point, exhaustion would blindside her.

Neril had watched the sun rise through bloodshot eyes prior to making the most regrettable phone call of her life. She'd felt dishonorable defending herself to Director Rozen, but as he painfully pointed out, Sharon had decided not to wait. Under the circumstances, there was nothing she could have done. Director Rozen had listened with a sympathetic ear. Losing a fellow operative extracted an emotional price. He also had bosses to inform. This would not sit well with them, especially following Ezra's death. He didn't order Neril home, which surprised her. Rozen advised she was in too deep now. Sending a replacement team at this juncture didn't make much sense. Besides, Neril couldn't definitively say Sharon's death involved

Yadin. She'd seen the profile of a man near Sharon, but dismissed him as a bystander because he hadn't matched the description Sharon texted her. She'd told the director there might be security video that could prove helpful. He promised he'd look into it. Meanwhile, Rozen was adamant that Neril remain on the job. Unless incriminating evidence surfaced, the mission concerning Yadin hadn't changed, but the rope was getting considerably shorter by the minute.

Neril's daylong depression got a jolt of optimism when she received an email labeled "Video." She sat up on the side of the bed to play the security footage from last night. The overhead angle captured the ramp from the garage to the street. The lighting was better near the street. A figure emerged from the garage. She rewound the video, zooming in as much as possible. She couldn't see the man's face, but he appeared to match the person Sharon had detailed in his message. The next couple of minutes were hard to watch. A stumbling, badly injured Sharon came into view. It must have taken every ounce of life he had left to make it up the ramp. Neril beat herself up again over not getting there in time. From the corner of the video, a man rushed to Sharon's aid. She took the video back to confirm what she'd spotted. When the moment approached, she hit slow motion mode and stopped the video. The good Samaritan had been clever in concealing the move, but the man who came to aid Sharon took his cell phone. He didn't take his wallet. That ruled out being an opportunist or pickpocket.

Neril played a hunch. She typed a text and sent it.

I know it was you.

She waited for a reply. Nothing. Frustrated, she tossed the phone on the bedside table. She had to get some sleep. She rolled into bed.

After several attempts, her head found a comfortable place on the pillow. Feeling she could finally close her eyes, she shot up when her phone dinged.

I didn't do it, Neril.

CHAPTER 70

THE PROBABILITY OF failure, the kind you don't return from, created a pit of uneasiness in Snow's stomach. He always got that feeling before he had to execute a contract. He had chosen a dangerous profession. The business model was not for everyone. You were successful until you weren't. There were few rules, but one he took seriously. Never overestimate your ability. If a job was too big, the odds too great, pocket your ego and pass. This contract rode the border of that doctrine. He'd nearly said no, but the challenge and huge payday had persuaded him.

He'd gone over the execution of the assignment in his mind countless times. Every plausible deviation he could think of to his plan had been considered. The goal was to strike strategically. If that failed, the body count would go up. One unexpected wrinkle had popped up. He'd anticipated the presence of Mossad, but not him. Not the one known as "The Devil." The man whose methods he'd studied for this job. The man the Iranians would say proved the Israelis were to blame for what transpired in Geneva.

Snow focused more on the four facial photos of the subject taped to the bathroom mirror. He matched every detail as he transformed into the person. He left nothing to chance, inserting contact lenses and dental veneers. He'd been out in the sun every day. That helped to get the skin tone right with the appropriate matching makeup. Now he applied crow's feet lines and rubbed in dark patches under the eyes. Thicker eyebrows made a telling impact on the overall look. When Snow secured the well-coiffed wig, he examined the finished product.

Perfection.

Orsette waited to undock and maneuver the boat into position. Snow had rechecked the equipment pre-dawn. That included reloading the ammunition spent during practice runs and making sure the GPS and Wi-Fi signals were strong.

Snow got dressed in the outer room. Saving the suit jacket for last, he adjusted the horizontal shoulder holster to hide the weapon's bulge. The next accessory was his security clearance badge, complete with photo ID. He took a final look in the bathroom mirror, comparing the makeover against the photos. Satisfied, he ripped them down and burned them in the sink. He pulled aside the bathtub shower curtain. He was now the lifeless figure in the tub, Bashir Torkan.

Minus the bullet to the head.

CHAPTER 71

MONTHS OF TENSION-FILLED, back-and-forth negotiating had led to this day of agreement. Dignitaries exchanged pleasantries as they arrived with their entourages in tow. Not all members of the P5+1 group stayed at the main hotel. China, Russia, and Germany passed through the heavily guarded hotel main entrance. The US, the UK, France, and Iran were hotel guests. Security clearances were checked again for entrance to the pre-signing reception hall. Last-minute changes or additions were subject to an extra layer of screening that included a firm reminder to countries of their accountability. France had to sub out one due to a severe cold. The other alteration was an addition involving the United States.

The DSS wasn't thrilled, but since Champion was director of the National Clandestine Service, and assigned by the president to the proceedings, his request was green lit. Alex stayed close to his temporary boss. He wasn't used to concealing a weapon again. However, it was comforting considering he was dealing with the unknown.

Champion pointed out the prominent players he recognized from each country as they assembled. He joked that if the shit hit the fan, Alex should take special care not to shoot Jake Lancellotti from the White House or Tom Stacy from State.

"Secretary Drake over there," Champion added in a hushed tone, guiding Alex to the robust, boisterous figure holding court, "he's fair game."

According to the timetable, they were about half an hour away from moving on to the next venue, where the signing was to take place. Once it was completed, a celebratory buffet meal would start, the offerings representative of each country taking part. Champion walked Alex to the room where history would take place. He wanted perspective from a fresh set of eyes. There were two entry doors set apart from the other, each manned by two guards. One guard consulted a list on a tablet; the other maintained a steady focus. Champion and Alex's photos popped up next to their names and country. The guard looked up for visual confirmation. He stepped aside to open the door, announcing into his communication device, "Two coming in."

The guards inside were not bashful in displaying their semi-automatic hardware. Champion and Alex garnered a head nod. The room was large enough to fit around sixty to seventy people, but was reduced in size by a long, rectangular table positioned in the center. There were sixteen chairs tucked in, spaced well enough to allow for ample elbowroom. A series of booklets, notepads and pens were the table's place settings. Within reach of every four chairs were large ice water carafes and a tray of glasses. The flags of each country proudly stood at the back of the room. A long row of seats, reserved for associates and intermediates, hugged the wall behind the table.

An interior door to the room got Alex's attention. It led to an adjacent staging area, stairwell, and service elevator for staff use. Champion saw Alex concentrating on the same area that had troubled him during an earlier tour. The large bank of windows offered a panoramic view of Lake Geneva that stretched beyond the harbor to the city on the other side. Apartment buildings and other structures framed the shoreline. They were on the second floor, above the cover of a tree-lined thoroughfare along the waterfront.

"Would have to be one hell of a shot from the other side," Alex thought aloud.

"I figured the same thing," Champion confirmed. "Plus, the windows are reflective from the outside. It's like looking into a mirror."

Security was being enforced on the street. No public parking for two blocks. The day was perfect for outdoor activities. From this vantage point, Alex saw that boaters were taking advantage of the conditions.

Back in the outer reception area, Champion explained the rules for each delegation. Every country would have one security person inside the signing room. Since the DSS ran point, its man would be inside.

"I'll just be over by the bar if you need me," Alex smirked.

"Yeah, the hell you will," Champion shot back. "I'll be in the room. If you hear anything out of the ordinary, I expect you to come charging through one of those doors."

"You nervous?"

"Me, nervous?"

"You look nervous."

"I'm not nervous."

"Okay." Alex gave him a pat on the back. "It'll be over shortly."

All participants were at ease in the reception area. This really was about to happen. A historic agreement aimed at maintaining some level of peace and stability in the Middle East. Unfortunately, not everyone saw it that way. Time would tell. But it was good to start somewhere.

Champion forced a smile and gave a thumb-up to someone across the room. Under his breath he asked, "Where is Nathan?"

"See, I knew you were nervous."

Champion exhaled, "Where is he?"

"This will not help you relax."

"Alex . . ."

"I have no idea."

The lights flickered, followed by an announcement directing all required individuals to make their way to the signing room.

"Now I'm nervous."

CHAPTER 72

YADIN AND NERIL were both on the outside looking for a way in. Their motivations, however, were far apart.

Neril contemplated the security footage for the hundredth time. The man who'd rushed to Sharon's side was more than a petty opportunist who stole his phone. He'd responded with understanding to the text message she'd sent to Sharon's phone.

I didn't do it, Neril.

He'd purposely mentioned her by name. The contact information listed for her in Sharon's phone was just a number associated with the letter *n*. No amount of guessing could have come up with "Neril."

In addition, she wrestled with the description Sharon had provided. Because of his training, he'd be accurate about that. The man Neril had caught a glimpse of at the scene did not match the one Sharon had described. This person left behind a wallet with cash— and a passport that provided fake cover.

I didn't do it, Neril.

What about the man who'd been first out of the garage? He'd hugged the shadows, so the footage of him was less than clear. Tough to tell, but he'd appeared to be closer to Sharon's description. Based on the sequence of events, Neril concluded he must have killed Sharon. If he wasn't Nathan, then who the hell could he be? A common criminal would have never gotten the drop on Sharon to that degree.

Neril's frustration grew exponentially the longer she sat nursing her drink at the bar, knowing what was taking place on the closed-off floors above her. She could feel Nathan's presence, but what he looked like was a complete mystery.

***

Yadin didn't spend the day dwelling over his response to Neril's message. Without further explanation, she wouldn't stop pursuing him. He did devote his time to working on an angle to gain access. It took a ton of persistence, and multiple phone calls, but eventually, the potential value of what he was selling had proven too tempting to ignore. The charade had required him to overspend on a rush order at a local stationery store.

With a fresh set of business cards, Yadin was welcomed to the hotel by the junior sales manager, who as luck would have it, was new to the position in the last month. His boss was busy attending to the needs of the hotel's "special" guests. Management tried to reschedule the impromptu meeting for the following day, citing a huge event at the hotel that would prohibit a total tour, but Yadin explained he had a late afternoon flight that day, and stressed that today was the only time that fit his schedule. Hotel management caved, deciding the prospective business of more than three hundred guests for nearly a week was worth discussing. The company Yadin represented was a music streaming service based in Europe. A study of the company's website gave him enough basic information to talk a good game. A preliminary conversation wouldn't get in depth beyond the expected numbers and needs.

At the start of the tour, Yadin handed over his business card, complete with company logo, and his title of executive corporate event planner. He dangled a carrot by hinting they would have to work on a deal to get streaming service to the hotel. Noticing the security in place, the visitor, with a touch of concern in his voice, asked whether something serious was happening. He received assurances there was nothing to worry about. The hotel employee wasn't at liberty to say what was going on, other than a huge event that required protection for the attendees.

"Good to know," the pretend exec replied.

"You'll hear about it later on the news," said the man from the hotel, a trace of pride in his voice.

The tour covered rooms and suites, presentation needs, drink and meal options. Yadin listened while taking mental notes of the premises. The sales manager used a security card clipped to his waist for admittance to the expansive ballrooms on the first floor. Yadin asked about the ones he couldn't see on the closed-off second floor. The sales manager provided descriptions, telling Yadin that exact details with photos were in the brochure packet. The manager fielded questions about food and beverage delivery to the various venues. Supplying the first floor was easy. Service elevators and stairs facilitated the second floor on a priority basis.

"So if we have a large group, and we will," said Yadin, admiring the vacant ballroom they were standing in, "you can replenish the food and drinks on the second floor quickly?"

"Most definitely. In fact, the hotel's most popular bars are up there."

Yadin gave his approval. "The whole thing is very impressive. The city works, lots of restaurants, nightlife, water activities. I'll sit down with our CEO and make my recommendation."

"Excellent." The sales manager smiled, shaking hands. "You have my details to get in touch. Hope to hear from you soon."

"Mind if I grab a drink before I go? I also want to make a preliminary call to the office while I'm thinking about it."

"Not at all. Let me take you to our grill bar, get you comped. The view of the Alps and Lake Geneva is quite the selling point."

What the sales manager didn't realize, after he'd set the potential client up with drinks, was that his security card was no longer in his possession.

CHAPTER 73

UNLESS SPOKEN TO, protection personnel rarely conversed on the job. Snow put stock in that protocol. He'd passed the immediate test of greeting the other Iranian guards, returning short responses in Farsi. He stayed active to avoid confrontation. When stationary, his stance incorporated a piercing gaze.

Weeks ago, Bashir Torkan's professional life got a dramatic boost for the better. He was chosen to be Iran's lone security guard in the agreement signing room, providing protection for his countrymen. Torkan told anyone who'd listen that the appointment was merit based. In reality, he got the assignment because among the list of candidates presented to Snow, he was the easiest to impersonate. They shared similar height, build, and facial structure. The rest came down to cosmetic alterations. Snow made it clear to his benefactors that Torkan's future had been determined by the decision. They accepted his fate as a necessary means to an end.

Forty-plus people in the room seemed like a daunting task to undertake for one man, but Snow understood the complexity of the numbers. He knew early on that a multifaceted device with pinpoint accuracy was paramount to achieving success. The doors were locked the moment the last person entered the room. Snow confirmed that the seating arrangements had not changed.

Torkan didn't wear glasses. No one in the room knew that. Like the other security officers there, he was a background ornament with an IFB earpiece. When Snow put on glasses, the simple act went unnoticed. The demands of this job required advanced innovation. The glasses were built primarily on bone conduction technology. Bob the farmer had outdone himself. The glasses were impossible to differentiate from a regular prescription pair. They operated via touch interface—tap, double tap, long press, and swipe all performed different functions.

Snow established a connection with the devices on the boat, putting them in standby mode. The glasses gave him control to achieve the precision he needed. When he acquired a target, he'd mark it by double tapping the glasses right temple. If the target moved, the tracker stayed locked on unless Snow canceled it.

The attendees at the main table ironed out last-minute details. When a question or observation needed clarification, it was quickly addressed. The chatter gradually diminished. The official document got passed around the table for signatures.

Snow reaffirmed his first target. He programmed more actions to take place in careful succession, then signaled the equipment on the boat. Standby shifted to ready status.

Four signatures to go . . .

CHAPTER 74

"YOU SHOULD BE sitting at the table," Champion whispered to Lancellotti. The foreign policy advisor for the vice president had performed a sizeable amount of the groundwork on this project. Yet, he was content to sit back and watch Secretary of State Ron Drake get the lion's share of credit. It was admirable that at his age, he understood how the system worked inside the Beltway.

Lancellotti got that Champion was being mischievous. His day would come. He'd done enough to warrant a move from the State Department to the White House in a short amount of time. This treaty made for a compelling addition to his resume. He didn't have to sit at the table—he was in the room.

"Happy to take a back seat," Lancellotti whispered back. "It's the greater good that matters."

Champion smiled. The kid definitely had a future. It was enough for Lancellotti to see Deputy Secretary of State Stacy, who'd also done a sizeable chunk of the work, at the main table. Secretary Drake sat next to him, his chest pumped out with pride.

France got the document next, and once China signed, the

dignitaries could have their feel good moment. They'd pretend for the rest of the day that everyone would try very hard to play nice in the world. An open bar could be a great influencer. Champion wanted to get the whole proceeding over. Staying on high alert was nerve-wracking.

China's representative put the pen down. The signed document made its way to the head of the table, where the EU foreign policy chief gave a final inspection. He added it to the other hundred-plus pages. The world would get a full-blown press announcement later, but for this moment, history came down to, "Ladies and gentlemen, we have an agreement."

Lancellotti led the wave of clapping from those seated in the secondary rows. It progressed into a standing ovation. Members at the table joined in, pushing their chairs back to stand.

All except for one.

An Iranian delegate was slumped over the table, motionless. The clapping lost momentum as recognition spread. The Iranian security guard rushed around the table at the sight of blood soaking the tablecloth. No one knew how to react, what to make of it. Champion was the first to notice there was a hole in the back of the man's dark suit jacket. The space behind him had been empty, and a shot hadn't been fired within the room. Champion looked toward the windows. The glass hadn't shattered, but he saw an unmistakable bullet hole. Champion leaned to line up the trajectory.

"Everybody get down," he shouted. This time the windows exploded. Smoke began to fill the room, diminishing visibility. Panic mode was in full effect now.

Security in the outer room had to hear the pandemonium. Champion expected the doors to burst open any moment. He'd cautioned Alex to be ready. Through the thickening smoke, Champion located Secretary Drake on his knees three chairs away. The doors to the reception room swung open with authoritative voices yelling, "Stay low!" A whoosh of bullets echoed overhead. Loud splats and sickening groans followed. The bullets shredded the first wave of guards attempting to enter the room. The heavy doors swung closed as more rounds tore into them, forcing the guards to back off. Champion worried one of the downed guards might be Alex, acting on his orders. He couldn't fixate on that now. He had to concern himself with safeguarding the room. The frantic movement from delegates scrambling for cover didn't help as bodies bumped into or tripped over one another.

Another round of gunfire filtered through the room. This time, it was different. The muffled sounds were coming from within. A body hit the floor behind Champion, and something with weight crashed into the table. Champion had pushed Lancellotti under the table during the initial attack. Hopefully he'd have the good sense to stay there. Secretary Drake was crawling just ahead of Champion. For some reason, he tried to get on his feet. Through a less dense patch of smoke, Champion saw the outline of a man holding a gun. He was taking aim at the secretary. There was no time to warn him. Champion lunged forward, firmly grabbed the secretary's right shoulder with one hand, and wrapped Drake's waist with the other, driving him hard into the ground.

Drake jerked and grunted before hitting the floor. "Shit, I'm hit! I'm hit!"

Warm liquid ran over Champion's hand. He patted Drake down for confirmation.

"It's just your arm," said Champion. "Now stay down."

Visibility was better on the ground. A fallen guard lay a few feet away, bloody, but still alive, his service weapon next to him on the floor. Champion took two large gorilla steps, lifting his knees to dive. He had the gun in his hand before crashing back down. He fired two shots into the air, hoping it would convince anyone from the delegation foolish enough to be standing to get on the floor. Champion then fired indiscriminately above the table. He waited for return fire. What he got was another onslaught of bullets whizzing overhead, biting into the wall and doors. Amidst the mayhem, Champion thought he heard a door fling open prior to the noise generated by the outer doors being breached.

"Stay on the ground and crawl out this way," new voices directed. The smoke followed the air stream of the open doors. Members of the delegation either scrambled to safety under their own power or were forcibly dragged out. A multitude of security personnel entered the room, ready to engage any threat. They searched the room, but came up empty. Outside the conference room, the less injured waited for medical help.

Serious concerns were addressed first by arriving emergency medical crews. The death tally included the two guards who'd originally attempted entry to the room. Four other guards who were inside the room had gunshot wounds, and one of them was in bad shape. The Iranian delegate remained slumped over the table. Lancellotti and Stacy were a little shaken, but unharmed. Medics led Secretary Drake away as he cupped his now-bandaged wound. Champion checked the identity of the unfortunate guards. Alex wasn't among them. He was relieved to find him standing in front of the blown-out windows, the wind ruffling his hair.

"Not possible for a sniper to pull this off," said Alex when Champion joined him.

Piecing it all together, Champion didn't know what to believe. "Never heard the first bullet. It didn't disintegrate the glass, but it came through the window."

Alex assessed the damage and noted the bodies behind him. "A lot more happened than one bullet."

"Yeah, shit hit the fan in a hurry. The windows shattered, the room filled with smoke, bullets came in hot. Amazing the death toll isn't higher."

"We heard gunfire in the room. Who was shooting?"

"Probably me. At least the shots you heard," Champion said, reflecting. He had a blank stare. "There was a shooter in the room.

He shot at Secretary Drake. With all the smoke and confusion, I thought at first he was trying to take out a perceived threat."

Champion bolted for the outer room, getting nearby security guards to huddle around him. At the top of his lungs, he shouted, "I need a head count of all the security personnel who were in the room with the delegation."

Officials looked around, puzzled.

"Now!" Champion reinforced.

The injured guards who'd been in the room from France, Russia, the UK, and US were getting medical treatment. Germany and China's reps were unharmed and accounted for.

"Iran?" a guard from the UK called out. "Iran?"

The Iranian security personnel consulted with their surviving delegate in the back of the room. Arms open, Champion demanded an answer.

"Bashir Torkan is not here," a guard reluctantly offered.

Champion ran back into the signing room with Alex and an Iranian guard on his heels. Torkan was not one of the dead men on the floor. Champion fixated on the inside access door.

"What is it?" Alex inquired.

"I heard a door open right before security burst into the room." Champion summoned the DSS member who'd been responsible for clearing the delegates and security personnel. He instructed him to pull up Torkan's identification on his tablet. Champion hadn't gotten a good look at him; he hadn't paid him or any of the other security personnel much attention. Torkan's face appeared on the tablet.

Alex didn't wait for direction. He withdrew his weapon and disappeared through the inside access door.

CHAPTER 75

A FEW DROPLETS of blood didn't equate to a roadmap, but they were a start. Alex estimated the assassin had nearly a ten-minute head start. Regardless, he descended the stairway with caution. He ruled out the service elevator even before discovering the blood drops. The possibility of being slowed down would have made that too big a gamble.

Blood on the door handle at the bottom of the stairwell let Alex know he'd guessed right. The door opened to a curved back hallway that fed into the kitchen area. Further down was house maintenance. A heavy door reduced the steady hum of industrial washers and dryers going full blast with the first loads of towels and linens gathered by housekeeping. Alex worked his way back to the kitchen. His unexpected, armed arrival drew uncertain stares. All activity came to a hushed halt.

He raised his security badge. "Has anyone out of the ordinary come through here in the last ten minutes?" he asked softly, trying to keep everyone calm.

A burly chef in uniform emerged, wiping his hands with a wet towel, which was impressive considering he also held a large butcher knife. He gave Alex the once-over. "No one's come through here," he answered, slinging the towel across his shoulder.

The answer and knife were good enough for Alex. He nodded his thanks and left. Next, he pushed through a door that let out in a common area. Searching the floor, he picked up a trail of blood spots. The spacing was farther apart, showing an effort to stanch the loss, but the droplets were bigger.

Alex wasn't sure how close the lobby was, but he could hear the wail of ambulance sirens and the din of excited voices. The blood drops headed away from that direction. Security would have safeguarded a path by now, restricting movement by putting sections of the hotel under lockdown. Access to this area appeared sealed off—it was quiet. The blood trail led to a restroom at the end of the corridor. Alex crouched and brushed the door open, ready to shoot. Hearing only silence, he stepped in to clear each stall. The restroom was empty. Heading out, he noticed watered-down traces of blood in a sink. He crossed over to a trashcan and ripped the top off. Bloodstained paper towels were on top, along with torn fabric from a suit lining. Underneath them was a wig, soiled towels with makeup smears, and fake facial hair.

Alex stopped analyzing the contents, because someone was behind him. Grabbing the top of the trashcan, he hurled it back, dropping to one knee as he spun to aim.

Finger on the trigger, Alex held off firing as Nathan held his hands in the air. Alex exhaled. "You could have said something."

"Sorry about that."

"'Sorry' almost got you shot."

Lowering his hands, Nathan sifted through the scattered contents of the trashcan. Alex watched him, remembering what Champion had said.

"How did you know I was in here?"

"I didn't. Blood on the floor in the corridor led me here. This stuff significant?" Nathan held up the wig. "What happened upstairs?"

Alex filled Nathan in on the havoc that had transpired there. The skill and boldness of the attack impressed the Mossad operative. The Iranians were right. If the assassin escaped, Israel would be placed in a very dark light, with no way to dispel allegations that they were involved. Too much time had already elapsed. The assassin could have used the ensuing chaos to slip away. Waiting to strike until the agreement was signed meant the mission had been a success. A virtual win-win for Iran. Killing the Iranian diplomat had to have been part of the plan. An excellent move to divert suspicion.

Alex received a text message from Champion, and shared it with Nathan.

Discovered Torkan's body in his room. He's been dead for several hours.

Nathan tossed the wig back into the trashcan. "So our mystery man could be anybody."

Alex gave it some thought. "Not exactly."

"What are you thinking?"

"Our guy is injured. Not enough blood loss to be problematic, but he wanted to get it under control. He comes in here, ditches the disguise, and cleans up his wound as best he can. I didn't see blood drops heading out of the restroom."

Nathan picked up the discarded fabric from the floor. "Used the lining of his jacket for a bandage?"

"Yeah. So what does that suggest?"

"Wouldn't use it to wrap his head. That would draw too much attention. If it were his arm, the jacket would serve as a sponge long enough for him to get somewhere else to take care of it. The leg?" Nathan shook his head. "I doubt it. Blood spacing isn't wide enough. Some of it would have soaked into his pant leg. You mentioned there was blood on a door handle."

Both nodded agreement.

"He's got a hand injury," they said in unison.

CHAPTER 76

SNOW'S WINDOW TO escape had closed rapidly. He'd intended to use the cover of gunfire, smoke, and confusion. The problem had been that the smoke worked too well in the closed environment, making target selection tricky.

The Iranian delegate's death was by design. He had betrayed his country by feeding information to the West. Monetary deposits to foreign banks weren't as sufficiently shielded as he'd thought. His death would serve the purpose of reminding others that loyalty was not just expected, but demanded.

His plan in motion, Snow had gained control of the room by creating mayhem without drawing suspicion. He'd needed to neutralize as many potential threats as possible. That meant incapacitating the guards in the room and keeping security on the outside at bay. Which delegates got wounded was his choice, but he had strict orders not to kill them. A man of his skill knew where to place non-lethal shots.

He had been in the process of facilitating his escape by remotely firing another barrage of bullets from the boat when someone in the room had started shooting wildly. The smoke made it difficult to pinpoint its origin, and he paid the price. He didn't duck in time to avoid a bullet that ripped open a sizeable piece of flesh on the back of his left hand. Once the shooter's magazine was empty, Snow had made sure everyone stayed on the ground by guiding in the last round of ammunition. Pinning down occupants of the room gave him time to reach the side door.

Snow feared he would have attracted unwanted attention if he'd been among the first to arrive on the main floor after having survived the attack. His injury looked bad, and would probably require stitches, but he was supposed to be a trained security guard, whose job required him to stay the course if he could physically do so. He'd hoped to blend in with the frenzy of diplomats being rushed to their motorcades and the injured, who were either getting treated at the scene or being loaded into ambulances for a hospital trip. He wanted to slip away unnoticed before anyone knew Bashir Torkan was missing.

The hand injury, coupled with an uneasy feeling, had forced him to abandon that plan. Changing course, he'd ducked in a restroom previously closed off to the public. He'd removed all things Torkan, discarding them into a trashcan. Next, he attended to his bleeding hand. Though he was fortunate enough for it to be just a deep flesh wound, he had to stop the blood leakage. Paper towels weren't pliable enough. Improvising, he tore away strips of his suit jacket lining to create makeshift bandages.

Once done, he'd sought a way outside. Police officers had already secured the hotel exits, and they ordered him to head back in another direction. Snow had tossed his pistol into a corridor trashcan. Keeping his injured left hand in his pants pocket, Snow was ushered to a holding area, where a group of distraught guests and hotel visitors were being detained at a distance. He eavesdropped on their nervous banter, picking the right moment to blend in.

"Have they said anything about what's going on? How long do

they plan on keeping us here?" Snow asked no one in particular. For now, this was as good as any place to wait it out.

Snow's presence drew the attention of another detainee. He was the right build. The way he moved seemed consistent too. Neril hadn't been able to get a good look at his face from the video feed, so she couldn't make a solid determination in that regard. She had watched the nightmarish footage of a figure walking up the ramp from the parking garage to the point that it was imprinted in her brain. On that same video stream, a mortally wounded man had taken his final steps.

As she eased through the crowd, each step convinced Neril she had found the son-of-a-bitch who'd killed her partner.

He perfectly fit the description Sharon had given.

CHAPTER 77

LIKE AN ANIMAL sensing impending danger, Snow's comfort level shifted. There was nothing in front of him to cause such angst. Heavily armed police officers and plain-clothed security details weren't taking any particular interest in the group he'd holed up with. He didn't have a grip on the source of his uneasiness, but it was closing in. He came up empty on his peripheral too, which left only one option.

Snow turned around to engage the nearest person. He eliminated possibilities as he went down the line of suspects. Two people gave him pause. On his right, a man, gray shirt and jeans. A woman, directly behind him, blue sleeveless shirt, white pants. He eliminated them both because of the person now in his sight line. He removed his glasses to rub his eyes, taking a closer look during the process. This woman—denim shirt, stylish athletic pants, and sneakers—had moved up from his left. Despite the surrounding turmoil, her interest seemed concentrated in his direction. The purse slung over her left shoulder was open, her opposite hand on top, holding it in place. She wedged in between several people to help shield her movement. Her face wasn't familiar. Snow wondered how and why she'd zeroed in on him. He wasn't about to let it play out.

He tapped his glasses to confirm a connection with the equipment on the boat. Three short-range rockets were at his disposal. Their design prohibited massive destruction. That kind of payload would have added too much bulk, sacrificing range and accuracy. Besides, he wasn't looking to create a mass body count. These rockets would make a ton of noise on impact, shattering windows and sending out shock waves capable of knocking those in proximity unconscious. Snow chose a point above and to the right of the main entrance. There was a cluster of guards assembled below, protecting the remaining diplomats and those less injured as they were being loaded into vehicles. Snow started to move, increasing his distance from the woman. He swiped the right side of his glasses. A launch confirmation vibrated his inner earpiece. Counting down, he spun around to make eye contact with the woman. Snow's eyes widened with fake fright.

Pointing at Neril, he yelled, "Gun! She's got a gun!"

CHAPTER 78

THE DECLARATION SET off a stampede. The maddening scene grew measurably worse as a loud, screeching boom disintegrated windows, sending glass fragments flying. One group of people covered their heads and dropped to their knees. The confusion had others trying to figure out where to run for safety.

Neril got caught up in the initial panic. She was bumped to the ground from behind by a couple that nearly tripped themselves. They stepped on and over her in a mad scramble. Neril shielded her head from more indiscriminate feet as they haphazardly rushed past. Gathering herself, she reached for her dislodged purse. Her pistol was in plain view on the ground. Neril scurried to retrieve the weapon. A shoe arrived ahead of her, sending the gun skidding along the floor. She looked up to see men in suits, their weapons pointed at her head.

"Don't move," they commanded. "Put your hands on top of your head."

Neril was grabbed in a hurry, then handcuffed and patted down. Rather than protest, she tried to locate the man who'd drawn her interest, cleverly shouting that she had a gun. He was nowhere within view.

"Let's get her out of here," a guard said. "Put her in the holding area for now."

"Wait!" Neril squirmed and resisted. "He's getting away. Let me go!"

More security personnel arrived, wanting to know the source of the hysteria. A face emerged among them that she'd seen the other night. He was the man who had come to Sharon's aid, the one who'd taken his phone and likely texted her back. He shadowed another individual, who had his gun drawn. The guards shoved Neril forward when she acted on a hunch.

"Nathan," she called out. "Nathan."

Vice grips on both arms lifted Neril off the ground. Being airborne gave her the chance to use her legs. She drove hard into the thighs of each man restraining her. They didn't release her, but her feet were back on the ground.

The lead guard had a handful of her hair and snapped her head back. "You want to be dragged out of here?" he growled, his tepid breath on the side of her face.

Neril tried to break free. "Nathan," she yelled.

"Have it your way," the guard responded in exasperation.

"Hold it," a voice commanded the guards, causing them to pause. They relaxed their belligerent stance when the man who'd dared to raise his voice to them held out his ID badge.

Alex looked at Nathan. "You sure?"

He nodded. "We're from the same office."

"Uncuff her, please," said Alex.

The guards were reluctant, but complied. "You sure about this? She had a gun."

"Let's give it back to her then." Alex smiled.

The weapon was returned without apology. The guards dismissed themselves to go help people affected by the blast.

"You shouldn't be here," Nathan said without fanfare.

"I'm only here because of you," Neril shot back.

Nathan leaned in so only Alex and Neril could hear. "They find out you're Mossad, you'll be helping the Iranians pull this thing off."

Neril had contempt in her eyes. "What the hell are you talking about? I was about to confront the man who killed Daniel before this shit happened."

Alex held up his hands. "I hate to break up this family squabble, but we're looking for the person responsible for what happened upstairs."

Angry at being interrupted, Neril said, "Who the hell are you?"

"I'm the guy who just saved your ass from hours of interrogation, and accusations your country doesn't want to deal with. Look, Nathan can get you caught up later."

Nathan gave his approval. "He's legit."

The atmosphere in the lobby was chaotic. Several people were down with injuries or visibly shaken. Between the attack upstairs and this, Alex had an increasing concern they might not find the person responsible.

Alex addressed Neril. "Any chance you see a guy with an injured hand? Might have a crude bandage on it."

Neril gave it some thought, coming up empty. Then she remembered. Perhaps it was nothing, but could they be searching for the same man?

"The guy I was telling you about," she said. "He kept his left hand in his pants pocket. He created a diversion before the explosion. Even then, he didn't remove his hand."

Alex looked around. "Did you see what direction he went?"

"I got knocked down when people panicked. I think he headed in that direction." Neril pointed toward a corridor. "Away from the blast."

"Come with me," Alex told Neril, taking off running. "You're the only one who knows what he looks like."

CHAPTER 79

THE ASSASSIN HAD a head start—he could be anywhere by now. Since Neril was the only one to see him face to face, she provided a detailed description. It helped, but the search remained akin to finding a needle in a haystack. The one advantage they possessed was that the suspect had a bandaged hand. On the run with limited resources, he couldn't sufficiently hide that.

The hotel's exit points were well secured by multiple police officers. If the suspect failed to get out in time, he had to still be on site. Because officers used them, the only remaining unsecure points were a stairway and elevators to the upper floors.

"You thinking what I'm thinking?" Alex asked Nathan.

"He has a room in the hotel," Nathan answered.

"We can have them all checked," Alex acknowledged.

Nathan reached into a pocket to retrieve the sales manager's master key card. "We can get a head start."

Neril stayed put to cover the ground floor should the assassin double back or appear from another direction. Alex and Nathan took the elevator to the third floor. Searching six floors with over four hundred guest rooms would take an eternity.

Stepping onto the third floor, Alex called Champion to explain what had to be done. He gave an updated description, requesting that all available security personnel help clear rooms on each floor.

Searching the last rooms on their floor, Alex received notification that a security team working the fifth floor had discovered a suit jacket with its lining torn, a pair of shoes, and bloodstained towels on the floor. Remnants of fine, short hair were in the bathroom sink. A change of clothes, plus a slight appearance alteration, would create a subtle difference, but the wounded hand would be difficult to sufficiently cover up.

The prolonged room search and heightened security dialed down Neril's anger. Leaning against a corner wall, she had the vantage point of seeing before being seen. She processed each face that crossed her horizon. Security had commandeered the elevators, so when the doors opened and a group of police officers exited, it was no big deal. She recognized a few of them—different shapes, sizes, sexes, their upper bodies bulked up by bulletproof vests and additional ammunition. She hadn't heard from Nathan upstairs. Her stomach churned with a dreadful feeling of failure. Had she failed Sharon a second time, allowing his killer to escape when he was within reach?

Neril snapped out of her remorse in time to focus on the officers who'd gotten off the elevator. They bunched together, heading toward one of the hotel's exits. She caught a glimpse of a profile. It was enough to pique her interest. She pushed away from the wall to follow. The officer was the right height and frame. She thought back to the man who'd yelled. He hadn't had a trimmed beard like the officer. He had, however, been wearing glasses, and they appeared to be the same ones. She tried to get a look at his left hand. Officers flanking him blocked her view. The group stopped to engage someone who appeared to be a superior. Neril ducked behind a corner, messaging Nathan that she might have eyes on the suspect. Nathan asked if he was wearing new clothes and a different hairstyle, and Neril relayed that he was in a police uniform. She couldn't confirm a hair change, because he wore an official hat. She added that he now had a beard. When the higher-ranking officer passed her in the hall, Neril poked her head around the corner. The officers were no longer there. The only place they could have gone was through an exit to the street.

Neril sprinted for the door, transferring her weapon to the back of her pants. She covered it with her shirt before stepping out. Looking to her left, she found the officers heading toward the waterfront street to join a blockade already in place. The man with glasses was not among them. She spotted him walking alone in the other direction. Neril crossed the street. She hung back far enough to hide behind a line of people who'd gathered at a safe distance to observe what was going on at the hotel. When she saw his bandaged left hand, there was no doubt. Neril informed Nathan of her discovery. He hated to do it, but he reminded her of what happened to Sharon when he got too close. Nathan also needed Neril alive to help clear his name with Tel Aviv. Not trusting Neril to keep her emotions under control, he took off to join the pursuit with Alex in tow.

CHAPTER 80

FOR A COUPLE of blocks, Neril took what Nathan had said to heart. But now, realizing where she was, her heart raced and her mouth was desert dry. Even though she'd been walking at a sweat-producing pace, her skin felt a rush of cold air, as if she'd stepped into winter without a coat. Neril tried not to look. The gravitational pull of guilt made that impossible. She had no other choice than to walk over the spot where her colleague had died. Following the man responsible for his death, Neril uttered, "I promise, Daniel. I promise."

She maintained distance as the suspect turned the corner onto Place de Cornavin. Having arrived in Geneva by train, she recognized that the main station was ahead. If that was his destination, keeping tabs on him with one set of eyes would be difficult. She didn't know how far back Nathan and this Alex were. She now understood the predicament Sharon must have encountered. The smart thing to do was wait for backup, but doing so risked him getting away, perhaps for good. She couldn't live with that.

The fake policeman made his way to the tram and bus depot. He lingered while pretending to do his job. With a tram approaching, he waited until the last second to cross the street, narrowly avoiding getting hit. Figuring out his intention, Neril backtracked. To facilitate all the cars attached for pickup and unloading, the tram blocked the intersection, making it impossible for vehicular traffic to get through. Neril crossed by sidestepping the idled traffic. She saw her policeman head for the Cornavin train entrance. Neril broke out in a dead run, verbally sending Nathan a message of what was happening.

Faced with a daunting task, Neril halted inside the station's main foyer. There were escalators and stairs straight ahead. To her far right, more stairs provided another option. Directly next to her, a set of escalators and stairs led down to the parking garage. On her left were numerous shops and ticket machines down a long hallway that fed into another part of the station. She stood there, unable to decide. Her eyes sorted through each possibility, but the policeman had vanished.

Breathing hard, Nathan and Alex caught up with the motionless Neril. Observing from her vantage point, they assessed what she was facing.

Neril didn't take her eyes away from scanning the horizon. "I was pretty much right behind him. Now, I've lost him."

They decided a course of action without discussion. "I'll go left and take the basement level," said Alex, peeling away.

Neril chose next. "I got the train platforms."

Nathan nodded. "I'll take the right and catch up."

Alex cleared the left side of the terminal, inspecting each shop, eatery, and restroom along the way. Then he tackled the garage area. If the assassin had a waiting car or motorcycle, it was game over with the limited resources they had. Alex headed back upstairs to take another pass.

Having less ground to cover, Nathan broke off to follow Neril's path after sweeping his area. Hopefully the man who was impersonating him would double back. That was a confrontation he wanted more than anything.

Neril had canvassed the various train platforms for nearly fifteen unsuccessful minutes. She didn't want to give in to the sinking feeling that Sharon's killer had boarded a train at the onset and was long gone. Complicating the search was day transitioning into evening, creating pockets of shadows. Neril was on the farthest platform from the terminal. She couldn't remember, but thought it might be track 7 or 8 on the Place de Montbrillant side. Her emotions at the breaking point, Neril rested against a rectangular billboard that separated benches on either side. Another approaching train distracted her before she saw Nathan staring at her from two platforms over. She hoped to see a positive sign and not the inquisitive look she got. Dejected, she answered with a shake of her head. Alex emerged from the main terminal to join Nathan. He looked exasperated too. Nathan made a hand gesture, asking Neril if she wanted to search the terminal again. She stopped leaning against the billboard, but didn't respond. Nathan thought she didn't understand. He tried again. She was looking directly at him, but gave no acknowledgement. Suddenly, Nathan knew why.

Their suspect stepped partially into view from behind the billboard, his bandaged left hand on Neril's shoulder. His other hand was behind her back. He no longer wore a police uniform, having changed into a black polo shirt and khaki pants. Nathan shared a penetrating gaze with his nemesis. Each understood who the other was. Snow was aware that the man standing next to Nathan had retreated into the terminal, undoubtedly trying to reach this platform.

Nathan readied for a more direct approach. He took a couple of determined steps toward the edge of the platform, but an arriving train impeded him from jumping off. Nathan tried to maintain visual contact by looking through the windows of the decelerating car. He thought about running to the end of the train to jump, but didn't want to lose sight of Neril. The train in motion again, Nathan saw Neril being forced to back up. With the platform clear, Nathan leaped and darted through the tracks to reach the next platform. Surprised people on the platform gave him plenty of room as he pulled himself up. Nathan saw that two trains were about to arrive—the first on his platform, the other trailing by a car and a half. It would arrive behind Neril. Nathan didn't wait this time. He got a running start and jumped. Landing, he lunged forward and rolled, narrowly avoiding being crushed. Pushing up from the ground, he saw Neril holding her right forearm. Her knees buckled while her eyes were cloudy and concerned. Seeing blood cascade over her hand, Nathan understood why. Hoisting himself onto the platform, he removed his belt.

Alex had appeared from the stairs leading up to the platform at the far end to see the attack happen. He took off, trying to make the finish line in a full-out sprint. The assassin assessed his choices with threats coming at him from two directions. He pushed Neril away after slicing under her arm with a knife and jumped onto the tracks, clearing the oncoming train. From what Alex could tell, there wasn't a lot of room on the other side of the train, just a railing and support wall overlooking the street. The train blocked him from making the jump to pursue, but Alex's first thought was to give aid to Neril.

Nathan was with her when he arrived, tightening a belt around her upper arm. The assassin had been precise about where he cut. Wounding her this way served him better than straight-out killing her. Inspecting the cut, and the degree of blood loss, Alex was sure Neril's brachial artery had been severed. Her inner elbow appeared slashed right before the division of the radial and ulnar arteries. Nathan worked fast to slow the blood loss, trying to keep Neril conscious, but she needed immediate medical attention.

The scene was drawing attention. People who glanced in their direction upon departing the train displayed confusion as they headed toward the terminal. Shouting and protesting from the street on Place de Montbrillant made its way up to the platform. The train inched forward. Alex withdrew his pistol, not knowing what to expect once it cleared. There was no one visible when the train vacated. Alex gave Nathan a knowing look.

"You stay with her. One-four-four is emergency services."

Alex hopped onto the track and hustled to the railing overlooking the street. He located the suspect taking off down the road on a bicycle. Because other people were around, he couldn't chance firing a shot. It was possible to climb down to the street, but the quicker method was to take the same route the assassin had. Alex slid over the railing and aimed for the dented roof of a taxi. His landing further caved it in. The driver, who'd been yelling at the man escaping, turned in disbelief to see his vehicle damaged even more. He approached Alex, spitting obscenities, arms flailing in protest. Alex brushed him aside and headed toward a bike shop. There were plenty of options to choose from parked along the street. Alex made a quick judgment of which bike looked the fastest. He climbed on, steadied himself, and hoped his childhood bravado of thinking himself invincible would kick in.

CHAPTER 81

LIKE MANY EUROPEAN cities, Geneva embraced multiple modes of transportation. Motorcycles, bicycles, trams, trolleybuses, cars, and trucks all shared the roadways. A tram nearly clipped Alex rounding a corner onto Boulevard James-Fazy, forcing him to angle out further than planned. The near miss triggered a car horn blast and screech of brakes. Navigating the bike lanes was tricky. On some streets, they put you right into the mix of traffic, squeezed between cars and spaces reserved for trams and buses. Alex exercised more caution than the assassin, who rode ahead with reckless abandon. Dusk being pushed aside by night compounded the danger. Alex couldn't count on motorists' reaction time to sudden, unexpected maneuvers by two-wheeled objects appearing out of nowhere.

Crossing the Rhone on the Coulouvrenière Bridge's long straightaway, Alex utilized his strong legs to make up considerable ground. He lost it just as fast when the light at the intersection turned red. The man he was chasing barely hesitated, taking a brief glance back to gauge his lead. Alex inched into traffic, forcing stoppage with an apologetic extended arm. Understanding that long streets put him at a disadvantage, Snow turned down shorter venues and alleyways when possible. If this turned into an endurance test, Alex liked his odds, but not knowing the difficulty each turn presented at these speeds was a scary proposition.

Approaching a busy intersection, they squeezed between two trams, merging into the flow of traffic on an angling turn upon exit. Snow bumped and bounced off a car, stripping away a line of paint. The angry driver tried to retaliate by swerving into Snow, but he avoided contact by breaking off onto a one-way street. The car hit its brakes, dictating an evasive maneuver from Alex onto the sidewalk. He braked hard to miss colliding with a couple. Had he not spun the bike to the side, the sudden stop would have catapulted him into a somersault.

Alex offered brief apologies to the couple and got back on track. The one-way street fed into two different challenges. One street had a gradual upward slope. The other had a steep decline into parts unknown. Snow didn't have confidence that his legs could hold off his pursuer if he chose the uphill route. He cast fate to the wind. They'd both have to deal with the extreme condition.

The man was suicidal, Alex thought. He considered letting him go, but he'd come this far and too much was at stake. It made no sense to let him escape now. The street curvature required a delicate balance of braking, steering, and acceleration. The speed increased exponentially when they hit a straight section. The path appeared to let out onto a wider, busier street that neither man slowed down to consider. Snow reached the street below at a ridiculous rate of speed. To avoid flying right into traffic, he had to lean right hard, his foot contacting the ground for leverage and support.

Alex noted how the man managed to not become roadkill. It required a hell of a lot of luck and extreme control. Alex tightened his grip on the handlebars. He engaged the brakes to keep the bike under reasonable control, his foot hovering along the ground at the ready. Alex came within inches of being struck by a car and counted his blessings that somehow, he remained vertical.

The assassin ventured across the centerline into oncoming traffic. He cheated a peek back, amazed that the bigger man made that turn. A piercing horn got Snow's attention, giving him a split second to dodge a head-on collision. The overcorrection sent him hard into the side of another car. The bike crumpled, dislodging Snow like a missile to the pavement. The oncoming car struggled to regain control after avoiding the crash and rear-ended the car in front of it. That chain of events redirected the car into Alex's lane. He had no room to negotiate on his right side. If he chanced moving left, there was no guarantee he could avoid an even faster moving vehicle. Alex touched the brakes, which slowed the bike a fraction. He lifted up to put one foot on the frame before he careened into the car. Alex's knee scraped the car's hood, ripping a hole in his pant leg. Flying with no control, Alex wrapped his arms around his head. He landed against the front side of a stopped vehicle and bounced off, his back slamming against a parked car.

Alex maintained the vice grip to his head, because everything was spinning. He stayed motionless. This wasn't the first time he'd experienced this. Concussions had caused an early end to a stellar career in the NFL. The faces hovering above him were out of focus, their voices a symphony of gibberish. Alex wiggled his toes. Thankfully, the response was immediate. His body hurt everywhere, but it seemed to be in one piece. Torn clothing exposed scraped flesh, and hidden areas were on fire. He could feel his weapon pressing against his back and wondered how it had managed to stay holstered.

The voices started making sense, and jigsaw faces became clear. His head resting on the pavement, Alex saw through gathering legs that his suspect was stumbling away. Bruised, in pain, and wobbly, Alex fought to his feet. Protesting strangers held on, telling him to stay down. Alex ignored their concerns and broke free to take off after the assassin.

The only weapon Snow had was a knife. He'd have to make do. He hurt too badly to survive an exhaustive physical struggle. The knife would suffice if he could draw the big man close or get the element of surprise. Snow scurried forward despite what felt like a fractured ankle. Each bounce sent shots of agony to his rib cage. He had to make a stand soon; he couldn't go much farther at this pace. Hobbling down a flight of stairs, clinging to the railing for support, he used the leg that didn't throb as much. Under the nighttime sky, the street ahead was poorly lit and had reduced foot traffic. Parked cars jammed the street, offering places to hide. This was where he had to make a stand.

Alex discovered that if he placed his weight down a certain way, a sharp, nerve-pinching jolt would run up his right side from above the knee to his shoulder. He kept flexing his left hand to keep it from going numb. The extent of injuries went beyond those, but determination was a strong partner. The man he was chasing was equally motivated. His mobility appeared to be even worse. For that reason, Alex took the bait and continued into an obvious trap. He didn't know if the suspect was still armed, but based on past performance, Alex assumed he was. He definitely was skilled with a knife. If the assassin had a gun, the parked vehicles could offer life-saving cover. The street empty, Alex withdrew his gun. The simple act of retrieving it hurt. A deep breath, and he started the process of elimination.

Halfway down the street, the sound of youthful laughter interrupted the silence. Approaching from a slight bend in the street, their footfalls grew closer. Alex worried his ripped pants and torn suit jacket would appear suspicious. The gun in his hand wouldn't help. He took off his jacket, folded it, and climbed on the hood of the nearest car like he owned it. The jacket covered the gun and the rip in his pants. When the two young women and their male companion discovered he was there, they were startled. A head nod from Alex eased their apprehension. The trio laughed at their embarrassment, then continued away from the creepy guy in a wrinkled suit.

Alex waited for them to pass, making sure they were out of harm's way. He leaned forward to push off the hood. Then he felt a blade slice below his right shoulder. He lunged for the ground with no regard for how he'd land. In his haste to prevent the knife from burrowing deeper, Alex hit the ground awkwardly. The fall crippled his right side. He couldn't get a shot off. His attacker followed up, ready to deliver a knife strike to his neck. Alex's assailant was shorter, and the feeling on his right side returned in time. Angling left, Alex bobbed to dodge the knife. Leading with the suit jacket padded in his left hand, Alex swung his hips around, staving off what would have been a deadly blow. He had an opening to raise his gun, but Snow was quick to knock it from Alex's hand with a kick that nearly made him lose his balance.

Alex moved outside of Snow's knife hand, preventing him from thrusting with all his weight. Snow switched to short jabs, but Alex deflected them with the wound-up suit jacket. Alex threw his bulk into Snow, pinning him against a car while grabbing his knife hand. He slammed it several times against the side-view mirror, but Snow refused to loosen his grip. Snow gave up trying to overpower the big man. He used his free hand to strike every potentially vital area he could, finding a vulnerable spot just above the hip to drive the larger man back. Alex's right side went numb again, leaving him unable to lift his arm. He had only his jacket-wrapped left hand to fend off the knife until feeling in his right side hopefully returned. He paid the price for being slow to react to a swipe at his legs, as the knife cut into flesh.

Alex couldn't afford to wait for his right side to come alive. Snow had hobbled away from the crash scene, favoring his left foot. Even now, he tried not to bear too much weight on it. Alex decided to steal a move from one of his favorite movies.

Sweep the leg.

When Snow came at him, Alex didn't hesitate. He took Snow down to the ground with a swift, hard sweep of his left leg. Alex pounced, expecting the recovery maneuver of trying to roll and strike. Falling to the side, Alex grabbed the assassin's shoulders as he turned to strike, using his momentum against him. Alex was now under him, limiting his mobility. He got his legs on top to prevent Snow from kicking. Alex's left arm closed around Snow's neck. He was trying to stab his way free when Alex's right side returned.

He restrained the knife hand, choking with his left. Snow struggled to regain movement. Alex was too strong. Applying pressure, he guided the knife against waning resistance above Snow's heart.

Down.

Down.

Then penetration, blood, and a final, forceful thrust. Snow let out a gasp of air, the power to fight gone. Alex rolled free, landing on his back. He exhaled deeply, staring at the sky.

He lay there for a moment, trying to regroup. Gingerly, he got his cell phone from a back pocket. The screen was cracked, but he could still dial. He called Champion to let him know they could call off the search. Alex approximated where he was, requesting medical attention and a body bag.

CHAPTER 82

CHAMPION ANNOUNCED HIS presence with a polite knock prior to entering Alex's hospital room. He caught Alex struggling to put on his shirt.

"I hear they'd like you stay a couple more days for observation," said Champion, practicing his bedside manner.

"Thanks, Doc, but I'm checking out."

"Okay, how's this? You look like shit again."

Alex lowered himself into a chair, where he fumbled to put on his shoes. After two unsuccessful tries, Champion took a step toward him. A cautionary hand went up. It was painful, but Alex got into his shoes.

"Why not just wait until the end of the week?" Champion tried again.

Alex clenched his teeth and rose to get up. "I'll be fine. I've got a pinched nerve on my right side, a spinal contusion, and fractures in my left hand. A mild concussion. Mild. Skin abrasions, and some stitches on my leg and shoulder. Plus, the knife wound is patched

304 Alan L. Lee

and ribs are bruised, not cracked. See, nothing serious. Like the Monday after a Steelers game."

"Joke all you want, but you need rest."

"Fortunately, I've got the perfect place for R&R."

Champion felt a twinge of guilt watching Alex move around like a man in need of multiple painkillers. "Sure you don't want to hitch a ride back to the States then?"

"On a plane with a bunch of bureaucrats? Appreciate the offer, but I'll pass." Alex waved. "I'm booked on a flight later today. Should be home by tomorrow afternoon."

Alex grabbed a bouquet of wrapped pink roses from a counter. "Any luck finding out who our mystery man was?" he asked.

"Not yet. Drawing total blanks through every database so far, but something will eventually surface."

"And what about the agreement? Don't tell me all this was for nothing."

"The treaty will hold, but with some additional concessions from Iran. Doubt if we'll be able to prove they were behind any of this. They're maintaining a good front, blaming Israel, and reminding everyone they suffered losses. For the moment, we take what we can get."

Champion almost gave Alex a pat on the back, but realized in time that it wasn't a good idea. He held out his hand. "Appreciate the help."

Taking Champion's hand, Alex could see in his eyes what was coming next, so he beat his former boss to the punch. "I know. I'll give it more thought. Once I'm healed up, and my mind is right, I'll get in touch." Alex smirked, patting Champion on the back as they headed out the door.

***

Roses in hand, Alex walked into a hospital room that mirrored his. "How's the patient?" Alex placed the flowers on a mantle.

"She'll be fine," Nathan answered. "She's heavily sedated. In and out of consciousness."

On cue, Neril opened her eyes—not alert, but aware. "Flowers, how nice," she slurred. She then returned to a peaceful slumber.

"Told you, heavily sedated."

Seeking privacy, they hung toward the back of the room. Nathan gave Alex the once-over. "How you doing?"

Alex shrugged. "Everything will heal. I'm heading out later."

"How do things stand with Ms. Mossa?"

There was no easy answer to that. "I don't know. I've tried calling her. Left a few messages. Haven't heard back."

Thinking of his situation with Lauren, Yadin understood how fragile and fleeting a relationship could be. Learning from Alex, he realized at some point, to move forward, he had to be upfront with her about what he was. Not exact details, but enough to make an honest attempt. He'd understand if she walked away.

"I am sorry," Nathan offered.

"I shouldn't have kept it from her." They let silence take over as Neril stirred. "What about your situation?"

"I've agreed to go back to Tel Aviv with Neril. She believes my story about the assassin and his role in all my mess. Hopefully everything will sort itself out."

"Well, I'm sure the devil is in the details," Alex said, preparing to leave.

Nathan threw him an appreciative look. "So, you figured it out?"

"Yeah, not as dumb as I look. But, your secret is safe with me. " Alex opened the door. "Good luck to you."

CHAPTER 83

ALEX SET HIS suitcase down just inside the front door. Unpacking was the last thing on his mind. He'd slept as much as he could during the three flights to get home. Between Nevsky and the assassin, his body had taken a beating. The prescribed pain medication never left the hospital in Geneva. It was deposited in a trashcan along with the torn-up prescription for more pills. Being a control freak, he didn't like the way painkillers made him feel, masking discomfort. He'd seen too many athletes and friends develop an unhealthy dependence. The healing process had begun the moment he stepped off the plane, with the warm, refreshing trade winds welcoming him back home to the Virgin Islands.

The first order of business was to kick off his shoes on the way to making a tall rum and Coke with lemon. He savored the first comforting swallow. Alex enjoyed the rest of it on the deck. He never took the magnificence of the ocean for granted, its waves providing a constant symphonic rapture. He closed his eyes and listened, fortunate to be alive to experience moments like this. Things could have gone wrong in Moscow, Paris or Geneva; that they hadn't was worthy of a refill. He tried to relax, but Nora weighed heavily on his mind. He knew he could be a stubborn, unforgiving ass. She'd been distraught over Erica Janway's death, but what had transpired in Paris was something different. If she was unwilling to even talk with him, he was clueless on how to address the situation to make it right. And he wanted to make it right. Sometimes, trying to spare someone's feelings wound up doing more damage. Life continued to teach lessons. You just had to pay attention to learn.

A steamy, drawn-out whirlpool bath was calling his name. Alex dimmed the bathroom lights, filled the whole house audio with a Monk/Coltrane collaboration, and sank into the tub. The smell of Epsom salts filled his nostrils and soothed his aches. For the first time in a long while, he achieved Zen-like relaxation and dozed off.

When he opened his eyes, the ice in his drink had nearly melted. He emptied the watered-down contents down his throat. This was a heaven he had no intention of leaving. He partially drained the tub to make room for a fresh flow of hot water. The music shuffled to the saxophone styling of Paul Desmond.

Alex didn't fight the relaxing effect of dozing off and waking up. The near-hypnotic state made him question whether he saw a sliver of light get interrupted behind the partially closed bathroom door. The house alarm was set, so his tired eyes were playing a trick on him, or perhaps a group of clouds had eclipsed the sun. He let it go until doubt got the best of him. What if Nevsky had survived and hunted him down? What if the Iranians had figured out Paris was unsuccessful and discovered his real identity? The nearest gun was under a shelf attached to his bedside nightstand.

Alex crawled out of the tub, draping a towel around his waist. Peering around the door, he neither saw nor heard anything unusual. As he stepped into the room, the alarm panel on the hallway wall showed the system was activated. That gave him a sense of relief. It confirmed he needed plenty of de-stressing rest. He turned back toward the bathroom, then heard a faint, rustling sound coming from the bedroom. He picked up a display football off a table and braced against the wall next to the bedroom. Counting down, he sprang into the room, ready to fire a bullet pass.

"Jumpy, are we?" the voice giggled.

Alex tossed the football. "Trying to scare the hell out of me?"

Nora caught the ball with one hand. She was in bed, the covers pulled up under her arms. "I hope you aren't thinking of making a comeback," she playfully said.

"How did you get in?" Alex sat on the edge of the bed.

"You haven't changed your alarm code."

He made a note to himself—change the code, and maybe get a dog. "I've tried calling you."

"I've tried not answering."

"What made you think I'd be here?"

"Your watch," Nora pointed out. "Duncan helped me monitor your movement. I've been in town a few days, noticed you were finally heading home."

They seemed unsure where to take the conversation next. Alex had rehearsed what to say. He wanted it to come out right.

Nora took the initiative. "I forgive you."

He looked into her beautiful eyes. "You don't have to forgive me. I'm sorry. I should have told you from the start. It wasn't right to keep that from you. I knew how much Erica meant to you. I just didn't know how to tell you."

"That means a lot to me," she said. "You were right to do what you did in Paris. Killing him wouldn't have served a purpose. I only would have made more trouble for myself."

Nora opened the covers, inviting him in. Alex let the towel fall away and did as requested, grimacing as he moved. He took a second to let the pain subside. Nora leaned on her side to look at him.

"Finish what you had to do?" she asked.

"Yep. Your boss is happy. And oh, we haven't seen each other in a few weeks. Especially not in Paris."

"I've got another week of suspension. I've been on vacation."

Alex took his time turning to face her. "You're wrong about one thing. I have the capacity to love," he whispered, reaching to stroke her hair.

They stared at each other, and then kissed passionately. When Nora tried to pull him closer, Alex flinched.

"You're pretty banged up."

"Between Moscow and Geneva, I'm feeling it. I need a lot of downtime."

Nora's hand searched below his waist. "You think you're up for this?"

Enjoying Nora's probing, Alex said, "That part doesn't hurt."

Nora smiled. "Perhaps I should do the heavy lifting," she said, sitting up to turn him on his back, exposing her nakedness. She leaned over to deliver a kiss, climbing on top of him.

Alex didn't have to convince himself that the pleasure he was about to feel would far outweigh the pain.

EPILOGUE

THE LAST TIME Michele Orsette sat in a lawyer's office, she cried at the bleak prospect of trying to make ends meet on what her murdered husband had left behind. He'd worked hard to provide for his family, but it would never have lasted for the long haul. As if getting help beyond the grave, her life had changed, especially financially. The trade-off was giving up a part of her moral compass to justify stability and opportunity for her children.

She remained in the dark over why she was sitting across from a lawyer whose name was up on the wall of the three-partners Southfield firm. She'd researched them after getting the phone call. They were legitimate and private, and didn't need to advertise for business. They offered a variety of services for a worldwide client base that included portfolio growth. Perhaps that was why she was here, but that made little sense when she'd thought about it. Her bank account and subsequent investments were comfortable, but not worthy of the attention from a firm like this.

The lawyer (she looked at his business card again—Bradley Flynn) had hardly spoken since offering her a seat and collecting her identification. He spent his time nodding periodically, thumbing through a multiple-page folder highlighted by colored stickers. He finally put his pen down and closed the file, then glanced up with a smile.

"I apologize for the cryptic nature of this," Flynn said. He handed her documentation back. "Our overseas associates asked us to handle this with the utmost discretion. This concerns the dispersal of funds from an account in which they list you as one of the beneficiaries."

The look of confusion on Orsette's face was genuine. "I'm afraid there must be some mistake. I don't have any relatives who have the money that would involve a firm like this. I don't even recall having any relatives who live overseas."

"You don't have to be a relative, not in this case," Flynn assured her. "We've done our due diligence in checking your background. You've confirmed that you're Michele Elizabeth Orsette."

"Yes, I am."

"Then all is fine."

He slid the folder over to her. "I'll need you to sign your name next to all the stickers. Simple as that."

"I still don't understand what all this is about. Who would leave me money?" She thumbed through the folder's pages.

"This financial arrangement was set up by ... I believe you knew him as Erik Snow."

The mention of his name caused Orsette to freeze. She hadn't heard from him in nearly three months, but in Geneva he'd told her not to concern herself with a lack of communication. He'd said it would be necessary to drop off the grid for a while. Was this his way of disappearing? Throwing his enemies off his trail? Or ... She didn't want to entertain the thought that another man she cared for had been taken from her. Her eyes got watery.

"Does this mean . . ." She didn't have to finish the inference.

"I'm sorry, but this more than likely wouldn't be happening if there was another answer. Do you need me to give you a moment?" Flynn provided a tissue.

Orsette mumbled a "thank you" as she took the tissue. She wiped away a tear, hoping this was just another of his clever maneuvers. The feeling that came over her, one she'd had for weeks in fact, was likely validated. She stared at the document, unaware that her right hand was trembling.

"Take all the time you need," Flynn said.

His words helped her gather strength. "Thank you, again. I'm fine."

Orsette began signing her name where indicated. Getting to the last page took strength. She wasn't prepared for this. Not again. She had a flashback of their last days in Geneva. He had been a hit man, a killer, but she came to know that he possessed a good heart. At least he had with her. Finished, she returned the folder to Flynn, who went over the contents one last time. Satisfied, he opened another folder and withdrew a cashier's check.

"This is for you." Flynn handed the check over. "Sorry it had to be under such unfortunate circumstances."

Staring at the check, Orsette's eyes widened. She hardly registered what Flynn was saying. He had extended his hand.

"This concludes our business. Use the room for as long as you need. If I can be of further assistance, you have my card," Flynn said, releasing her faint grip.

Orsette was at a loss for words. She didn't acknowledge Flynn leaving the room, softly shutting the conference room door behind him. She was mesmerized. The check had to mean he was dead. Another man in her life gone, never to return. This time, though, she wouldn't have to stress over her financial future.

Considering what she'd already saved and invested from the enigmatic man who had been her employer, her lover, her savior—the two-million-dollar check was a generous severance package.

###

ACKNOWLEDGMENTS

To the readers, a heartfelt thanks for all your encouragement, support and patience. I know it's taken me a moment to follow up *Sandstorm*, but life has a way of dictating its own storyline. Looking forward to continuing this adventure together.

One of the joys of the journey is intersecting with people that have a profound impact on your life. Special thanks to the gone-too-soon influences who inspired me with their kindness: Robert Ludlum, Vince Flynn and Elmore Leonard.

I'm also extremely fortunate to have a relationship with two of the best Brads in the business. Their talent stands out among the rest, but most importantly, they're exemplary human beings who never hesitate to offer guidance and friendship. Thank you, Brad Thor and Brad Meltzer.

Dylan Garity, your editing was on-point and thankfully, light-handed with just the right amount of gentle nudging here and there.

Thanks to designer Jerry Todd. Back and forth emails and mock-ups resulted in the perfect cover art.

As always, tremendous gratitude to the men and women who tirelessly keep watch, doing the kind of work that allows us to follow our dreams and sleep well at night.

An *overt* thanks to the Central Intelligence Agency for always getting back to me with an answer.

My sons, Spencer and Drake, you're more than I could ever have hoped for. Extremely proud to be your dad.

Saving the best for last, to my wife, Sean. Couldn't have done this without you. The editing starts with your red pen, the support comes from your heart for helping me achieve my dreams. Rest your left hand because more work is coming your way.

Made in United States
North Haven, CT
14 March 2022

17111620R00193